"This was all I ever wanted. To be close to you, even with you knowing what I am."

Faran looked down into her face, his human eyes as impassive as the wolf's had been.

Lexie's hands found his chest, bringing back a flood of sensory reminders. Suddenly she felt flushed and aching with memory. Her first thought was to push him away, but the crack in his voice stopped her. Her heart was pounding so hard she felt breathless. "I'm sorry."

Her hands slid down his shirt, feeling the quivering muscles beneath. He was holding himself in check so hard, it felt as if he might explode.

And then her hand found hot, sticky wetness. She gasped. "Faran, you're bleeding."

He exhaled, his breath warm against her cheek. "That wasn't what you said in my fantasy of this moment."

POSSESSED
BY A WOLF

SHARON ASHWOOD

Published in Great Britain 2015
by Mills & Boon, an imprint of Harlequin (UK) Limited,
Eton House, 18-24 Paradise Road, Richmond, Surrey, TW9 1SR

© 2015 Naomi Lester

ISBN: 978-0-263-25418-1

89-0515

Printed and bound in Spain
by CPI, Barcelona

Sharon Ashwood is a novelist, desk jockey and enthusiast for the weird and spooky. She has an English literature degree but works as a finance geek. Interests include growing her to-be-read pile and playing with the toy graveyard on her desk. Sharon is the winner of the 2011 RITA® Award for Paranormal Romance. She lives in the Pacific Northwest and is owned by the Demon Lord of Kitty Badness.

To my Grandma, who taught me the joys
of the kitchen (and the occasional tall tale).

Follow love and it will flee,
Flee love and it will follow thee.
—English proverb, 16th century

* * *

The Royal Family of the Kingdom of Marcari

King Renault

Dowager Queen Sophia

Princess Amelie

* * *

The Royal Family of the Kingdom of Vidon

King Targon

Crown Prince Kyle

Prince Leopold

There are very few monsters who warrant the fear we have of them.

—Andre Gide

Chapter 1

Something cracked, a snapping sound that shot up Lexie Haven's spine with an icy, instinctive foreboding.

She looked up from her Nikon, still absorbed in photographing the wedding ring on its black velvet pillow. Her concentration had been absolute, and it took a moment to come back to reality and wonder what had disturbed her. Curious, she glanced around the room, but the portable lights she'd rigged up sank everything and everyone else into darkness. The night outside turned the floor-to-ceiling windows into mirrors. She was far away, but could see herself move—a figure in an emerald silk tunic and slacks, her pale face framed by a hip-length tumble of fiery hair. And then someone moved, blotting out her reflection.

"What was that?" she said to no one in particular. No one replied. She looked around, almost ready to dismiss the noise from her mind. She had work to do.

The dim room crowded with party guests made it next

to impossible to take good photographs, but royalty paid well. In return, Lexie took plenty of shots of the attendees and their bling, and that included the celebrated wedding band. Although not every palace official wanted a photographer at the party, Lexie was the compromise choice between no coverage and a tabloid free-for-all. Hers would be the first photographs to hit the press. The royal couple had unveiled the ring only half an hour ago.

Which was why Lexie was standing beside the marble fountain, camera pointed at the display case where the ring was being shown. For Lexie's convenience, the case's glass top had been removed and the security alarms switched off. Nevertheless, security guards stood to either side of the case. Until that moment they'd been polite yet bored, but at the cracking sound they stiffened like dogs catching a scent.

Other people must have heard the noise, as well. Voices rose above the splashing of the central fountain, no longer the polite murmur of ambassadors and celebrities deemed worthy to visit the Palace of Marcari. The hundred-odd A-list guests were now just ordinary people, shrill and afraid. Only the classical pianist carried on as usual from his Steinway in the corner, but then musicians were trained to keep going no matter what.

Another cracking noise came, sharper this time. A woman screamed—a short, horrified yelp of surprise. Lexie switched off the portable lights, bringing the rest of the room into better view, and stopped cold. The three south walls of the octagonal room were almost all glass, giving a view of the gardens. A spiderweb of fractures radiated across the center pane, leading away from a tiny hole. *Gunshots*. That's what they'd heard. Fear came like a crashing wave, and Lexie's whole body turned cold. Who was out there in the darkness, looking—shooting—in?

Both the guards drew their guns and joined the scatter of security bolting toward the prince and princess, who stood just in front of the fountain. Lexie's hands had gone slippery with fear, and she set the Nikon down, some part of her still sane enough to worry about dropping it. She grabbed the edge of the display case to steady herself.

The crowd was scattering—or trying to. The west doors that led to the rest of the palace were flung open, but rather than offering escape, more gunshots rang outside the open door. Someone shut the doors again, and the noise of the crowd escalated.

"What's going on?" Lexie's friend, Chloe Anderson, appeared at her elbow. She was dressed in a silk suit with her fine hair swept up in a twist. Her normally fair coloring had turned ghostly pale.

"Someone is shooting. We need to get people out of here." Lexie's voice shook. The room suddenly felt smaller than it had a minute ago, as if the walls were being sucked inward.

"There's got to be another exit." Chloe's eyes were wide with shock. And no wonder—she was the princess's wedding planner, responsible for making sure the event went off without a hitch. Whatever was going on definitely wasn't part of Chloe's plans.

"I think we're trapped," was all Lexie could say.

The room was packed, making it hotter than it should have been. Lexie swallowed hard and forced herself to breathe. A jittering edge of panic danced at the edges of her self-control. She slammed it down. She needed her wits sharp. Lexie passed a hand over her forehead, trying to ignore her clammy skin. *Get it together.* She made herself stand straighter. "How are we going to keep these people calm?"

She was just a photographer, but job titles didn't count

at moments like this. Fortunately, she wasn't the only one thinking ahead. Right then, the knot of security around the prince and princess broke apart. Princess Amelie of Marcari had one hand on her future bridegroom's arm. Kyle Alphonse Adraio, Crown Prince of Vidon and future king of both countries, was waving a hand as if insisting the guards leave his side and help deal with the shooters. The guards, who wore the green uniforms of Vidon, didn't look happy. Nor did Prince Kyle's younger brother, Leo, who had gone the pale gray of moldy cheese.

Another shot punched through the window and smashed one of the crystal chandeliers, making Lexie jump. In the next moment, the central window shattered into tiny fragments. Cries of fright and pain tore the air as shards smashed to the marble tiles, sending up a dazzling shower of glass. Lexie grabbed Chloe and ducked behind the display case. Needle-sharp glass fragments left a stinging kiss against her skin.

The crash still echoed as an enormous wolf leaped through the gaping window frame. The beast cleared most of the fallen glass in one graceful bound, landing a dozen yards away from Lexie, its claws skidding as it turned to face the broken window with a savage snarl. The creature had pale gold eyes, its coat shading from white fur at the muzzle to black at the tips of its ears. It was huge, at least four feet at the shoulder.

There were wolves in Marcari's mountains—they were on the crest of the royal family—but this one's size gave him away as something more. The beast was not just a wolf, but a werewolf, and she knew his markings. More than that, she inexplicably *knew* it was Faran Kenyon as clearly as if he had called her name.

Faran. Her ex-boyfriend really was the big bad wolf.

The room—even the piano—fell into a horrified, fixed

silence. Lexie's heart, already speeding, nearly pounded through her ribs. Memory speared her, adding old terror to new. She'd seen those razor-sharp fangs tear a limb off.

The silence ended as every one of the prince's guards drew their weapons and pointed them at the beast. Lexie leaped to her feet and thrust out a hand. "Stop!"

Her voice rang with command. Everyone turned to stare. Even the wolf looked surprised.

So was Lexie. *Why am I saving Faran? I ran across a continent to get away from him.* And yet, there was nothing else she could bear to do. With a terrible, desperate surge of dismay, she understood that not even a world of distance had broken the essential bonds between them.

"Be careful!" Chloe said in alarm, though Lexie couldn't tell whether it was the guns or the fangs that worried her.

"I know what I'm doing," she replied tightly. It was an utter lie. Lexie's heart was pounding so hard she felt dizzy, but she moved until the guards would have to shoot through her to get to the wolf. And then she turned and faced him. The wolf—Faran—was watching her with his cool yellow gaze, sniffing the air. Lexie wondered if he would recall her scent, and how he would react when he did. She'd never been sure how much humanity Faran kept in wolf form and besides that, their parting had been awful.

Glass clung to his coat in glittering fragments, his muzzle scratched and oozing blood. There was a wound in his flank, too—deep enough that the fur was matted and dark. Lexie felt a wrench, guessing that was where at least one bullet had gone. The wolf rose, taking a step toward her.

"No," she said sharply. "Sit. Stay."

He sat, ears going back as if she'd ticked him off. Faran never had liked being told what to do.

Too bad. Lexie was shaking. She had memories of watching him fight, teeth and claws rending flesh with unthinkable, wet sounds. The sight of blood didn't bother her much, but the warmth and smell of it had undone her that night. She'd never heard a man scream like that before. They weren't memories she'd ever shared much less tried to figure out. It had been easier to run, and keep running. *I knew there was a chance he might be in Marcari. I should never have come.*

But there were other memories of Faran Kenyon. Like the fact that he'd brought her champagne in bed and listened to her talk about the career she'd have one day, the beautiful photographs she'd take. *We did love one another.* Until she'd found out what he was.

Their history was a painful tangle, but this moment—here, now—was simple. She refused to watch him die.

"Ma'am," said one of the guards, his weapon raised. "Step away."

"I don't think so." She stepped closer instead, wiping her sweating palms on the green silk of her tunic. Her stomach felt like a bag of writhing snakes.

At the sound of the guard's voice, Faran snarled again, showing long, curving canines. He began to stand, but Lexie ordered him down with a gesture. There was no question Faran would protect her, but that would just put him in harm's way again.

Why had he come through the window, and who had shot him?

"Listen to Ms. Haven," said Princess Amelie from across the room. "Unless the creature attacks, do not harm it."

"Your Royal Highness, please!" one of the guards protested, glancing at the prince for direction. "There is enough danger without this!"

"You will respect her wish," Prince Kyle ordered in a tone that brooked no argument. The prince and princess were well aware of Faran's secret.

A whisper ran through the crowd, and not a happy one. They saw only a wolf.

Lexie swallowed hard. Panting, Faran regarded her with that unreadable yellow gaze, giving away nothing. She could feel the eyes of the guards on them both, waiting for an excuse to shoot. A sudden image of Faran's smile, the private one he'd kept for her alone, stabbed through her.

Chloe was still crouched behind the display case. She spoke, low and soft. "I hear dogs."

So did Lexie, and the baying was getting louder, breaking into the deep bell of bloodhounds and the growling snarl of coursers bred to bring down prey. Lexie's breath caught. She raised her chin, forcing authority into her voice. "That's a hunting pack. What's it doing on the palace grounds?"

One of the guards looked up, his eyes cool. "I don't know, ma'am." Since the wolf wasn't moving, a few of them stepped away, trying to get a better look out the windows. Lexie watched them suspiciously. Had the guard just lied?

And why are they—whoever they are—chasing a werewolf? she added silently. *And who is doing the shooting?*

Faran was looking at the broken window and giving off a slow, steady rumble of threat. Enough light spilled across the lawn that Lexie could make out what was happening outside. The pack was just beyond the gaping hole where the window used to be. Despite the gunfire, some of the guests had been escaping through the shattered opening. Now they scattered out of the way. At least two dozen dogs were coming fast, straining at their leashes. Their handlers also wore the green coats of the visiting Vidonese.

That was the clue Lexie needed. "Oh!"

Chloe shot her a curious look. "What?"

Lexie dropped her voice. "Does Vidon still hate the supernatural?"

Chloe blinked and gave a single nod. The wolf made a chuffing noise that sounded sarcastic. Lexie swore under her breath, doing her best to still the trembling in her hands.

Until Faran had finally taken her into his confidence, Lexie's knowledge of the supernatural was limited to B movies and horror novels. Only a handful knew that the King of Marcari had vampire soldiers at his beck and call, or that the King of Vidon had a company of knights sworn to destroy them. *And they're still fighting. Brilliant.*

The disagreement between Team Vampire and Team Slayer had kept the two tiny countries at war since the Crusades. The marriage between Amelie and Kyle—a true love match, by all accounts—was supposed to unite the kingdoms and end the hostilities. That was why all this—the party, the ring and the photos—was happening.

But if the Vidonese were hunting a werewolf on Marcari soil, all bets were off.

The hounds spilled over the window frame, howling in fury. Faran was on his feet, suddenly between Lexie and the dogs. The guards flinched, and the wolf froze, stopping just out of reach of his opponents. But he growled so deep and low that she felt it through the floor.

The hounds exploded toward him, but the rush didn't last. At the last moment, the handlers realized there was a sea of broken glass. Swearing, they hauled on the leashes. The dogs whined and yipped and howled, denied their prey.

Faran stalked back and forth just beyond the litter of shards, limping from the wound in his side. Blood spotted the floor behind him. Still, his jaws dripped with saliva, upper lip curling to show long ivory fangs. One particularly ambitious hound strained forward, front paws rising as it fought the leash. Faran snapped, taunting the howling dogs. Guarding Lexie.

The tension in the room spiraled upward. Several of the Vidonese guards looked ready to start shooting, no matter what the princess had said. "Wolf," Lexie commanded, fear sharpening her tone. "Heel!"

He gave her a look that sent ice down her spine. "Heel your alpha ass," she muttered under her breath, dizzy with terror but showing none of it. "Now. Please."

Faran stubbornly remained standing, but he fell quiet.

"Get those dogs out of here!" Prince Kyle thundered. "This is a palace, not a kennel."

The west entrance to the rest of the palace slammed open again, the heavy oak doors swinging as if they were no more than paper. Lexie realized that the gunshots both inside and outside the palace had stopped. A tall, dark-haired man with a rifle stood poised on the threshold, looking stern and businesslike in a perfectly tailored black suit.

"Sam!" Chloe exclaimed softly.

For the first time, hope warmed Lexie. Sam Ralston was Chloe's fiancé and like most of the warriors serving *La Compagnie des Morts*—the Company of the Dead— Sam was a vampire. He was also utterly reliable, exactly the sort of good guy one wanted on one's side when the world turned upside down.

Sam was one of Princess Amelie's personal bodyguards. Lexie frowned, doubt eroding her sense of relief. Why hadn't he been at the party, guarding the princess? Why were the only guards here Prince Kyle's?

Sam had clearly been fighting, the collar of his jacket ripped and the front of his shirt smeared with dirt. He strode forward, looking disheveled but in control. His cool regard took in the wolf, the hounds, the royals, and only faltered when he saw Chloe huddled on the floor. His expression grew even darker. A handful of other armed men arrived in his wake, all wearing black. They were vampires, too, judging by their pale faces and graceful movements.

Princess Amelie watched them approach with a somber expression at odds with her bright yellow party dress. She was delicately beautiful, with long dark hair and wide violet eyes. Prince Kyle kept a protective hand on her waist.

At the prince's order, the handlers had removed the dogs. The baying of the hounds was fading, but many of the green-coated Vidonese had remained. Now they stepped forward. They were less graceful than the vampires, but made up for it with coiled, angry tension. And then one of the green-coated men pushed forward, gesturing to the others to fall in behind him. Clearly, he was their captain—and it wasn't just his air of authority that set him apart. An elaborate design of a serpent and crossed daggers was embroidered in gold on his jacket sleeve. *Those aren't just ordinary guardsmen*, Lexie realized with a fresh bolt of alarm. *They're Knights of Vidon!* Both sides of the supernatural war were right in front of her, facing off before her eyes.

The knights were closest to Kyle and Leo, the vampires to Amelie. The two groups—so clearly representing the kingdoms of Vidon and Marcari—seemed to pull the couple apart with the weight of their hostility. Anger hung in the air like lightning waiting to strike.

Sam stopped before the princess and dropped to one knee, the gesture reminiscent of a warrior of old—which he was. He bowed his head, and the room fell silent once more.

Faran moved to stand close to Lexie, the heat from his body like a warm blanket. His rough fur brushed her hand. For a moment, with him beside her, she forgot to be afraid—forgot that she'd done her best to break the bonds between them.

Then Sam spoke.

"My lady, we have been betrayed."

Faran sent up a howl, long and heartbroken, that stole Lexie's breath.

Chapter 2

Lexie watched the closed faces of the knights and vampires and wished for her camera—and not just to take pictures. Somehow she saw things more clearly through a lens, and right now she desperately wanted to understand what was going on.

Apparently, she wasn't the only one.

"Explain yourselves," Kyle said, his gaze roaming from the captain of the knights to Sam and back again. The room felt unnaturally quiet in the ringing emptiness left by the wolf's howl.

The prince was young and athletic, looking more like a striker for one of the Italian football teams than he did royalty. His brown hair curled past his collar, and normally his mobile mouth was ready to laugh. But right now, he was furious. "Tell me why there is violence here? Why you are making accusations on a night when my bride and I should be toasting a united and peaceful future?"

Nobody spoke for a moment, the vampires still as wax-work. It was Faran who broke the silence with a low woof. He roused himself, his ruff brushing against Lexie's hand as he limped slowly toward the royal couple. With a touch of panic for his safety, she reached out, her fingers tangling in his coat. Faran paused, looking over his shoulder. His eyes caught the light, reflecting an unearthly yellow glow—but the wolfish stare gave nothing away.

Gooseflesh rose along her arms. She had left him for good reasons—only some of them to do with his furry side. Her courage suddenly draining away, she dropped her hand.

The wolf huffed and carried on, padding wearily forward. He was safe now, Lexie decided. With so much tension in the room, no one was drawing a weapon without good cause. Still, everyone in Faran's path moved away as if pulled by an invisible string.

The wolf sat down next to Sam, ears pricked forward as if ready to join the conversation. Sam put one hand on his back, a gesture of solidarity. To the onlookers, it appeared as if the wolf was Sam's pet.

"Your Royal Highness," Sam said, addressing Princess Amelie. "The Knights of Vidon struck at the loyal members of the Company. They claim our presence here is treason. We were forced to defend ourselves."

Before anyone could respond, the captain of the Vidonese Knights gave a sharp, military bow. "There was clearly a mistake, Your Highness. When it became clear to me that the orders had been given too soon, I commanded our men to stand down. The hostilities have ceased."

Too soon? Lexie's entire body chilled until she was light-headed. Did that mean there was a *correct* time to open fire on Sam and the rest of Marcari's trusted body-guards?

The princess wheeled on the knight. "Captain Gregori, when is it ever suitable to fire on my people? Who gave those orders?"

A shocked murmur ran through the room. Lexie moved quickly to Chloe's side, grasping her friend's hand. Chloe returned her grip as if she needed comfort just as badly.

"Where is my father?" the princess demanded, fear sharpening her tone.

Captain Gregori gave a slight bow. "Your Highness, the Kings of Marcari and Vidon have been in a private conference at the summer palace."

"I know that. Where is he *now*?"

"They are still there, Your Highness."

And they didn't even break for their own heirs' engagement party? Lexie wondered. Both the queens had passed away, which made the absence of the royal fathers even more pointed. *What's so important that it's keeping them locked away in the countryside?*

The storm of voices grew louder. Kyle held up a hand for silence, waiting out the crescendo of exclamations until the room fell quiet again. "Many of our honored guests have left, but some still remain. Captain Gregori, would you please order your men to see those still here safely back to their rooms. You, however, will remain. Once this chamber is cleared, we shall receive your full report and a *thorough* explanation."

"Shots have been fired," the princess protested. "My people attacked. I want more than words!"

Prince Kyle gave a firm nod. "So do I, my love. But we must think first of the safety of our guests. Captain Gregori, order a sweep of the grounds. Ensure there are no more misinformed marksmen lurking in the bushes. And bring those dog handlers to me. I want to know what possessed anyone to bring a dog pack into the city. The last time I looked, downtown was woefully short of wild boar."

Although the prince's words were polite, his tone said heads would roll. Still, there was an uncomfortable pause where no one moved a muscle. But then Sam pointed to two of his own men. "Start helping."

Obediently, the dark-suited members of the Company turned and approached the shocked crowd of onlookers.

It was like a switch flipped. Suddenly everyone moved, the scene dissolving into commotion. People streamed past Lexie as they pushed toward the doors, many not even waiting for an escort back to their rooms.

Lexie swept up her cameras and equipment, packing as quickly as she could. Now that the threat of danger was past, an intense weariness flooded her. Unfortunately, it wasn't the kind of tired that promised a good sleep. She could already feel nightmares coming on.

Winding an extension cord, she looked around the room. Even though she was moving at top speed, she was one of the last ones out. Even Faran was gone, vanishing when her back was turned. There was only a trail of blood from his wound.

She still felt a treacherous pang of disappointment. Knowing Faran, that would be the last glimpse she'd have of him. Once he'd made a decision, he stuck to it. Her vision blurred a moment, but she blinked the tears away. She'd already cried enough over the way things had ended between them—enough to last a lifetime.

"Ms. Haven," said a male voice beside her, making her start.

She looked up. It was Prince Leo. He wore a dark suit, his style and manner as impeccable as an aftershave commercial. He was holding another extension cord, neatly bundled. He gave her a faint smile. "I thought you could use some assistance."

She accepted the cord. It was a polite way of hurrying her out the door, but it was graciously done. "Thank you, Your Highness."

"Have you got everything?"

She put the cords in her bag and glanced around. "I think that's it."

His fingertips brushed her sleeve. The contact was barely there, but it made her shiver, and not in a good way. The gesture reminded her of her brother, who'd been the perfect gentleman in public and something else when her parents' backs were turned.

"Then I bid you good night, Ms. Haven. I must say I admire your spirit. I'm not fond of large dogs, to say nothing of wild animals." Without waiting for a reply, Prince Leo gave a brief nod and went to join the other royals.

Her *spirit*. Just a suave way of saying that her particular brand of crazy had some entertainment value.

Lexie bent and zipped up her duffel bag, then hitched the strap over her shoulder. It was heavy, but the familiar weight was a comfort. Chloe, who had been speaking with Princess Amelie, finished the conversation and joined her. Together they left the reception room for the corridor, the heavy oak doors slamming behind them. The sound echoed along the marble palace floors.

"I can't believe any of this," Chloe said, pale with anger. Her heels clicked on the marble floor, the sound like snapping teeth. "Their wedding is just weeks away."

Lexie frowned. "What was all that about Kyle's knights going after the Company? Did you follow any of the conversation?"

"I don't think it was Kyle's idea. He looked ready to strangle Captain Gregori."

And then they stopped walking. The corridor was crammed shoulder to shoulder with people—guests, palace employees and medical personnel tending to those with cuts from the broken glass. Lexie hated enclosed spaces. "We'll never get through this."

Chloe glanced around, noticing that Lexie was standing motionless behind her. "You can dive out of an airplane, but you hate a crowded room."

Lexie shrugged. "I want somewhere private to hash this all over. A jam-packed hallway isn't the place."

"Follow me." Chloe took a left turn and led her down a different, less populated corridor. Eventually they came to a narrow door. She pushed it open, revealing the palace garden beyond.

Lexie followed her out. A walk across the soft, springy grass wasn't ideal—Lexie's bag was heavy and Chloe had to take off her spike heels, but the open air was a relief. The dogs were absent, and a few guardsmen patrolled at a distance. Otherwise, it was quiet.

"Well?" Lexie asked after a moment. "Do you have any idea what's going on?"

"There is a disagreement between the two royal houses," Chloe said, keeping her voice down although there was no one close by. "Sam won't tell me anything."

At that, her cheeks darkened to a brighter pink.

"Has he even hinted what it's about?" The breeze whipped Lexie's hair across her face. She brushed it away.

"I don't think he knows the details, but it's to do with the wedding. It's all wedding, all day. No one thinks about anything else."

Lexie shifted the strap of her bag. "Still, it's a *wedding*. What's so wrong that they're shooting at each other? Did someone order the wrong napkins?"

Chloe gave a derisive laugh. "This isn't like an ordi-

nary marriage, sweetie. With royal families involved, it's
as much a treaty as anything else. The politics are above
my pay grade, but even I know everything could fall apart
in a blink."

The wing of the palace where they slept was just ahead,
and Lexie's spirits began to recover a little. They walked
without speaking, the way old friends could, and she
caught the scent of the sea. The Mediterranean was visible from the upper balconies of the palace, but here there
were only trees and pale stone walls.

"Who's that?" Chloe asked, pointing ahead.

Lexie squinted. Someone was sitting on a rock wall,
hunched over as if he was resting. The waist-high wall—
according to the official palace guidebook—was part of an
ancient fortification no longer in use. The breeze gusted
again, rustling leaves. The ambient light caught a shock of
fair hair. Lexie stopped, dumbfounded for a second. *Faran.*

Chloe gestured with the hand that held her shoes. "I'm
sure you two have something to say to each other. I should
go."

"Don't you dare!" Lexie reached out to catch her arm.

But Chloe was too fast. "I'll see you in the morning.
Maybe Sam will actually tell me something by then." She
retreated across the lawn.

"No, wait!" But Lexie's feet were glued to the earth, and
it felt as if that earth was opening up to swallow her whole.
Defeated, she set her bag of equipment on the ground.

Slowly, Faran slid from the wall and landed with easy
grace, although he seemed to favor his right side. Lexie
felt the same tug of recognition as when she'd seen him
inside. Now that he was in human form, he was terrifying
in a completely different way.

Faran had shaggy fair hair and strong-boned features
that reminded her of a Viking. But it was the memory of

what she couldn't see beneath the black T-shirt and jeans that made her mouth go dry. Faran Kenyon was tall, with a warrior's lean and muscular body that had made Lexie reach for her camera time and again because she barely trusted what her naked eyes told her. She could have made a fortune from those photos. For a moment, she drifted in memory, recalling the hot, hard feel of him beneath her hands.

They'd met in Cannes when she'd been photographing a swimwear collection. He'd been catering private events, and looking as sexy as sin fresh out of the box. When he'd turned on the charm, it had been a full-on sensory assault.

Two months later, they'd been living together in Paris. She'd had no idea he'd been working undercover the whole time, hunting down a ring of rogue vampires who dealt in the traffic of runaway girls. Not until the end, when she was halfway out the door.

"Hey," he said, watching her warily. It was too dark to see the color of his eyes, but she knew they would be blue now, and not wolfish gold.

"Hey," she returned, hot embarrassment stealing over her. She groped for something to say that wouldn't be inane. "You got dressed fast."

So much for sounding cool and collected.

His eyebrows gave a slight lift. "The guardhouse has lockers."

"Oh. So you're prepared."

He gave her an exasperated look. "Normally I'm a prepared kind of guy. Though I didn't expect to see you here."

There wasn't anything to say to that. "Are you hurt? Did they use…" she trailed off. "I should stop talking now."

His mouth flattened with anger. The next words came out hot and fast. "Silver bullets? Yeah. Thirty-eight hollow point ammo and hunting dogs. Way to make a guy feel special. I was lucky it wasn't a direct hit."

"What are you saying?" she asked in a small voice.

"I've been patrolling the grounds every night after dark. They knew I was coming. I ran to the one place I could think of where they would have to stop shooting."

"Inside the palace." She realized they were talking as if years hadn't passed since their last conversation.

"Leaping through the window was not my best move, but I'd tried everything else and I'd been hit." He ran a hand through his fair hair. "I appreciate that you stood up for me."

"No problem." She wasn't sure what she expected, but *appreciate* felt lukewarm. Then again, she was talking to a werewolf ex-boyfriend who'd never been a stickler for etiquette. "Do you know what's going on?"

"No." His voice held a ring of bitter truth. "But it's nasty."

He touched his ribs, probing gently. His breath hissed inward, surprising her. Faran rarely showed pain or any kind of vulnerability, so it must have really hurt. Her hand rose, automatically reaching out to comfort him, but she dropped it before he noticed.

"I thought you healed when you changed form," said Lexie.

"Wounds from silver are different."

"Do you need a doctor?"

He gave her a narrow look, his expression changing as if he suddenly remembered how everything had ended between them. "In a human hospital? That would go well, don't you think?"

She took a step back. "I'm sorry. I didn't think." Hollowness opened up in her, recalling everything that she'd lost when she'd slipped out of their apartment, leaving no more than a note behind.

His tone grew sharper. "What are you doing here, Lexie?"

"Chloe hired me as the wedding photographer."

"I don't mean that, I mean…" He gestured from her to him. "I mean why are you talking to me? I don't exist for you."

"What is that supposed to mean?" she shot back, irritation rushing in to salve her hurt. "If I close my eyes, you'll disappear?"

His glare reminded her of why she had left him. Beneath his charming exterior was a predator. That beast was fully present now.

"But one day I did vanish, didn't I?" The resentment was thick in his voice. "The day you learned what I really was, you just stopped seeing me. It didn't matter if I was standing right in front of you."

"That was years ago, Faran," Lexie said, fresh shock rising in her. She'd expected time to blunt emotion, but clearly that hadn't happened for either of them. "Why are you still so angry?"

He stood with one hand over his side and a stubborn glower on his face. "Why am I still angry?" he repeated softly. "Do you have to ask?"

She matched stubborn for stubborn. "Yes."

He closed his eyes. "Lexie, what does happiness look like to you?"

The question caught her off guard. "What does that have to do with anything?"

"Just answer me."

"I'm an artist," she said automatically. "Taking pictures is what makes me happy."

He moved so fast she never saw it. All at once, his hands

were on her arms, pulling her close until their bodies all but touched. Werewolves ran hot, their body temperatures a degree or two above humans'. A long line of heat vibrated between them, tantalizing Lexie through the silk of her tunic and slacks.

She didn't like being trapped in his grip. It was far too unexpected and intimate for comfort, putting him in control in a way that sent every alarm bell ringing. She squirmed, but his fingers were like iron.

Faran looked down into her face, his human eyes as impassive as the wolf's had been. She could almost touch his resentment. He wore it like a scar over the hurt she'd left behind. "This was all I wanted. To be close to you, even with you knowing what I am. I thought maybe you could eventually get past the wolf."

Lexie's hands found his chest. It was familiar territory, bringing back a flood of sensory reminders. Suddenly she felt flushed and aching with memory. Her first thought was to push him away, but the crack in his voice stopped her. Her heart was pounding so fast she felt breathless, her face nearly numb. "I'm sorry."

Her hands slid down his shirt, feeling the quivering muscle beneath. He was holding himself in check so hard, it felt as if he might explode. Her fingers became clumsy, unequal to whatever it was she was trying to do. Comfort? Fend off? She'd lost all sense of direction.

And then her hand found hot, sticky wetness. She gasped. "Faran, you're bleeding."

He exhaled, his breath warm against her cheek. "That wasn't what you said in my fantasy of this moment."

"Faran…"

He pulled away, walking backward. Cold air flooded in to take his place. "Go home, Lexie. Get out of here. Whatever's going on is just going to get worse. Believe it or not, I don't want to see you hurt."

Of course she believed him. Whatever else he was, Faran had never been cruel. "But aren't you in danger?"

He stopped moving, his hand over his injury again. "That's got nothing to do with you."

Lexie couldn't help feeling that he was very, very wrong. "What are you going to do?"

He didn't answer. Instead, he turned and walked away. It was exactly what she'd done to him back in Paris.

It was what she wanted.

She was absolutely sure of it.

Almost.

Chapter 3

"You're lucky you left the scene when you did," Sam said to Faran. "The discussion in the reception hall went from bad to worse."

It was just before dawn and Faran was exhausted. Sam didn't look much better. He had gone from the palace to a long meeting with the Company's top brass and hadn't even bothered to change out of his torn suit.

Now they were sitting in one of the break rooms at the Company's headquarters, which was a compound hidden in the hills outside the capital city. It had been decorated by vampires, and looked like a cross between a country club and a crypt—all dark, heavy furniture and oxblood wallpaper.

"What did I miss?" Faran asked. "Please tell me Prince Kyle did more than send Gregori to bed without his supper."

"Amelie was ready to flay him alive for threatening her personal guards."

"I'm touched."

"I'm in awe. She has her father's temper."

Of course the members of the Company were more than just bodyguards. They were supernatural operatives, and the King of Marcari encouraged their participation where and when the international community needed them.

Faran was one of the Four Horsemen, the Company's crack unit named after the riders of the Apocalypse: Death, Plague, Famine and War. Sam was called War and the doctor, Mark Winspear, Plague. Faran was Famine and the only one not a vampire. Jack Anderson—Death—had been killed in action. He'd been like the father Faran had never had.

Even one man down, the Horsemen were the best. They took the call after the CIA, the FBI, MI5 and all the rest of the big boys failed to get results. Then they slipped in and did what needed doing. They were ghosts, action heroes and James Bond all wrapped into one fabulous package—at least on a good day.

This had not been one of Faran's better days. "I would have stayed, but silver bullets aren't exactly my friends. Once I got the bleeding under control, I came back here."

"I would think so."

Faran slumped as far down in the armchair as he could without pulling his stitches. "Still, I hated to miss the punch line."

The whole time he'd been in the reception room, Faran had felt his strength fading, his vision going dark. He'd been bleeding out, but every instinct had refused to let him show weakness. Not in front of the enemy.

Not in front of Lexie.

"You drove like that?" Sam asked, changing the subject abruptly.

"I turned human first. Easier to reach the gas pedal."

The vampire gave him a look. "I'm surprised you managed without passing out."

Faran grunted. "Not a big deal."

"Right. You could have asked for help."

"Whatever." Being the token werewolf in the group wasn't easy. As tough as he was, keeping up with vampires demanded his best game. There'd been a few bad moments in the locker room when he'd struggled into his shirt. There were so many tiny movements that went unnoticed until a person had a hole ripped through his gut. And the walk to the parking garage a few streets away from the palace had been no treat, either. But he'd rather shave off his fur than admit it.

"Did anyone see you?"

"Chloe," he answered automatically, but then he hesitated. "She was with Lexie."

Sam cocked an eyebrow. "Any problems there?"

"No." Not in the way Sam meant. Lexie would never betray the fact that he was a werewolf. She'd been true to her word about keeping his nature and the Company a secret. By Company law, she should have had her memories wiped, but he hadn't been able to ask that of her. Lexie clung fiercely to her independence, and obviously that included control over her memory. That bargain—her silence for his trust—was the one unbroken promise between them.

Faran leaned his head against the chair back, closing his eyes. "Lexie and I talked for a few minutes and then I left."

Her voice—always low, always a little throaty—had resonated through him, stirring up the memory of so many midnight conversations. A hopeless, empty feeling yawned inside him, reminding him that she'd recoiled from the very core of what he was. Faran pressed his hand against the wound in his side, as if that would keep his soul, as well as blood, from leaking away.

He opened his eyes. Sam was watching him. Faran was used to the undead, but there was something about that motionless, storm-gray gaze that put him on the alert, predator to predator. "You're giving me the vampire stink-eye."

"I remember the mess you were in when you two broke it off before. Right now, we need your head in the game."

Faran didn't argue. "Not an issue. We're barely on speaking terms."

"She faced down men with guns for you. That took a lot of courage."

"She didn't mean anything by it." He'd learned his lesson the first time. "Our love life was filled with sound and fury, signifying nothing."

Sam didn't look convinced, but he let it drop. "Shall we move on to the hounds and bullets part of the entertainment?"

"Why not?"

"We need to talk about what happened tonight."

"I've heard that one before, but the girl was half-naked and holding a bottle of Veuve Clicquot."

"Don't joke. Not now." Sam's worried expression sobered Faran.

Faran tried to sit straight and regretted it. "What's up? Give me the quick and dirty version first."

"The Vidonese insist on using their own security for the wedding. In fact, they're insisting that the entire capital be patrolled by their own guard."

"So where do we fit in that picture?"

"We don't. No nonhumans allowed."

Faran's anxiety burst into full bloom. "That doesn't sound like Prince Kyle. He likes us."

"It's not Kyle, it's his father." Sam pushed his dark hair

out of his eyes. "Now that the prince and princess are unit-ing the two kingdoms, there has to be a compromise about the Company and the Knights of Vidon."

"What does that mean?"

"The Company is banned from the palace. From the city itself." Sam was expressionless, which usually meant he was about to explode.

"Since when?" Faran growled. "How come this is the first I'm hearing about it?"

"No one knew. The kings signed the agreement ear-lier tonight, but their negotiations have been kept under wraps. No one could afford a leak, especially with all the international media around for the wedding. Both sides agree that the supernatural should remain a secret from the general population."

"And this agreement is why the knights suddenly started shooting at us?"

"The Vidonese expected our resistance. Their orders were to clear us out, at gunpoint if necessary."

And of course—knowing nothing about any agree-ment—the Company had fought back. Anger hunched Faran's shoulders. "Did anyone plan on informing us we weren't welcome anymore?"

"The king wanted to speak to us, and to Princess Ame-lie, himself. The Vidonese representatives agreed that would be best."

"That's not what happened. Amelie and Kyle looked as surprised as anyone else."

"His Majesty was going to tell us tomorrow. But the order to treat the Company as hostile went out tonight. Vidon is claiming an administrative error."

Faran swore. "Yeah, right."

Sam's mouth was a tight line. "Marcari's human guards

will stay at the palace, but no members of the Company. None of them except you."

Faran looked up in surprise. "Why me?"

"The Vidonese don't know your human face. Were-wolves don't show up on the Knights's security sensors the way vampires do. You can still walk freely though the palace and the city."

It was true that Faran hadn't worked at the palace very often. His comings and goings involved a lot of sneaking around, posing as a tourist, and once showing up with Sam holding his leash. They'd both been the butt of jokes after that one.

"You're saying I'm to be the Company's eyes and ears?" Faran said, a mix of apprehension and excitement stirring inside him. "Who knows about this?"

"Company HQ, the king, Amelie and Kyle. That's it."

"Even though Kyle is from Vidon?"

"He knows you, and he loves Amelie. He wants her to be safe."

Faran narrowed his eyes. "Why wouldn't she be?"

"Vidon just forced Marcari to give up its greatest pro-tection. The two nations have been at war forever. You have to admit, it looks suspicious. There are even whispers of Vidon's collusion with outside forces. King Renault is willing to go along with the agreement up to a point. He wants the marriage and alliance to work, but he wants a hotline to the Company if things go wrong. That's you."

"I see." Faran shifted uneasily. He was ideally suited for the task, but was—at least compared to the centuries-old vampires—a junior agent.

Sam ducked his dark head. "Tell Chloe all this, will you? With the wedding so near, she's sleeping in the pal-ace. She needs to know why I cannot come to see her."

"Of course," Faran agreed, wishing he had someone expecting him.

He dismissed the thought, even if the emotion behind it snagged in his soul like a barb. Wanting Lexie—a woman who saw him as a slavering beast—was no way to keep his head in the game.

Pounding woke Lexie out of a fitful doze. She cracked open her eyes, squinting into the darkness. For a long, foggy moment she couldn't figure out what had dragged her to consciousness, but then she heard it again. A fist thumping on the heavy wood door to her guest suite in the palace.

Foreboding brought her fully awake. She groped for her phone and checked the time—five o'clock. Her anxiety deepened, making her clench her fingers around the phone.

The pounding started afresh.

No one pounded on a door before dawn for a happy reason. She shoved the covers aside and got up, pulling on a robe. Her feet found slippers somewhere between the bedroom and the tiny sitting room.

"Who is it?" she called.

"Open the door, Ms. Haven," a male voice demanded. "It is Captain Valois of the Marcari Police Department. We would like to ask you some questions."

Lexie hesitated, her fingers on the door handle. The officer was speaking English even though the country's official language was French. It was a courtesy she'd encountered everywhere in the tiny kingdom, but for once it seemed sinister. Whatever questions the captain had to ask, he wanted to be clearly understood. With a hard swallow, she opened the door.

Valois didn't so much as blink at her disheveled appearance. "May I come in?"

Lexie stepped aside. The captain was somewhere in his forties, with nondescript brown hair and worry lines. But his uniform was neatly pressed, as were those of the guards who stood to either side of him. All three marched into the tiny front room, immediately overcrowding the small space.

"What can I do for you, Captain?" she asked. Her voice was thick with sleep, but firm.

"Please remain here with me while we search your quarters," he said evenly.

"Search my things?" Lexie exclaimed. "What for?"

Valois gave a nod to his henchmen. One started for her bedroom, the other picked up her bag of camera equipment. Lexie darted forward protectively, but the captain grabbed her arm. "Let my men do their work, Ms. Haven. I promise you they will not be unnecessarily destructive."

Lexie pulled away, feeling utterly ambushed. She ran her hands through the rough tangle of her unbrushed hair. "What's going on?"

Valois clasped his hands behind his back. "A distressing circumstance has emerged. We are questioning everyone who was in the reception hall last night."

She suddenly noticed the dark circles under his eyes. Valois appeared to have been up all night. "Distressing circumstance? You mean the shooting?"

He gave a slight shake of his head. "Not that. You were photographing the wedding band." It wasn't a question.

She winced as something clattered inside her equipment bag, and the man searching it swore under his breath. "Yes, I was."

Lexie pictured the heavy gold band set with the magnificent fire rubies of Vidon. The stones were part of Vidon's crown jewels—and some of the finest specimens in the world. Kyle had ordered them reset for Amelie as a symbol of unity between the two kingdoms. The sight of them in the swirling gold band had dazzled the guests at the reception. "I was about halfway through when everything happened."

"As I understand it, the security detail had disabled the alarms and opened the case to make the process easier."

"Sure. They were standing right there. The ring was perfectly safe." Lexie stopped short, realizing what she was saying. Her irritation at the intruders faded beneath a mounting dismay. "But they left the ring unguarded when they went to protect the princess."

"Exactement," he said grimly. "The ring is missing. We can only assume that it has been stolen."

Lexie's mouth dropped open. "Surely there were security cameras on the display case!"

"Indeed there were, but it seems that they malfunctioned at exactly the right moment. There were a number of incidents last night that had unusually bad timing. The chaos caused by a pack of hunting dogs, for instance, that just happened to be available right when Sam Ralston's pet wolf ran by. Or the fact that an order to dismiss the Company guards was given to the Vidonese at a time when it was guaranteed to cause a riot."

Bewildered, Lexie struggled to take in everything Valois was telling her. A sick feeling spiraled through her, especially when she knew how unusual it was for someone like Valois to reveal so many details to a civilian. There was only one reason he would do so—which was confirmed in his next words.

"But you know all of this already, don't you, Ms. Haven?" the captain asked with an icy glint in his eyes. "Once we established that the ring hadn't simply been knocked aside during the chaos, we put our heads together and thought about that familiar threesome: means, motive and opportunity. You were the one closest to the unguarded ring, and you had a perfect excuse for being there."

Lexie felt the blood drain from her face. "What are you saying?"

Relentlessly, Valois continued. "It would have been nothing to take it when everyone's attention was riveted by breaking glass and howling dogs. There are your means and opportunity, and motive isn't hard to figure out. The ring is priceless. With your connections in the fashion and art worlds, it wouldn't be hard to find an unscrupulous buyer for such treasure."

A suffocating sense of injustice howled through her. She wanted to rage at him, but the words stuck in her throat. Instead, she fell into one of the overstuffed chairs, her skin prickling with rising panic. His theory was too perfect. There wasn't even video evidence to prove she hadn't done it.

"I think you had better get dressed, Ms. Haven. I'd like to take you to a more secure location for the rest of our tête-à-tête."

Chapter 4

"Stop right there," ordered the green-coated guard at the gate to the palace grounds. His scowling glare traveled from Faran's shaggy blond head to his well-worn boots.

Faran stopped, suddenly wary. It was barely noon the next day, but already the palace guard had been replaced by soldiers from Vidon.

"Step back here, please," said the guard.

He moved slowly, hiding the stiffness from his wound. According to Sam, he should still be in bed. Whatever. Faran needed to sort out his shiny new position as palace spy, and he was counting on Chloe to help him develop a cover. He'd left a message on her cell phone he hoped wasn't cryptic to the point of nonsense.

"Identification?"

Wordlessly, Faran handed over his passport and waited patiently in the pale January sunlight, the distant rumble of midday traffic competing with the splash of the courtyard fountains. The formal gardens separated the Palace of Marcari from the street. The building itself rose in the middle distance, a confection of pointed turrets and carved stone balconies. It crossed his mind that Lexie would be there as well, but it was a big place. He'd just have to put on his big boy fur and keep to himself.

Never mind that his inner idiot yearned for another glimpse of her. Last night she'd been even more beautiful than he remembered, with that flame of hair tumbling down her back. He longed to bury his face in it and smell the perfume of her skin. *Like that's ever going to happen again.*

The guard looked up, jerking him back to reality. "American. From California."

Tourists wandered past, cameras clicking.

"Yes," Faran replied, watching the man scrutinize his passport. Ironically, this was his real one. Faran had plenty of fakes he could have used, but he'd decided a simple approach would be the best.

"Hmm." The man nervously brushed the double row of gold braid on his uniform. Despite himself, apprehension pooled in Faran's stomach. Cops of any kind made him feel guilty—no doubt a knee-jerk reaction from his misspent youth.

"What is your business at the palace? There are no tours today."

"I'm here to see Chloe Anderson."

"Step over there while I confirm," the guard said, pointing. Obediently, Faran moved to a spot beside the black iron fence that surrounded the palace grounds. There were three more Vidonese soldiers waiting there, weapons already drawn. Faran tensed, last night still fresh in his memory. The guards saw him flinch and gave an unpleasant laugh.

The gate guard said something that Faran didn't quite catch. Whatever it was, it made the one with the gun step closer, shoving the barrel inches away from Faran's ear. "You're not on the schedule."

Faran laughed. "You're going to shoot me for that? Seriously?"

Mocking wasn't the best idea. The closest soldier spun Faran around and pushed him against the fence. Pain burned through Faran as the stitches pulled over his wound. The pat-down began, professional but thorough. Fury rose like an incoming tide, knotting Faran's shoulders. He clenched his teeth against it, willing himself to be silent.

"I think you had better come with us," said the guard who had frisked him. He took one of Faran's arms, the other soldier grabbed the other, and they began walking toward the palace. "Captain Valois has a special place ready for unexpected visitors."

Oh, goody, Faran thought as they led him away.

As it turned out, the Vidonese didn't take Faran to the cells built into the—thankfully modernized—palace dungeon. Instead, they took him to a room that looked vaguely like an old-fashioned kitchen, complete with huge enamel sinks and a massive table in the middle. Benches ran along either wall, and they were full of other people. Faran glared around him. The wolf in him wanted freedom, dominance and revenge—not necessarily in that order—but the rest of him knew smart strategy was going to make or break his cover.

The benches were already full of people awaiting questioning. Faran sat in the one empty spot.

"The cells are already packed," said a tall, thin man next to him. He spoke English with a cultured British accent that belonged on a polo field and not at all with his wardrobe. He had ink-black hair to his shoulders and was wearing a black T-shirt stenciled with *Old Goths don't die, they're just Nevermore*.

"Why are you here?" Faran asked, but he thought he knew. If the man wasn't immortal, he should have been. No one but a vampire had the right to rock that much eyeliner.

"I am suspect because I am Maurice." The man stretched out his arms as if addressing the entire world. His fingernails sparkled an electric blue.

"Is that so?"

The man shrugged. "They're idiots. The captain isn't— he's real police—but he's working with those green-coated fools. Eventually they'll figure out my most criminal act was a diminished seventh chord during the final moments of my last concert. It was at the end of the tastiest riff, just hanging there with buckets of unresolved longing. *Mwah*." He kissed his painted fingers like a satisfied chef. "Stole the hearts of my audience. Every single one."

"Right," Faran said, humoring the guy. Memory sparked— a clip from a recorded concert involving a light show, live horses and a snowstorm of glittering feathers. The guy was some kind of musician, if one used the term generously.

Faran didn't have a chance to ask more questions. The door flung open and Chloe stormed in, her heels clicking on the tile. Two Vidonese officials trailed in her wake.

She took one look at the room and spun on the guards. "I was told my friend is being interrogated. Clearly, you've shown me to the wrong room."

Faran got to his feet. "Chloe!"

She looked around a moment before spotting him. Her blue eyes widened. "Faran! I got your message. What are you doing here?"

"I need to confirm that I have an appointment with you."

Chloe blinked, but caught on at once. She turned to

the guards. "Let him go, he's with me. Now where's my photographer?"

An argument started, Chloe insistent and the guards defensive. Faran tried to eavesdrop, but Maurice tugged on his sleeve. "Do you know if they ever found the ring?" he asked.

"What ring?" Faran answered.

Maurice grinned a ragged smile. "The wedding ring. What did you think I was talking about, hobbits?"

Faran grimaced. "I'm so not going there."

"It's gone. Stolen." The man waved a long-fingered hand. "That's what this is about. The green-coats showed up at my rooms last night looking for it."

"And they think you have it?"

"I'm not sure what they think. I was having a party. You know—a few musicians, a few fans. Some lush young lady in a school uniform. Don't think she was in school though, if you take my meaning. The green-coats showed up with faces like the Grim Reaper in need of a laxative."

"And?" Faran said.

"One of the guards was clearly unused to such sights of revelry. He fainted dead away."

"A Knight of Vidon passed out on the job? That's hard to believe."

Maurice shrugged. "I can't be responsible for the effect I have on common mortals."

Faran couldn't think of a reply to that one. Fortunately, Chloe's argument with the guards ended right then. She grabbed Faran's wrist and dragged him away—which felt odd since she was more than a foot shorter.

"This is a nightmare," she murmured. "They think Lexie stole Amelie's wedding band."

"They think everybody stole the ring," he replied, gesturing to himself and Maurice.

"You'll be fine," Chloe replied, sounding exasperated. "The guards have nothing concrete on you or Maurice. They're just making a big show so they look like they're doing something. But Captain Valois is focused on Lexie because she was standing right next to the case when it vanished. It's circumstantial, but he counts that as a real lead. I just found out he's taken her for questioning. He's had her for hours."

"What?" Faran snarled. Lexie was many things—some of which made him furious—but she was no thief. "Is she all right?"

"They won't let me see her." Chloe's blue eyes were dark with worry. "Thank heavens you're here. They've sent Sam out of the city."

"You know Lexie and I aren't together, right?"

"What does that matter?" Chloe demanded. "She saved your life last night."

Chloe had a point, but that didn't make things any less awkward. He folded his arms. "Where are they holding her?"

Silently, Chloe pointed to a door at the end of the hall.

He flexed his fingers, wishing they were claws. "Have they allowed her to call a lawyer?"

"It doesn't work like that in Marcari. You know that."

But what he knew and what he demanded for Lexie weren't the same thing. His vision went fuzzy around the edges as he went from anger to fury. Faran was storming down the hall before he realized it.

Within moments, he heard Chloe's voice raised in another argument. Clearly, she was running interference with the guards and buying him time. She might have been Lexie's best friend, but Faran owed her a long list of favors, too.

One of the guards called after Faran, ordering him to

stop, but he blew through the command as if it was no more than a wisp of steam. There were a few things the world didn't understand about werewolves. They didn't need the moon to change. They were a different species, not victims of a disease caught from a bite. And they were insanely loyal when the occasion demanded it.

The door was locked but he wrenched the handle. It made a sick crunch and ping and then the door swung open. Lexie was sitting alone at the table, her head in her hands. She looked up, her hazel eyes widening as she saw him. "Faran!"

His chest constricted. She was alone and forlorn, the only vibrant thing in the dead room. He crossed the room in two steps, stopping on the other side of the table from her. "Time to go."

Her hands settled on the table, looking pale against the dark wood. "What are you talking about? Captain Valois is holding me for questioning."

He knew Valois. A good cop, but this time he had the wrong suspect. "You don't belong in custody. I won't have it." A tiny voice inside Faran whispered that he was losing it. He wavered a moment, realizing that the wolf in him had bounded past some invisible line of good sense. Lexie brought that out in him as surely as if she short-circuited his brain. But then he decided he didn't care.

She opened and closed her mouth before sound came out. "You shouldn't be here!"

"Why not? You need help."

She held up her hands, palms out. She looked appalled. "You've got to leave. If you break me out, you're just digging us both in deeper."

"Don't you want to get out of here?" He leaned across the table. She pulled back. Whatever softness he thought he'd seen in her when they'd met in the garden was gone.

Her fingers were trembling. He could scent fear on her, sharp and sour. His own nerves coiled, unnaturally alert. Fear meant prey. "Come with me."

"Think, Faran." Her expression was fierce, but tears glinted in her eyes, silvery in the hard light of the room. He had always loved her combination of bravado and vulnerability—but at times like this, her stubborn refusal to take the easy way out drove him crazy. She lifted her chin. "Cooperating is my best chance for a clean getaway."

She was probably right, and that made her refusal sting all the harder. *Getaway.* She was already planning to leave him behind. Again. Frustration bit like fangs. He slammed the flat on his hand on the table, making her jump.

"Stop it!" she protested. She was breathing hard, a pink flush bright on her cheekbones. "You're not going to bully me. Not ever."

He instantly felt worse. She'd been terrified of him ever since he'd saved her that night in the alley. He didn't understand. He'd never hurt her. Ever. "Your solution is to run. I want to make it so that you don't need to run ever again."

"That's not your decision!" Her voice cracked, but there was anger there as well as fear. "And you're not being logical."

But he was far past rational thought. The ground seemed to drop away under his feet, and suddenly he was back in Paris, begging her to stay. "How do you expect me to help you if you keep pushing me away?"

She took one last deep breath. It came out on a sigh. "I didn't ask for your help. I can clear my own name. Or maybe running is what I want, but I'll manage it on my own."

And there was the rejection again. *You wrote me off as a freak and cut your losses.* "Sorry I stopped to care."

Lexie didn't answer. Instead, she looked up, her eyes

shifting to a point behind Faran. He whirled, past and present blurring in his head. And then the present hit him like a brick.

Captain Valois was in the doorway, a scowl on his face. Odd, but the captain looked shorter from this vantage point. Faran had only ever seen him when in wolf form.

"What happened here?" Valois asked, his voice mild. Faran wasn't fooled. There was a core of steel in that softness.

He didn't care. "The door was in my way."

Valois's eyebrows rose.

Chloe appeared at the captain's elbow, linking her arm around Valois's as if they were very old friends. Faran knew it was a trick she used to calm her clients when they were on the edge of a bridal meltdown. "They're fighting," she said in a stage whisper. "Like wild dogs."

"What about?" The captain looked mildly interested.

"It's personal," Faran and Lexie said almost at once. She shot him a sour look.

"Is that so?"

"It's domestic," Faran said with some annoyance. The word didn't sit well on a wolf.

"Sad when a marriage goes like this," Chloe added, clearly improvising.

Lexie made a strangled sound.

"What's your name, sir?" Valois asked.

"Faran Kenyon."

"What's your business in the palace?"

There was an uncomfortable silence as Faran's brain froze. He'd lied his way in and out of hostage takings, terrorist cells and crime dens, but Lexie had flash-frozen his brain. "I had to see *her*," he said with asperity.

"They work together, too," Chloe volunteered. "He's her assistant *and* her husband. Always a bad combination."

Faran's eyes met Lexie's. For the first time in years, they were in complete accord: Chloe was out of her mind.

Valois gave a slow nod. "You should leave, Mr. Kenyon, and I suggest you do it quickly."

Faran barely stifled a growl.

"But don't go far," Valois added. "I'll need to speak with you later."

Faran took a last look at Lexie. "I won't be far. I'll come if you need me."

"Go," she said. "Just go."

Even now, she didn't want him. Especially now, when he'd let the wolf get the better of him. With a curse, Faran pushed his way from the room.

Chapter 5

"The ring isn't in your chamber," said Valois. "It is not in your belongings. So where did you put it?"

Lexie was exhausted, but sat with her spine straight and her don't-mess-with-me face intact. Her watch said it was just after two o'clock, but it felt as if she'd been in that tiny, windowless room for days. She was bored with the grimy walls, the scarred tabletop and the gritty floor. She'd never thought it was possible to be bored and scared at once. Added to that was guilt. Faran had pushed her buttons and she'd lashed out. He'd been trying to help and deserved better than that. If Valois ever let her go, she'd try to apologize.

"I don't have the ring," she said. "I never took it. I don't know who did."

"Is that right?" Valois tapped his chin with his forefinger. "And yet I wonder about a woman such as you, one who grew up in what might be considered luxury, and now lives more or less out of a suitcase. With all those advantages in childhood, why is it that you work and live like a nomad, when you don't truly need to work at all?"

Lexie stiffened. "I choose to work. I earn my own living in my own way. I don't need to live off anyone else."

"What does your family think of that?"

"I've never asked. They don't control me anymore."

His eyes narrowed at that. "You don't miss them?"

"No." She tried to say it without venom. Her brother had been the golden child, as vicious as he was perfect. They had both been restless, intense children, but he'd channeled his unsettled energy in dark ways. Her mother had doted on him, even after his death. "We're not close."

Valois didn't waver, although he sat back with a weary air. His fingers twitched against the tabletop, though his expression was exactly the same as it had been when he'd knocked on her door early that morning. "Tell me about your husband. When we checked your background in preparation for your employment here, your marriage was not mentioned."

Lexie's mouth felt sticky with stress and bad coffee, as if she'd been drinking glue. He'd grilled her over and over about every minute detail of the evening, but he hadn't touched this topic yet. Did that mean he had a fresh layer of hell in store for Mr. and Mrs. Werewolf? What the blazes had Chloe been thinking, coming up with this story? And why?

She sighed. "What about him?"

For a moment Valois almost looked amused. "He seems very protective."

"He is." That much at least was true.

"The front gate scanned his passport. I asked them to do a little digging just now." Valois examined his nails.

"There wasn't much to find at first glance. No mansions or art schools like you had."

"No."

"In fact, there is little information about his early years. It is almost as if he had no childhood. Can you explain that?"

"He doesn't talk about his childhood much." *And that would be the first clue he's different.* His secrecy should have rung an alarm. "I don't think he had a happy youth. Not that it's any of your business."

For the first time, a flicker of interest crossed the policeman's eyes. "From your tone it seems you are just as protective of him."

"So?"

"You're not exactly inseparable. No evidence of a common address. No common name."

"I'm a fashion photographer. My work keeps me on the move." The room felt as if it was growing smaller. Sweat trickled down the small of her back.

Valois flicked his fingers dismissively, as if suddenly changing his mind. "Perhaps you are telling the truth. There was an application for a marriage license in Paris some years ago. There is every chance that none of this is relevant."

Marriage license? Lexie's limbs numbed with shock. She blinked stupidly, trying to mask her surprise. Valois was regarding her coolly, studying her response.

Her hands rested in her lap, but they felt clumsy and cold, as if they belonged to someone else. *Faran was going to propose back then? Was that why he told me his secret?* Her heart jerked painfully at the memory, but she gave a careless shrug. "We have a unique relationship. It works for us."

"Is he violent?"

"No!" She looked away. *Not to me.*

Valois caught her hesitation. "Interesting."

Lexie didn't reply, but rubbed a scar along the back of her hand. A gift from Justin, her golden brother. It was far from the only one. She forced herself to turn her gaze back to Valois. He was still regarding her intently, searching for something to expose.

There was plenty there. The earlier scene with Faran had been achingly familiar, a replay of their last days together. Him burning with intensity and her wanting to duck and run. They were lucky all that broke this time was a lock.

"What has any of this to do with the ring?" she asked coldly.

"Your Mr. Kenyon has known associates in the jewelry business."

"Oh?" Lexie strained to keep the curiosity out of her voice.

"It makes for interesting reading." Valois stroked his lip. "But as his wife, I'm sure you know all that."

She didn't. Faran had kept so much from her. Tiny flames of anger licked along her bones. At the same time, she saw the yawning pit opening up beneath her feet. Faran's history—whatever it was—made him vulnerable. No doubt Valois would invite her to save herself by selling Faran out.

Her stomach turned sour at the thought. *The secrets I know aren't the ones Valois expects. He's looking for a thief, but I could hand him a monster.*

Valois watched her reactions the way a cat studied an aquarium. "You know, I can't put my finger on you two. You are either master criminals or helpless fools. Should I arrest Mr. Kenyon?"

"We don't have the ring. You're not going to find it by talking to me. Or him."

"Are you so sure about that?"

"Yes." Refusing to budge, Lexie dragged her fingers through her hair, but turned the nervous gesture into a leisurely stretch. She wasn't giving Valois the satisfaction of seeing how much he'd rattled her.

And she'd keep the act up as long as she had to. Faran was innocent. Last night he had been in wolf form and thieves generally required opposable thumbs.

"How do I know you're not lying?"

"That's up to you. I have no idea how I can prove our innocence to you."

Valois removed a roll of antacids from his jacket pocket and began peeling away the paper wrapper. "I'm forced to agree with you there. Guilt is a far easier thing to prove, Ms. Haven. Or should I call you Mrs. Kenyon?"

Faran sat outside the corner bistro three blocks away from the palace. After leaving Lexie—and after Chloe had told him to go cool his jets—he'd slipped into the guardhouse and cleaned out his locker. Now he wore a light trench coat and had the local newspaper folded in front of him on the small glass-topped table, looking like any other young professional caught between appointments.

He was trying not to brood, but it was far from a complete success. It was as if he had an idiot button, and Lexie pushed it every time they met. But some instincts were more than human society could handle—and that was the whole problem.

Back in Paris he'd gotten himself on the bad side of bad men—a hazard of working undercover. Stupidly, one of them had tried to get to Faran by hurting Lexie. That was a very bad choice. There were some lines no one got to cross—and hurting Faran's mate was one of them.

But that night Lexie saw what a rage-filled werewolf could do. She was gone by the next day, leaving no more than a note. His need to protect—as much a part of him as his head or hands—had driven her from his side.

And now Chloe had saddled him with a cover identity as Lexie's husband and assistant. Chloe had meant to give him a plausible excuse to be in the palace, but that meant Lexie would be close to whatever trouble Faran might stir up. *This is going to be no end of fun.*

Regret stewed with anger in his gut. It was true what they said about love and hate being one step apart. He'd never hate Lexie, but his love had edged to that painful point where it was hard to tell the difference. He was a lone wolf, orphaned and raised up rough. Self-worth had come hard, and trust even harder. Lexie hadn't destroyed him, but she'd left a hole that still hadn't healed.

Disgusted with everything, Faran took another swallow of coffee, feeling the sugar and caffeine already buzzing along his nerves. The wound in his side was a steady ache.

Instinctively, he watched the street. Crowds walked by, some locals and some clearly visitors. No one seemed to notice the green-coated Vidonese guards everywhere, replacing the usual patrols like a spreading stain.

They were, however, looking at the red-haired woman striding down the street like the hounds of hell were at her heels. Faran set down his coffee. He knew that set of her mouth. She was swallowing back tears. He had to go to her. Now.

Or not. Hadn't he tried the whole rescue thing once already today? And yet, he had to know what Valois had said about the ring. There was every chance its theft was connected to the scene last night. He had to talk to her, whether he liked it or not.

Faran abandoned the coffee and strode after her. He caught up in seconds.

"Lexie!" he cried, grabbing her arm. "What happened after I left?"

She turned, her hair whipping around her face. In the thin sunlight, the long waves were the color of turning leaves—not one shade of orange or red, but all of them—like a riot of flame. He dropped his hand as if the hue alone could scorch.

To his utter surprise, she fell against him with a strangled noise, her arms around his neck. Not sure what else to do, he held her. The way her tall, slender frame fit against his was all too familiar. They'd stood like this a thousand times, her cheek against his shoulder, the curve of her back under his hand. He tensed, afraid to remember too much—even if his body knew her soft skin and sweet, womanly scent.

It was just as well he held back, because the next instant Lexie pulled away, her eyes wide as if she couldn't believe what she'd just done. "I'm sorry."

"No problem," he replied.

She scanned his face, her expression cautious. It rankled.

"What happened in there, Lexie?" he asked, keeping his voice neutral. "How come they let you out?"

She didn't answer, just studied the pavement.

"What happened?" he asked again in a flat tone.

She heaved a slight sigh. "Valois can't prove anything right now, but I think we're still in trouble. More trouble. I was actually— I was actually going to find Chloe and see if she knew where you were. But I kept getting her voice mail."

"Okay," he said, his voice careful. This was a complete reversal from telling him to get lost. "Now you've found me."

With jerky movements, she looked around. "We need to go somewhere private."

"How private?"

Lexie angled away, her shoulders tight. "Away from the palace. I feel like there are eyes everywhere."

She was probably right. Besides, staying put wasn't in Lexie's nature. She didn't even like going to the same restaurant twice. Faran nodded, but not too eagerly. He'd learned his lesson about overenthusiasm that morning. "Let's go for a drive. That always makes me feel like I'm getting somewhere, even if I'm not."

They could be alone in a car. Lexie gave him a look just shy of apprehensive, but nodded. They went to the garage at the far end of the palace grounds where her rented Peugeot was parked. Since it was her car, Faran was content to let her drive. Sort of. Lexie was an excellent driver, but she'd never met an accelerator she didn't like.

Soon she was tearing down the service road that wound behind the myriad stables, garages, work sheds and other utilitarian buildings that kept the Palace of Marcari functioning. At the bottom of a sloping hill, she turned right onto the scenic coastal highway.

"So tell me what wasn't safe to say on the street," Faran ventured.

Lexie ran through the interview blow-by-blow. "Valois is suspicious. He pulled a lot off the computer about both of us. I think that's why he kept leaving the room. He wanted to check on the progress of his computer minions."

"Minions?" Faran echoed.

Lexie frowned. The expression looked dangerous with all that red hair. "Men like Valois have minions. He hinted about your associates in the jewelry business. What was that about?"

"That file was supposed to be buried deep." The Company had pulled him out of a bad life and given him choices. Part of that had been wiping the official slate clean. Faran looked out the window. "I was a kid. It was stupid kid stuff."

"Something illegal?" she asked in a quiet voice.

"You could call it that." Some were still doing time for their last score, but Lexie didn't need to know the details. "I was on my own. Some people had uses for a small kid with exceptional agility. I could get around obstacles they couldn't."

"You were a cat burglar."

"I don't like cats."

But the label was accurate. He'd received an education in thievery, especially precious stones. It had been a crack team, going after the best pieces. With Amelie's ring missing, no wonder Valois was interested.

"Why didn't you ever tell me?" Lexie asked.

Because you already had one foot out the door. "I'm not proud of it. There's never a good time to start a discussion about your juvenile arrest record."

She shifted gears to take a hairpin curve. "Before we moved in together would have been good."

But by then he was too far gone in love to risk losing her. "I didn't plan to screw everything up."

"We never do," she said quietly. "I'm sorry for all the ways I hurt you."

The soft words surprised him so much he forgot everything else. "You are?"

She didn't answer, but the blood rushed to her cheeks. He looked away, knowing that if he pushed her to say more the moment would be ruined. In the brief silence, his gaze drifted to the passenger-side mirror.

The back of Faran's neck tingled in warning. "Don't look now, but someone is doing an amateurish job of tailing us."

Chapter 6

Lexie looked anyway. There was a dark gray sedan behind her—which was not by itself a suspicious fact, but when she changed lanes, it changed with her.

"Told you," Faran said. "I'd give him five and a half out of ten."

"Yeah, whatever." Even before she'd known he was a real spy, he'd liked to give a play-by-play review of the covert ops on TV. "What do I do?"

He cocked an eyebrow. "Do you know who it is?"

"No."

"Think you can lose him?"

Irritated and apprehensive, Lexie looked behind her again. The sedan was still there. "Maybe."

"Go for it."

Conversation died. Full of curves and switchbacks, the scenic road had been used in more than one sports-car commercial and Lexie needed all her concentration. The first chance she got, she made a left turn off the highway, picking up a smaller road that wound through the hills. The sedan didn't change course.

"Wait a minute," she said, oddly disappointed. "Did we completely misread the situation?"

"I dunno," Faran said, but he didn't sound convinced.

Disgruntled and feeling as if she was missing some punch line, she let the road take her along a twisting loop that wandered back toward the city. It wouldn't take long to reach the suburbs—Marcari's capital was small. No place was more than ten minutes to the countryside and bad roads.

Lexie looked for another turnoff to take her back to the highway, but there was nothing in sight—not that one could see very far in front or behind with so many twists and turns.

"I don't like this," Faran said. "It's like driving blind."

"I'll get back to the highway as soon as there's a turnoff."

But there were just lanes here and there leading to farms or the wealthy estates that were hidden along Marcari's coastline. She drove along the hilly, bumpy terrain, sometimes surrounded by clumps of scruffy pine and other times overlooking the blue sea and whitewashed houses below. Another day, she wouldn't have minded getting semilost, but right then she wasn't in the mood.

Apart from everything else, Faran's presence in the passenger seat was reminding her of too many road trips that had ended up at little wayside inns. There had been magical evenings—sometimes with long walks or music festivals or just a local dinner and bed. They had all started out in a car going nowhere in particular with the whole world ahead of them.

Those scattered images of their past made the space between them far too small. Faran had a formidable presence, but Lexie was especially aware of his square, practical hands resting on his knees. Those hands had often told her so much more than his words. They were capable of incredible tenderness, but right now their nervous fidgets said he was every bit as uneasy as she was.

"Lexie!" Faran shouted, snapping her out of her thoughts. "Behind you!"

She glanced in the rearview mirror just in time to see a car speeding into view around a steep curve. Instantly, she swerved to avoid it, but the road was too narrow. The car clipped her back bumper, jolting her against her shoulder belt. The Peugeot lurched forward, the front tire sliding off the road and slewing into a sapling. Wood snapped as Lexie cranked the steering wheel hard, forcing the vehicle back onto the road before it skidded completely out of control. She felt the bump as the car regained the solid surface, and only then saw the gray sedan speed past. Furious, she leaned on the horn. Faran swore.

The sedan disappeared around the bend, going far too fast for the sharp curves. Lexie fell back against the seat with a gasp, almost deafened by the thunder of her own pulse. She lowered the windows a few inches, allowing the cool breeze to chill her sweat-soaked skin.

"Good driving," Faran said. His voice sounded almost normal, but his fingers gripped her forearm as if he would never let her go.

"If you hadn't spotted him, I wouldn't have been able to get out of the way."

"That was a close call. He meant to run us off the road."

Lexie's hands turned to ice. It wasn't just the idea of being targeted that bothered her—she'd lived with her brother's malevolent temper for years. She just couldn't understand how a random attack on the road connected with anything. "What's going on?"

"I wish I knew. A warning, maybe. Against what, I don't know." He cursed again.

She put her hand over his, trying not to meet his eyes.

At first she simply meant to reclaim her arm, but his touch was electric, as if that small span of skin against skin was all it took to loan her a bit of his unnatural strength.

"It's okay," Faran said finally, though which one of them he was reassuring wasn't clear. Slowly, he uncurled his fingers.

She didn't reply, not trusting herself. Words never worked well between them. With every heartbeat, she became more aware of the purr of the idling motor, the chirping of the birds hopping from branch to branch in the trees. The world was still there.

"I should check the bumper," she said.

"Don't get out," Faran said, his voice tense. "Not yet. Drive slowly until we get someplace where we can turn around and go back the way we came."

Spooked again, she inched the car forward, looking for a wider spot and wishing she could see more than a few car lengths ahead. She cautiously rounded a fork in the road. Tall poplars framed both sides of the avenue, turning the late winter shadows to a purplish blue.

"There," Faran said, pointing. He indicated a dirt lane that led through an old arched wooden gate in a high fence. Judging by the thick growth of grapevines shrouding the gate, it probably went to one of the local wineries. "Careful, though, visibility sucks."

She slowed, thinking she'd drive past and then back into the lane to turn around. It would take good aim, but the Peugeot was nimble. Even though she was on high alert, she didn't see the dark gray sedan speed out of the gate until it was too late.

With a yell, Lexie slammed on the brakes, swerving the car to the side. It was the only thing that saved them. The Peugeot skidded and slid, finally bumping to a stop.

A horrible noise followed, like a giant pop can crunching in an ogre's fist. That had to be the other car.

Lexie sat frozen, hands clenched around the steering wheel. Breath came in short, sharp gasps, her pulse pounding in her throat. At first she felt nothing, just a remote sort of panic. How bad was the damage? Was she hurt? Faran? What about the other driver?

The other driver had turned and waited to ram them on purpose. Why? Her vision focused and found the sedan. It had crumpled against one of the poplars, which was now leaning at a dangerous angle. The motor was silent, the door open and a man sprawled out of the driver's side.

"Oh, God!" she breathed.

Faran reached over and killed the motor of the Peugeot. "Are you okay?"

Lexie made a mental check of her limbs. "Yeah."

"Stay here." He opened the door and slid out, drawing a gun from beneath his coat.

Lexie watched him prowl toward the other car. She managed to wait five seconds before she followed. Her door jammed on the uneven ground, but she wriggled out, sucking in air as if she'd been drowning. As she stood, the smell of dust and gasoline assaulted her, and then she fell against the Peugeot, her knees weak with shock.

Faran circled the driver, gun pointed at the downed man's head.

Lexie drew in a slow, shaking breath. Her mind raced as she forced herself forward a step, eyeing the driver. His face wasn't visible, and he was wearing a plain black suit that told her nothing about his identity. It looked as if he was alone in the car.

Who was this guy? Her fear was draining away, pushed out by a rising anger. She'd been dragged out of her bed, questioned, locked up and now run off the road. If the driver hadn't been flat on the ground already, she was furious enough to put him there. She marched toward the sedan, wanting answers.

Faran kicked a stone toward the unconscious man. The prone figure didn't flinch. "Take the gun and cover him," he said to Lexie. "I'll check for a pulse."

"I hate guns." And she was in no mood to take orders. Despite Faran's protest, Lexie came forward and crouched, pressing her fingers to the man's neck. She gasped and yanked her hand away. "He's icy cold!"

His gun still aimed at the man's skull, Faran bent and felt for himself. His mouth flattened into a grim line. "This one's been dead awhile. No wonder his driving sucked."

"Is he one of yours?" Lexie asked in a tight voice.

"I don't recognize him," Faran replied. "Besides, he followed us from the palace. Vampires are banned from there now and, in case you hadn't noticed, it's broad daylight. Not even the old ones like moving around in full sun. This one has a tan."

"Are you saying he's not a vampire? Then what is he, a zombie?"

"He doesn't smell bad enough." Faran holstered his gun. "Stand back while I turn him over."

This time Lexie didn't argue, and she retreated a step. The countryside fell eerily silent. Only the ping of the cooling engines interrupted the shushing breeze. "Why do you think he followed us?"

"That depends on who he's working for." Faran grabbed the man's hip and shoulder and flipped him so that he was faceup. The limbs splayed lifelessly. Faran gave him a critical look, then bent and peeled back his upper lip. There were no fangs. "Not a vampire for sure. Let's look for a name."

"I'll check his pockets," Lexie said. "You take the car."

Faran raised an eyebrow, but left her to it. Caution and curiosity warred inside Lexie. She folded her arms, fingers curling into fists as she knelt beside the man. There was something compelling about the still form, which was why she wanted to be the one to check him over. Maybe it was because she finally had the upper hand in this bizarre chain of events. Maybe it was because she felt as though she was on the brink of an understanding she couldn't define. The guy was weirdly familiar. Not his face but…

She gave up trying to capture the thought and got to work. Gingerly, she reached over and pulled his wallet from his pants pocket, snagging a wrapper for salted peanuts along with it. He must have been a pack rat, because the wallet was stuffed with more wrappers and receipts. There was a Vidonese driver's license showing the same bland, round, brown-haired face.

"His name is Serge Gillon and he's thirty-two," she said.

Faran looked up from searching through the sedan. "Probably fake but it's a start."

Out of force of habit, Lexie pulled out her phone and snapped pictures of Gillon, the cars and the scene. She knew she'd forget half the detail any other way. She pocketed her phone again and tried to stuff the wallet back into his jacket pocket. A crumpled snack food bag blocked the way—apparently Gillon liked salty treats. She tossed that aside and tried again. As she reached into the satin lining of the pocket one more time, her fingers brushed something cold and metallic. With a sudden leap of suspicion, she grasped the metal object and plucked it free.

"Faran!" Her brain stalled as she gaped at Amelie's ring. Dumbfounded, she staggered to her feet, holding it up to the sunlight. The rubies sparkled like fresh blood. She slid the band over her finger, afraid she'd drop it otherwise.

Faran stepped over Gillon's body and grasped her

hand, angling it to see the ring better. There was a flash of bloodred fire. "That's the ring, all right. There can't be two sets of rubies like that." They stood like that for a long moment, hand in hand but for all the wrong reasons.

Finally, Faran spoke again. "Who was this guy and why did he have the ring?"

Lexie didn't have a chance to reply. With a sudden grunting roar, Gillon surged from the dirt and grabbed Faran from behind. Faran's eyes widened with surprise, but he twisted in the dead man's grasp and grappled with him. With a snarl, Faran rammed Gillon against the tree with enough force that Lexie heard a crunch of splintering wood. It would have knocked an ordinary human senseless, but Gillon just wrapped his hands around Faran's throat and started to squeeze.

Lexie had no weapon, so she dove for the cars to find one. The trunk of the sedan had popped open in the crash so she scrabbled inside, peeling up the carpet and grabbing the tire iron. She took a two-handed grip and whirled to face the two men.

Whatever Gillon was, he was as powerful as a werewolf. Faran was wrestling himself free of the choke hold, but it was taking all his strength. Gillon had him against the tree now, and Faran's hands were on the man's shoulders, holding him off. A fierce, feral snarling came from the combatants, but Lexie could not be sure which one was making the sound.

Faran's foot snaked out, hooking Gillon's knee. Gillon stumbled and Faran pounced, but the dead man kicked, launching Faran through the air. With animal grace, Faran twisted in the air, landing on all fours. Rocks and leaves skidded from beneath his feet, but he was up in an instant, braced for the next attack.

It came with terrible ferocity. Gillon bounded through

the air, arms and legs arched the way a leaping spider splays its legs. His lips drew back from his teeth in a savage rictus. He might not have had fangs, but it was no less threatening.

But just as he leaped, Lexie skidded forward and swung the tire iron, putting all the weight of her body into the motion. It caught Gillon right in the ribs with a loud crack. For a moment, she thought the sound was her shoulder joints separating as the force of the impact shuddered all the way to her spine. But then Gillon seemed to fold in midair, ripping the iron from her hands as he fell.

That gave Faran all the time he needed to draw his weapon. The instant Gillon hit the ground, Faran fired two shots into his skull. The sound tore through Lexie, but that was not what shocked her most.

Gillon's head exploded. Instantly, an acid smell hit Lexie's senses, making her cough. Through stinging eyes, she could see the shadow of his bones appear through his flesh. As she blinked, the shadow grew darker, seeming to pulse from behind skin that grew more and more translucent. His hands and the remnants of his face—anywhere flesh showed from beneath his clothes—quivered like something made of gelatin. And then, with a sickening slurp, Gillon's flesh oozed away into a glistening, yellowish puddle. A moment later, bones, clothing and even Faran's bullets dissolved in an ashy smoke.

"That's new," Faran said, his voice brittle with disgust.

Lexie's lips moved in a silent curse. She took a step toward Faran. His arm circled her waist and pulled her away from the smoking ruin. He'd gone pale, but his hand was firm and warm against her. They stopped a few yards away, Lexie stumbling against Faran. She leaned into him, grateful for the solid wall of his body. Lexie wanted to bury her face against him like a child and wish the world away, but instead she simply stood with her head bowed, her back against his chest. His support, at least, was something she could accept.

For that instant, she could almost believe that everything would be all right. They'd stopped fighting each other and conquered a common enemy. But now her nerves were jittering, flooding every muscle with the need to move. She curled her fingers, nails biting into the palms of her hands. It was as if a spring was overwound inside her and fighting that energy would only make her crack.

In the distance, Lexie heard the wail of distant sirens. Had somebody on one of the nearby farms heard the gunshots? "Do you think that's the police? Are they coming for us?"

"Do you feel like trusting our luck?" Faran replied in a weary tone.

She looked at the crumpled car, the stinking smear on the ground where Gillon had been, and at the glittering—stolen—rubies on her hand. Even with no actual dead body, there was no way this would end well.

Her hand gripped Faran's. "You know how I like to run?"

Pressed against him, she felt as much as heard his reply. "Yup. I'm right behind you. Let's get out of here."

Chapter 7

Faran studied the image of Serge Gillon on Lexie's phone, anger prickling his skin. "Now that I look at him again—when he's not strangling me—I do recognize him. That's one of the guards who chased me last night. He has to be connected with the Vidonese."

They were sitting on a bench in one of the back streets near the palace, counting on the afternoon shadows to hide their dirt-streaked clothes. Both of them had needed a moment to regroup. Faran's side ached; the wound had reopened during the fight. They'd driven back in the Peugeot, this time with Faran at the wheel. He'd taken some questionable goat paths to avoid the emergency vehicles summoned by the gunshots, much to the distress of the vehicle's paint job. But it wasn't as though the car didn't already need repairs after being run off the road, and a mechanic's bill was the least of their worries.

Lexie's face was wan, making the scattered freckles

stand out along her cheekbones. For an instant, Faran thought she might throw up. "Are you all right?" he asked.

She sat back, swallowing hard. "I don't deal well with violence."

"I know."

Lexie shook herself, visibly sliding her tough-girl mask back into place. "I don't suppose anybody does."

Faran shrugged. "No one is supposed to."

"But you're used to it?"

"No one likes an emo werewolf." He gave her a bitter smile. "I'm one of those things that go bump in the night, remember?"

She turned a shade paler, licking her lips. "I do. You're good at violence when you need to be."

"Yeah, well, it comes with the package." Sadness burned like silver.

Her mouth tightened. "Why do you think Gillon was after us? To get to you?"

Faran dragged his brain back to the problem in front of them. "Maybe. It would be flattering to have my own personal assassin. How thoughtless of me to break him so soon."

She heaved a sigh. "So what do we do next?"

"I think we need to return the ring, and then you need to get out of Dodge. Whether it was me he was after or not, it's not safe for you here."

She ducked her head, but then raised it slowly, her hazel eyes dark with something he couldn't name. "You're getting rid of me?"

Faran couldn't stop a wry smile—even though his insides lurched. "I don't know what that thing was back there. I'd rather you were far away right now."

"Do I get a choice?"

But you're so good at walking away. Why stop now?

Faran mentally slapped himself. He might be angry, but he had to be fair. As little as she hated violence, Lexie had fought bravely that day, as coolheaded as any Company warrior. Whatever else, she was good in a crisis—and with a tire iron. "Do you want to stay?"

Her fingers twisted in her lap. "Will it help if I do?"

Faran could see the reluctance in the set of her mouth, but there was also determination there. Lexie clearly wanted to do the right thing, and he had to respect that. "One step at a time. We should deal with the ring right away. The sooner it's back with Amelie, the better."

"Okay," she said, shifting impatiently. "Then let's go."

They rose from the bench and began walking. Pigeons fluttered away from their feet as they stepped off the curb and took a cobbled alleyway between bookstores and an antiques emporium. Faran cast a glance around, memorizing faces. He wasn't going to let his guard down again.

Lexie hunched her shoulders, slowing to a stop. "I need to see Valois," she said in a low voice. "His men seized my camera equipment."

"Why?" He stopped as well, turning to face her.

"I think they assumed the ring was hidden inside."

Faran winced. Although there were other, more pressing dangers than damage to her cameras, Lexie was madly protective of her equipment. Small wonder, since some of it was insanely expensive. "Once your name is cleared, there's no reason for Valois to keep your things. Is there any danger they'll erase the photos you've taken?"

"No," she said, sounding relieved for the first time. "There are too many publications who'd pay top dollar for pictures of this wedding. I've been keeping the memory cards with me."

People were starting to notice them standing there, deep in conversation. He urged her forward with a hand on her back. She shivered slightly, and he released her. His old anger—the one that resented her fear of the wolf—flared up, but he forced himself to let it go. They'd fought together. They were solving problems. That had to suffice for now.

But his old feelings refused to be silenced. This uneasy truce would never be enough. He loved her.

And yet she'd left with no more than a note scribbled with two words: *I'm sorry.* There was no reason to think anything would ever be different.

Lexie hugged herself, looking miserable. "If Valois suspects us already, if we just walk into the palace and hand the ring over, won't they think we took it?"

"You're asking for my advice?"

"I'm asking for your help. The prince and princess know you and they trust the Company. I'm asking you to go with me and help me clear my name." She brushed her hair back in a gesture he knew all too well. "I have no right to, but I am."

Faran cleared his throat. He should have been happy, or vindicated, but what he felt was too complicated for that. He'd assumed he'd go with her, but as usual Lexie had been planning on her own. She'd never thought like part of a couple. "Of course," he kept his voice cool. "I owe you for last night. It's the least I can do."

"Okay." Lexie's eyes held something almost like regret. She parted her lips to speak, but then pressed them tightly together. The clouds had thinned and the winter sun washed her in a clean white light that recalled another moment long ago.

She had stood in the middle of their Paris apartment, wearing nothing but a wispy white silk robe. The late morning sun had turned her long waves of red hair to molten gold. He'd spent the night tangling it with their lovemaking, and it had been wild as a fairy woman's locks. At that moment, he'd decided she was the one love he'd want forever.

The whole thing had been a terrible idea—a foolish, romantic, awful idea that had proved how young he was, despite all his years on the street. He'd been a grubby urchin clutching at a work of art.

He sucked in his breath, forcing the memory away, but the emotion lingered. "Let's get this over with." It came out almost as a growl.

She gave him a startled look, but he ignored it. He'd have to ignore everything about her if he didn't want to go mad. He couldn't bring back the past, and why would he? It had fallen apart in his hands.

This is just business.

Returning the ring right away meant getting a private audience with Princess Amelie on short notice. Since Chloe was in constant communication with Amelie and her staff about the wedding, she was the logical one to help. Chloe's schedule made her hard to reach, but by the time they reached the palace, she'd finally returned Lexie's call.

"I'll see what I can do," Chloe said briskly, back in wedding-wrangler mode. "You and Faran stand by."

"Stand by?" Lexie sighed, putting her phone away. She didn't want to wait. She wanted desperately to thrust the ring at Amelie and then jump on a plane. "That requires doing something with ourselves in the meantime. Without being arrested again."

"I can't see how we can possibly manage," Faran replied in a dry tone. "Perhaps if I stand very still. Oh, wait. That's loitering."

"With you it's more like looming."

He gave her a wounded look that seemed too real. "I don't loom."

Barely an hour ago, Lexie had seen him twist in the air and land like a cat. The memory of it still made her shiver. "Lurking, then. You've got to stipulate to the occasional lurk."

"I'll plead you down to hovering with intent."

He was hiding behind jokes—and that had always driven her crazy. Yet now it was weirdly comforting. Everything was in turmoil, but Faran remained stubbornly who he was.

They waited for Chloe in the Queen's Gallery, which was a long, wide hallway that stretched from one side of the palace to the other. The walls were molded plaster, the ceilings high and painted with designs of cherubs and clouds. Hung with selections from the royal family's considerable art collection, it was one of the attractions open to the public. Normally it would have been packed, but there were no tourists that day, since security was on high alert. They had the place to themselves.

It was the first time Lexie had been able to see the pictures without being elbowed by the crowd and, despite her mood, their beauty pulled her in. She wandered slowly from one canvas to the next, so lost in the study of colors and textures that she almost forgot everything else. Art was an almost physical pleasure for her, the sight of it as tangible to her a bubble bath or silk against her skin. It was one of the few things that could make her stay still.

And it mercifully stopped the image of the melting *thing* in the woods from replaying on an endless loop through her mind, though nothing drowned out her hyperawareness of Faran's prowling, restless presence.

She stopped before a portrait of a rugged young cavalier sprawled in an armchair, dangling a broad-brimmed hat in one hand, the feather sweeping the floor. His eyes were half-closed, as if he was amused and bored and maybe a little drunk. He might have been one of the three musketeers. Strangely, there was no card to identify either the subject or the artist.

"He looks familiar," Lexie said. "I know it's not possible, but I could swear I'd met him."

Faran had finally sat on a bench, his hand pressed to his ribs as if his wound hurt. "Take away the moustache and beard."

She squinted, studying the shape of the eyes and nose. "He looks a lot like Chloe's uncle." Chloe had lived with Jack Anderson after her parents died, and Lexie had been to her house plenty of times during their college years. Jack had been funny, dashing and kind. Of course, as a vampire hundreds of years old, Jack was an ancestor rather than an actual uncle—not that either girl had known it at the time.

"Jack lived in Marcari in the old days. He was one of the king's favorite companions," said Faran.

Lexie let out her breath with a whoosh of surprise. "Of course."

Unfortunately, he'd been burned to death in a car crash not all that long ago. A really hot fire was one of the few ways to kill a vampire—even the Horseman named Death.

"He used to call me Little Red," said Lexie. "He thought I was skinny and kept trying to feed me whenever I visited Chloe."

Faran rose to stand beside her. His mouth turned down in a rare show of emotion and was silent so long she wondered if he'd say anything more. When he did, his tone was wry. "He arrested me when I was sixteen and gave me a choice to clean up my act or else. He never said what that *or else* was, but I was scared enough that I listened. Jack could be…daunting."

Arrested? So that was the end of the cat burglar story! "He must have been something to impress a sixteen-year-old."

Faran gave a lopsided smile. "I thought he was a stuck-up corpse with delusions of social reform. I thought he was torturing me."

"Why?"

"He made me go to school—I had to do both academics and a trade. Pure hell. It was a long time before I appreciated any of what he did."

Lexie had never heard any of this before. The moment felt rare and easily lost, as if she held a feather that would fly away if she so much as breathed the wrong way. "Is that how you got your chef's papers?"

Faran cast her a sidelong look, his blue eyes bright. "Yup. I had to work at an honest job for years before he let me near the spy game. He made me learn discipline. Horrible man. He probably saved my life."

"And you learned to make those crispy shrimp things. You know, the ones with lemon."

"You remember those?" A flash of pride flickered and was gone almost before she caught it.

"Uh-huh." Lexie was adrift in memory and salivating just a little. "You turned out okay."

Given their history, it was the wrong thing to say. His back stiff, Faran turned away from the portrait of his mentor. "I manage functional adulthood at least once a week."

"And the rest of the time?"

His eyes scanned the ceiling. "Same old stuff. I save the world. Day in. Day out. It's a living."

"Does it really need that much saving?"

"Look around. You see paintings, but my mind goes automatically to how I could crack the security system. I know the kind of people out there because I've been one of them."

Lexie was speechless. Coolly, Faran checked his phone. "Still nothing from Chloe."

Confession time was over. Disappointment itched. Lexie wanted to say something to smooth the sharp edges in his tone, but she was fresh out of clever words.

Any answer she might have made was drowned out by a burst of noisy conversation echoing off the gallery walls. A gaggle of young men in tennis whites burst through a side door that led into the private part of the palace. The way they walked—as if they owned the world and everyone in it—made Lexie tense. They reminded her too much of her brother, Justin, and her body gathered itself for flight. As if he sensed her apprehension, Faran closed the gap between them until he was almost touching her shoulder.

The man in the lead was Prince Leo, looking in surprisingly good spirits despite the events of last night. "Why, it's the heavenly Ms. Haven," he said, changing course in her direction.

She had to admit Prince Leo looked good in whites, the crisp, bright clothes showing off his dark coloring. He had the same classic good looks as his brother, but they were muted—as was his popularity and his talent in school and on the playing field. It was as if he got a smaller helping of everything than the heir of Vidon.

Leo stopped and gave Lexie a slight, gentlemanly bow. "I trust you are recovered after the frights of last night."

Both Lexie and Faran returned his bow with respectful nods. "I am, my lord," she said.

"I am delighted to hear it." Ignoring Faran, he picked up her hand and pressed a kiss to her knuckles. Lexie thanked her personal angels that she'd taken off the ring and put it in her pocket.

"I am an admirer of your work," said the prince, doing

a reasonable smolder with his dark eyes. "I would like you to take my portrait while I'm here for the wedding."

Lexie tugged at her hand, wanting to keep things professional. "That's very kind of you. I'd be honored."

A look of satisfaction crossed the prince's features. "Perhaps we could combine dinner with our session, make an evening of it. There is no harm in matching a little pleasure with business."

Leo was still holding her hand. She drew it away. He reached for it again.

Faran cleared his throat.

Prince Leo looked at him coolly. "And you are?"

"Faran Kenyon, Your Royal Highness." He bowed slightly, but with grace. It showed the required level of respect, but not one bit more.

Lexie slipped her contested hand around Faran's arm. "My husband," she said brightly. She felt Faran's muscles tense as if he braced for a blow, but he didn't deny it.

Leo's expression puckered, as if he'd swallowed a bug. "I had no idea."

Neither had Lexie until that moment, but Chloe's fiction suddenly seemed ideal. Faran drew himself up to his full six and a half feet. He did loom marvelously well.

Prince Leo's mouth curved into the facsimile of a smile. "Well then," he said. "We'll be in touch."

"I'll be happy to set up a shoot," Faran said pleasantly, although his tone spoke more of semiautomatics than shutter speeds.

Giving Faran a murderous look, Leo walked back to his friends and picked a ball from one of their sports bags. He tossed it in the air, catching it. "Good to know who's qualified to handle the delicate equipment."

Lexie flinched at the double meaning.

"Now, I think I need to go take a shower." Leo gave

a wicked grin and sent the ball speeding toward Faran. "Ball's in your court."

Quicker than Lexie could see, Faran snatched it out of the air just as it was about to smash into Jack's portrait. A low rumble came from Faran's throat, but by then the tennis players were too far away to hear.

But Lexie heard, and it spooked her. She stepped away from Faran, suddenly wanting distance between them again.

"Are you going to take Leo up on his job offer?" Faran asked with deceptive smoothness.

"I don't know," she said. "But don't worry, I'm used to keeping clients in line."

His eyes glittered. The color didn't change from their startling blue, but she could glimpse the wolf just beneath the surface. The look said she was his territory to guard. "He's slime. The dinner date is out of the question."

His tone suffocated her, pushing every button. She wasn't putting up with orders, not even from a wolf. "Now you sound like a husband."

"Heaven forbid." Faran stuffed his hands in his pockets and began striding away.

Lexie cursed under her breath, remembering the proposal that never was. She had no idea where Faran was going, except that it was away from her. "Get over it. Leo was just playing games."

He kept walking.

She folded her arms. "And calm down. We've been pretending to be husband and wife for five minutes, and already we need counseling."

Faran spun to face her. Lexie's stomach dropped, but this time it wasn't out of fear. He was yards away, but she could see emotion in every line of his body. There wasn't just possession there, but feral desire. He'd wanted her before—lustily, heartily—but now she realized that he'd been showing only a tenth of what he felt. That knowledge rang through her like a tolling bell.

She felt the tug of his need deep in her belly, and heat pooled inside her. He'd walked away from her last night. He'd tried just now. It couldn't happen again. *But wanting him back doesn't change what he is.*

The wolf terrified her, but the intensity she saw in the man before her was even more formidable. She was most comfortable dancing on the surface of life, hopping a plane before she had the chance to set down roots. That was her nature—restless, yearning, never knowing what it was that drove her like a leaf in the wind. Faran demanded more from her, and she'd never known how to give it.

Wolves mate for life.

That scared her every bit as much as the fangs.

Chapter 8

Lexie looked shell-shocked. Faran knew the expression—
he'd seen it plenty of times from plenty of people when he'd
let the wolf peek out. That was why Faran tried to keep
the world at a distance with an easygoing smile and quick
wit. The only one who'd never flinched away had been
Jack, but he was gone. Lexie was right there, looking as
if she'd just encountered a nightmare. *Way to go, wolf boy.*

Mercifully, their summons to Princess Amelie's quarters came before the situation spiraled any closer to the
drain. The princess's apartments turned out to be spacious,
decorated in gold and burgundy. Glass doors opened onto
a balcony with a view of the sea.

Private was a relative term when it came to the court,
but Amelie had dismissed everyone but herself and Prince
Kyle. He and Lexie were alone with two members of the
royalty. All at once Faran's role as lifeline to the exiled
Company felt real.

"What happened to you two?" asked Princess Amelie. "You look like you've been rolling in the dirt." The princess looked tired, as if last night's debacle had sapped her energy. She was seated at one end of a dainty sofa, her attention on Prince Kyle, who paced near the balcony doors.

"My apologies for our appearance, Your Royal Highness," said Faran. "We felt it was most important to come here directly. I trust you'll understand once you've heard what we have to say."

"Which is what?" Kyle asked. There were dark circles beneath his eyes. "I've been hearing odd reports from Captain Valois. A car chase. Gunshots. A wreck found in the woods. It seems your rental car appeared at a local garage, Ms. Haven, rather the worse for wear."

Lexie colored. "It's been an eventful day, my lord."

"I think you'd better tell us the whole story from the beginning."

Lexie did, starting with her interview with Valois and finishing with the crash and how she'd found the ring. Faran added a word here and there, but Lexie's account was thorough. Before she got to the fight with Gillon, however, she searched in her pocket and pulled out the wedding band. The princess took it with a cry of surprise.

Kyle drew near, a crease between the dark line of his brows. "I feared we would never see the rubies of Vidon again. You say you found this on the dead man?"

"I did, Your Highness. This is his face." She took out her cell phone and showed him the picture.

Kyle looked at the image, and frowned harder. "What happened to his body? None was found at the scene of the wreck."

Faran and Lexie exchanged a look. Faran licked his lips. "He melted."

Kyle blinked. "He what?"

"It was like…" Faran groped for a comparison. "Do you ever watch late-night horror movies, my lord?"

The prince raised an eyebrow. "Not since I was thirteen."

"I do," replied Amelie.

"You do?" Kyle asked in surprise.

The princess gave a delicate shrug. "My bodyguards are vampires. They like mocking the dialogue."

"Um." Kyle rubbed his forehead and returned his attention to Faran. "Explain exactly what happened with this melting man."

Faran did his best. "I fully confess that I shot him, Your Highness. Lexie had no part in that."

"I just clubbed him with a tire iron," she said helpfully.

"Very well." Clearly agitated, Kyle returned to his post by the balcony doors. "You defended yourselves and you retrieved the stolen ring. I would ask no less of any agents I hired in my name, or in that of my betrothed. You need not fear reprisals for what you have done today."

Faran exhaled silently, but with heartfelt relief. Although the Company operated with considerable latitude, he was taking nothing for granted.

"But who is this Gillon?" Amelie asked. "What was he doing with the ring and why was he following you?"

"He was one of the men who chased me last night," Faran replied. "Though why he had the ring, I don't know."

"He was a Knight of Vidon?" Amelie asked, her voice tense. "A slayer?"

"It seems so," Faran agreed.

"I don't know what to make of that," said Kyle. "The Knights are loyal to the old ways and often I disagree with them. But they would hardly hire a—whatever he was. They object to all things supernatural."

"My lord, in the past the Knights of Vidon have dabbled in strange scientific experiments," Faran put in. "I've seen the results."

"That element was purged from their ranks," Kyle said firmly. "In all likelihood, Gillon, or whoever hired him, stole the ring because of its value, or to create complications that might upset our wedding plans. Not everyone wants peace between our nations."

"Couldn't it also have been a crime of opportunity?" Amelie added. "The ring was unattended for a moment, so he took it."

Kyle gave her a grim smile, but his eyes were soft when he regarded her. "Perhaps, although you must admit the miscommunication about the Company's withdrawal from the palace caused a perfect distraction. That smacks of planning to me."

"But who is behind this?" Amelie asked, her voice cracking. "Too much is going on that I don't understand. The ring is just the start of it. Why has the Company been sent away? Why was this Gillon following you? And what manner of creature was he?"

They all fell silent for a moment. The princess had neatly summed up their questions. The two people who might have had real answers—the kings of Marcari and Vidon—had been conspicuously absent for days. Kyle sat beside his betrothed and gently took her hand. His look, the language of his gesture said everything about how deeply he cared for her. "I don't know, either, but we'll get to the bottom of it."

"That's my job," Faran said. "If I am the Company's man on the inside, I have to figure this out."

"Agreed," said Amelie, "I will tell Valois that you have found and returned the ring and that Ms. Haven's name is cleared. That is a good start."

Faran stole a glance at Lexie, who sat with her long,

thin fingers laced together in her lap. Her wrists were so slender, they looked like the bones of a songbird. The thought of someone threatening her brought a harsh ache to his chest. "Until we know what is going on, Lexie should leave Marcari."

Lexie turned, her hazel eyes sharp. "Not so fast. I think I'd like to stay."

Faran shook his head. "You're in the clear. There's nothing more you need to do here."

Amelie shot him a quelling look. "A lady speaks for herself."

He nearly choked on the need to object, but his job with the Company demanded obedience. "Yes, Your Highness."

Amelie lifted her chin. "Where are your rooms, Ms. Haven?"

"They are in the adjoining wing, my lady."

"And, of course, you are staying there also, as you are her husband," Amelie said to Faran. Her eyebrows arched, as if daring him to argue. "I've heard about your virtual marriage of convenience. Chloe filled me in. I think it is quite a brilliant strategy."

Lexie shot Faran a glance filled with alarm. The words *husband* and *marriage* sliced through Faran, like a blade so sharp one barely saw the cut. He cleared his throat. "I have rooms at the Company Headquarters."

"Outside the city? That is too far, if you are here to keep watch over us," Amelie said with a wave of her hand. "You must stay in the palace. I expect it, and Captain Valois expects you to be with your wife."

Sleeping in the same suite of rooms as Lexie without sleeping *with* Lexie—that would be torture. "My lady, you're going to tell him she's innocent," Faran reminded the princess.

But Amelie had her mind made up. "He is an old bloodhound and will have lingering doubts. Let us keep him calm and quiet. And this way, you will be there to watch over my prized wedding photographer. Use that protective instinct of yours. Whatever else is happening, I am still getting married, and I need her in one piece."

The princess unhooked her necklace, strung her wedding ring over the chain and fastened it once more around her slim neck. "And doubling up is just as well, as every last room already has a guest. The palace is packed to overflowing."

"Your Highness…" Lexie began in a reasonable tone.

Kyle cast a cautious look Lexie's way, and then to Faran. "You are, of course, free to refuse such an imposition. We will honor your choice without question."

Which was nonsense, at least for Faran. He worked for the Company, and the Company worked for Amelie's father. He would have to have a monumental reason to do anything but comply. That was just business.

It was all up to Lexie, who was biting her lip in a most distracting fashion. He wanted to kiss her, but he wasn't sure he could stop with just a taste of her mouth. He was even less sure what he wanted her answer to be.

Some dangers had nothing to do with magic or bullets.

"Why did we agree to this again?" Lexie asked unhappily. She looked around in search of stray bras and other items too personal for comfort, and then snatched up a thong from the floor where one of Valois's men had scattered it during that morning's search.

They were standing in the front room of her tiny suite. It was little bigger than a hotel room, with a small sitting area, a bedroom and a cramped bathroom. A sash window overlooked the south side of the palace grounds. The decor looked like a royal rummage sale—old, substantial and mismatched. The photographic equipment she'd rescued from Valois's clutches was everywhere.

"We agreed because Amelie is a princess. She has that royal way of making everything she says sound utterly reasonable," Faran answered, his voice flat with stress. He looked stranded in the middle of the floor, clearly unsure about settling in. "I'll leave if you change your mind."

Lexie almost jumped on that, but squashed the impulse. They had a mystery to solve, and their best chance was to work together. Back in the princess's apartments, this seemed like the perfect solution. Now she wasn't so sure.

With a sigh, he sank onto the edge of the sofa. "I'll think of something to tell her. Do my best to stay out of the dungeon. Do you suppose they have an actual iron maiden?"

Lexie folded her arms, needing something to shield her vulnerable parts. "Somewhere in all that are you saying you don't mind sleeping here?"

He gave her a lopsided smile that looked as tired as she felt. "I don't know. Do you? What *are* we doing here? Am I the gentleman or the scoundrel in this script?" An awkward silence followed. Faran regarded her with a long-suffering air.

"We're solving a case," Lexie said at last. In truth, she had no idea what she was doing. "We need rules."

"Oh?"

"I get the bedroom. You get this room. There's a door in between."

Eyes unreadable, he waved an arm at the mess that stretched over the coffee table, couch and half the floor. "What room do your cameras get?"

She shrugged. "You're the photography assistant. Don't you want to get to know them up close and personal?"

His expression drew a line in the sand. "I think the

tripods and I will get along just fine without sleeping together on the couch."

"Right."

He rose. "I need to get some clothes. I'll be back in a while. Lock the door."

"I'll, um, clean up some of my stuff and make room." She palmed her face. "I can't believe we're doing this."

Faran smiled a little sadly. "This will be okay. Neither of us is an impulsive kid anymore."

Lexie didn't buy that. In that moment, she might have been twelve, unsure and awkward. What did it matter if she photographed fashion models and princesses and slept in a palace? She was still faced with a werewolf sleeping on her sofa. One who looked impossibly gorgeous.

She wanted to kiss him—for starters. She had to be honest, at least with herself. When she'd agreed to Amelie's plan, her motives had been utterly fuddled.

Dusk was falling, and the room was unlit. Everything had soft edges, like a photo that had bleached with age. She never understood why twilight made everything seem quiet. Light had nothing to do with sound, and yet a hush fell over the room.

She could feel the warmth from Faran's body, a balm of heat against her weariness. "You realize that today I've been arrested, interrogated, in a car chase, had a royal audience and been unofficially married to my old boyfriend?"

"I love chasing cars," Faran said mildly. "That part was fun."

She looked down, chuckling even as she ached with exhaustion. "How did we end up here?"

He put a finger under her chin, lifting her face. He kissed her forehead gently, the lightest brush of his lips against her skin. "Like I said, we'll be okay. And now I have to go get my stuff."

Okay wasn't good enough. The warmth, his gentleness, was too tempting and familiar. Lexie leaned forward, catching his mouth with hers. He flinched with surprise, but she clutched his lapels, not letting him back away.

He tasted just like she remembered, male and spicy and unique. She'd been starving for him ever since she'd seen him sitting on the garden wall. She ran her hands through his hair, feeling the rough thickness of it between her fingers, drawing him down for more.

His hands went to her waist, holding her as tenderly as if she was a bird. His mouth moved against hers, kissing her back, but it was guarded. The Faran she'd known had thrown himself into lovemaking the way other men jumped out of a plane—with a kind of determined recklessness. This wasn't the same.

She drew away, grateful and chagrined at once. "I'm sorry."

"Don't apologize," he said. "I enjoyed that. But I don't know where it falls in with the rules."

There was no rancor in his voice, just a caution that matched her own. "Consider it a time-out."

He nodded slowly. "Is that likely to happen more than just this once?"

"I don't know." She wanted to give in to the pounding heat inside her, but wasn't sure she knew how anymore. She'd seen what he really was—a vision of violence.

She needed to know that he'd stay on his side of the lines. Regardless of what had just happened, she wasn't ready to let him past. Not even close. *And yet you're not willing to let him walk away.*

"You realize I'm a little confused?" he said as if reading her mind. His voice was mild, but he couldn't entirely hide the heat of emotion beneath all that control.

"You're angry."

"I'm tired. What am I to you? Monster? Lover? Did I miss a memo?"

"I know, I know," she said softly, tears crowding at the back of her throat. "I don't think this is going to be as easy as saying we're all adults here."

Faran touched her cheek, the gesture gentle but not forgiving. "Let me know when you make up your mind."

Lexie drew back with a quick inhale of breath, but there were no words. He was right. She didn't know what she wanted from him anymore.

And so he left. Again.

Chapter 9

Faran was still thinking about the kiss when he returned with a backpack full of clothes. He'd been delayed at the Company Headquarters—like any bureaucracy, they wanted paperwork and explanations—and it was past midnight when he got back.

The night was clear and cool, and he took his time walking through the gardens to one of the side entrances closer to Lexie's rooms. Faran liked action more than reflection, hands down. Still, he had to figure out what he was doing with Lexie. For a long time he'd believed the end of their story was just that. But now she was acting as if she wanted more, and that set off a host of warning bells.

It also forced him to be honest.

Back in Paris, Lexie had been halfway out the door long before he'd introduced her to his four-footed alter ego. She had trust issues, especially when it came to men— something he guessed came from her family background, although she would never talk about it. For some reason, he'd thought revealing the wolf would prove she could count on him. He could protect her in ways no other man could.

Apparently that was the wrong move. Apparently he'd seen everything through the filter of his own needs and not taken the time to discover hers.

And yet something had changed. Was that scene in her bedroom tonight a sign that Lexie wanted him after all? Maybe. Or maybe he'd hung out with vampires too long and getting to work in daylight for once was making him unreasonably optimistic. Either way, if he wanted a happy ending to this drama, he'd have to go carefully.

Something moved in the shadows ahead.

Reflex made Faran duck close to the palace wall. He took in a long breath, steadying the sudden thrum of excitement along his nerves. He was on the south side of the grounds, not far from Lexie's room. A figure in dark clothing was standing about ten feet from the wall, his face tilted toward the windows above. Faran drew into deeper shadow, suspicion prickling the back of his neck. Whoever it was knew enough to avoid the patches of light spilling out from the windows, which made his features hard to make out.

Faran waited, perfectly still, barely breathing. Werewolves weren't psychic, but they had extremely good senses. He listened for the telltale squeak of leather and cloth that marked the rhythmic step of the palace patrols, but heard nothing. They should have been by every few minutes, but the minutes slid past with no one else entering or leaving the south lawn. Meanwhile, the figure— clearly male by his build—approached the wall, examined the surface judiciously and began to climb.

It was a daring move. Only an expert would attempt the wall without equipment.

A barely audible growl escaped Faran. There were only bad reasons why someone would be heading straight for Lexie's window. This had to end *now*. Faran dropped his pack and ran, shedding his jacket as he went.

The man's head turned toward Faran, and it became clear why his face was hard to see. He was wearing a tan balaclava beneath the hood of his jacket.

"Hey!" Faran cried. "Stop right there."

The man dropped from the wall, landing in an easy crouch, and then sprinted away. Within seconds, he was out of sight. But now Faran was annoyed. There were still no guards in sight—an illuminating fact all on its own— and the figure had chosen one of the few blind spots where the security cameras didn't reach. *Not suspicious at all.*

Faran stopped in the same blind spot and kicked off his sneakers. It took barely seconds to shed the rest of his clothes. Changing to wolf form was more a mental trick than something physical, much like switching to a different language. One moment he was bracing against the chill air and imagining himself in beast form, and then he leaped forward, landing on all four paws.

The world was suddenly alive with scents and sounds he hadn't experienced moments before. The grass was cool and springy beneath the pads of his paws, the wind sweet but for the pungent scent of human sweat. He drew in a deep breath, bunched his muscles and ran after his quarry.

Speed and power came at will, obstacles merely turning the chase into a game. Faran's human half wanted to question and punish, but the wolf in him would get to enjoy the capture. He caught sight of the runner on the other side of an ornamental pond. He had to stop him before he got into the maze—someone could hide in there for hours. Faran sped toward the pond, letting a snarl rip from his chest. The runner looked behind him and gave a cry of surprise.

A normal crook would run. This one stopped.

Alarm sang through Faran's veins as he saw the figure pull a long weapon from underneath his hoodie. Already crouching to spring, Faran sailed across the pond toward him, feeling the sharp pull as his wound tore open. The pain skewed his landing, and paws splashed when he fell short of the other side.

His bungled landing saved him. Faran jerked as a bullet whizzed inches from his nose. There had been no muzzle flash, no crack of the gun. Just a faint pop and whine and a thump in the soft ground—the bullet tearing past right where his skull should have been. Summoning all his speed, Faran burst from the water and disappeared behind the corner of a hedge, heart pounding.

That was no cat burglar's weapon. Whoever this was had killing in mind.

Faran crouched, belly to the ground, and peered beneath the branches of the box hedge. Hot blood was trickling down his side, mixing with the cold pond water dripping from his coat. His quarry was three bounds away, weapon poised. Faran could try for a frontal attack, but he didn't like his chances. The question was whether the man would decide to play hunter himself, or cut his losses and escape.

The figure looked around slowly, but human eyes weren't up to the inky dark near the hedge. "Come on, come on," the man muttered in French. It was hard to tell from two words, but the words sounded more polished than the rough accent of Marcari's streets. It wasn't much, but it was a clue.

Faran forced himself to stop panting, but cocked his ears forward to catch every sound. Cloth rustled as the figure lowered the weapon, then put it away. Feet scuffed the grass as the man turned and jogged toward the main path.

Faran rose silently, trotting behind the man but weaving in and out of the bushes and statuary like a ghost. His side burned, but he ignored the pain. The job ahead wouldn't be long or difficult. All he needed was the chance to take his prey by surprise. The figure reached the main path that led out of the palace grounds and settled into an easy jogger's stride. Faran quickened his pace, knowing there wasn't much time before they reached a populated area where black-ops werewolves couldn't go.

Opportunity came when the path neared the croquet lawn. It was a patch of open ground surrounded by stone benches. The pale strip of the path looped around the corner of the lawn, but like so many, Faran's quarry cut across the grass to save time. Impatient and all too aware they were nearing the traffic-clogged street, Faran burst from cover and bolted, meaning to take the man from behind.

But to Faran's horror, they weren't alone. Shadows and wind direction had played him false. Another figure was rising from one of the stone benches, looking on in blank surprise. It was Maurice, unmistakable in eyeliner and a long caped coat. He yelped in surprise as Faran all but barreled into his feet.

Faran wheeled and raced ahead. Yet the cry had alerted the runner, who veered off course. Faran's next pounce caught nothing but empty air. He gave a disgusted woof and spun to try again, but the prey was gone, vanished around the curve of the path. Faran scrambled forward and stopped with a growl, muscles quivering in frustration. He could see the dazzle of headlights and hear the babble of late-night tourists. The balaclava lay by the side of the path, but there was no one in sight.

Faran mentally recited a litany of curses, some not in any human language.

"Whoa, boy!" said Maurice. "Where are your manners?"

Faran suddenly felt a hand patting his head. As an oversize apex predator, this was not a common occurrence. He turned with an offended whine.

"You shouldn't chase joggers. It's bad karma." The tall, gangly man crouched in front of him.

Faran snorted. Maurice regarded him seriously, elbows braced on his knees. He'd changed his nail polish to silver sparkles and something feathery hung from one ear. "Where do you call home?"

Instinctively, Faran backed away. Home was a complicated puzzle, and Faran had given up trying to solve it long ago. But at least there was a place he was supposed to be. Somewhere he was needed.

With a faint rumble, he spun and loped across the lawn, back toward Lexie.

Lexie was in bed with the door shut when she heard Faran come in. She had her laptop open on the covers and was just starting to download yesterday's images from her camera. She'd known it was Faran just from the way he'd rattled the door handle. There was a rhythm to his movements—footfall and thump and the way the room key hit the table—that was unmistakably his. Faran always sounded like a man in a hurry to join a party, even if the party was just her.

She slid deeper under the covers and stared at her computer screen, not wanting to make a noise. It would be easier to avoid him than to engage, especially after that kiss. She'd set rules and she should have stuck with them. Now there were questions and possibilities hanging in the air like treacherous mist.

Silence availed her nothing. A light tap sounded on the door. "Lexie?"

She should have turned the light off, but it was too late now. She wished the bedroom door had a lock. "Yes?"

"Just checking. I ran into something outside. Wanted to make sure you're safe and sound."

"What? Why?" she asked.

He sounded tired. "I'll tell you in the morning."

She heard him move away from the door, and then the sound of a knapsack unzipping. Lexie stared at her laptop screen, not seeing the image in front of her. She should wait until morning, when there wasn't the temptation of the darkness, or beds, or the suggestion of what happened in beds. Of what might happen if they were both in the same bed. Waiting was the sensible way to go.

Lexie lasted one minute, then two, then five. She got tired of pretending to work on her pictures and put her equipment away. She thought about reading and discarded the idea. Eventually she heard water running in the bathroom. Faran was going about his business. Good.

But surrender was inevitable. With a grunt of disgust, she slid out of bed, pulling on a robe. Curiosity was her worst enemy.

She whipped the bedroom door open. "Okay, *what* did you run into that was so alarming?"

She barely got the words out before her brain registered what she was seeing. On the table was a clutter of first-aid supplies, toiletries—including condoms, good luck with that—and a thriller novel. Standing beside it was Faran, wearing a toothbrush and nothing else. She'd seen it all before, but there was a lot of hard, muscular real estate to admire. The corn-silk gold of his hair darkened as it traveled down his flat abdomen, interrupted only by the fresh-looking bandage covering his right side just below the ribs. As he tensed in surprise, the movement of muscle under skin was wildly distracting. She made a noise somewhere between a gasp and a prayer.

The toothbrush clattered to the floor, and suddenly there was a wolf with a mouthful of minty-fresh toothpaste foam. For once, the sight of the beast, almost as large as the sofa, didn't alarm her. It had been too long a day, with much worse to worry about.

"You look rabid like that," Lexie said. She stalked back into her bedroom, closing the door firmly behind her. Crawling under the covers, she switched off the light and turned her face to the wall.

A minute later, the door creaked open. She rolled over enough to see a human Faran outlined against the glow from the sitting room. "Someone tried to climb up the outside wall to your window," he said.

She sat bolt upright, turning the bedside lamp on low. "What?"

He shrugged. To her relief, he was now wearing loose sweatpants, though they rode perilously low on his hips. "I chased him off, but he got away."

"No clues?"

"All I got for my trouble was another encounter with Maurice."

Lexie spluttered. "*The* Maurice?"

"Is there more than one?" he asked dryly. "I kind of hope not."

"He's a huge star in Europe and some kind of relation to the royals. I took his picture at Fashion Week."

"Oh." He sounded displeased. "Isn't he a little sparkly for your tastes?"

Lexie made a noise of disgust. "Why are we talking about him instead of the nut job climbing the wall?"

"Because I've nothing to add. I didn't see his face. I'd know his scent again, though." He said it so casually, it almost sounded normal.

"So he, um, didn't smell familiar?"

"Not necessarily. I don't always pay attention. You don't remember every outfit you encounter in a day, even though you see them perfectly well."

"Just asking."

He shrugged again. "Never mind. I'll be on the alert from now on. I think it was someone from the palace."

Lexie wrapped her arms around her knees. "Why?"

"He's familiar with the security arrangements." He took a step into the room, then stopped dead. "May I come in?"

She shrugged.

"You burst in on me." Irritation in his voice, he took another step. "Fair is fair."

She swallowed hard. "Please, Faran."

"What do you think I'll do?" he asked, his voice dropping. "We *lived* together, remember?"

"That was…"

His cheeks flushed. "I know. Before you knew about the wolf."

"It changed things."

"Drama aside, I don't know why."

"Faran…"

His words were angry, as tightly controlled as a hunting dog straining against its leash. "I never raised a hand to you. I always put you first. I told you what I was—even though it went against all the Company's rules about civilians. If they had their way, your memories would have been wiped. Taking you into my confidence put us both at risk. Maybe you could bend just a little."

He was absolutely right, but he was also missing the point. "It was never just about you, or the fact that the Night World—all that supernatural stuff—exists."

"Oh?"

"Some of it's the world you live in. The danger. It was what I saw you do in the alley—attacking that man."

"Who was attacking you at the time."

"It was the last straw, but there were a couple of bales of it in my life already. I just broke. I couldn't absorb one more shock." She rested her forehead on her knees. "You think I'm being unreasonable."

Faran sat down on the edge of the bed and grabbed her foot through the coverlet, giving it a squeeze. His voice softened. "You said that was some of it. What was the rest?"

"Me." She didn't like the defensive edge to her tone, but she couldn't help it. "I get this feeling—like when I saw Gillon on the ground. I can't explain it. It's like I'm hungry and restless and lonely all at the same time. I have to run—get away from it—because it's the only thing that makes me feel better."

Lexie had never said that to anyone before. She wasn't even sure she'd known it herself before that instant. She raised her head to look at him.

He studied her for a long time, saying nothing but giving her the full force of his blue eyes. His expression wasn't hostile, but it was sad. "Did you ever love me?" he finally asked.

"Yes." Her mouth went numb. Not dry. It just ceased to be. *How can he think I didn't? That I don't?* She didn't want to consider that. Her heart hammered as if her rib cage was suddenly too small. She gave a slow nod. "I'm a mess."

"Yes, you are." He smiled to take the sting from his words. "And you kind of made a mess of me."

They'd run up against the wall she'd been dodging for so long. Tears stung her eyes. "I'm sorry. I know that's not enough. I—"

He put one finger to her lips, stopping the flood of apology. "You can't help what you feel. There's no blame here, but we need to be smart about this. I need you to tell me the truth. Don't tell me what your head says—tell me what the rest of you knows. That's what a wolf thinks like. That's always honest."

"I don't understand," she protested.

"Stop thinking."

Chapter 10

Faran leaned forward, sliding his hand up the side of her thigh, to her hip, to her waist. Lexie's limbs froze, not sure whether to lean in or pull away. "I can't think when you do that."

"Good."

There were layers of bedclothes between his palm and her skin, but memory supplied the feel of his touch. He'd always been able to ignite her like a match to tinder. Raw desire had never been the problem between them—just what her mind did with those feelings.

"I..."

"Shh."

Faran's breath fanned warm against her face. His lips brushed hers, barely there at first, and then with hunger. He pulled her closer, drawing her into his embrace. Her hands found the smooth skin of his shoulders and trailed over the bulk of his chest, delighting in the clean, hard lines. And then his arms tightened, folding her in the strong circle of his embrace. She felt the power of him, the sheer brute strength banked in all that hard muscle.

She tensed. He froze.

"What does your body tell you?" he asked.

"Danger." The word was barely more than a whisper.

He released her slowly, his brows drawn together in puzzlement. "Talk to me."

Lexie inhaled as if she'd been fighting for air without realizing it. "I know holding me like that's supposed to make me feel protected, but it doesn't. Not right now."

"What do you think I'm going to do?"

"Nothing—it's like there's something buzzing inside me when you get close." She couldn't exactly explain what she meant. She felt like a horse kicking down the barn door to get loose. She'd heard about people who got caught between a car and a wall and were slowly crushed to death— and in that moment she knew what it felt like. Helpless, immobilized, vulnerable. Desperate for air.

His fingertips traced the line of her cheek. "Claustrophobia?"

"That's part of it, but it's only part. Call me crazy."

His lips thinned at her evasion, but he pressed on. "I don't remember you ever mentioning feeling like that before…" He trailed off. *Before the wolf.*

Lexie knew she was hurting him. She had to give him something. "It was fine at first. It got worse the closer we got. The more I wanted to be with you, the worse it became."

"Why?"

"Like I said, it wasn't just you. Maybe I'm allergic to relationships."

Her tongue felt like a shriveled, dead thing. Faran waited, but she couldn't say any more. There were layers of emotion involved, and she barely understood half. Shame, habit, reflexes born of years of punishment muzzled her. She could see Faran thinking through the problem. He always wanted to fix things—but this wasn't a simple repair.

"Are you willing to try?" he asked softly.

"I want to."

"Good. That's all I ask." He lay down beside her, rolling onto his back with a come-hither grin. "So now you're the one in control."

Lexie looked down at him, feeling suddenly lost. "What?"

"Ravish me. You know you want to." He put his hands behind his head. It did great things to his arms.

"Uh." She bit her thumbnail. Lexie's first instinct had been to kick him off the bed, but suddenly she didn't want to. Faran looked like sin. She wanted to forget everything and just launch herself at him like a starving woman, but she felt tangled in the net of her own anxieties.

Her hand drifted to settle over his heart. It beat strong beneath her palm. He was so warm and alive, nervous energy almost crackling the air around him. Her own body responded, quivering in response. It made her short of breath.

"Do you still make those crispy shrimp things?" she asked, grasping for something safe and light to calm herself.

He responded with a lazy blink of his blue eyes. "I think I still have the recipe somewhere. I remember you like those."

She bent and kissed his mouth, feeling his heart kick slightly as she did it. It gave her a twinge of ridiculous pride. "You want to know what I like? I like that." She kissed the spot over his heart. "And that."

He reached out, taking her hand in his. His fingers were so long, they engulfed hers. Her breath caught.

"But you don't like that," he said.

She pulled away. "I need to know I can get free. I like being touched, but only if I'm in control."

"Why didn't you ever tell me?"

Tears rushed up the back of Lexie's throat, and she clamped her teeth hard to keep them in. *Because I'm fearless. I'm the one who lives without a care.* She'd told herself that a thousand times, but it was a lie. She'd just hidden it until she couldn't anymore. "It's old stuff. Baggage. Damage."

The admission left a bitter taste in her mouth.

"Lexie, what happened?"

She sucked her breath in, shaking her head as if to push away the groundswell of memories. "I think that's enough fun and games for one night, don't you? It's been a really, really long day."

She was running without even moving, and she knew it. Faran knew it, too.

The air between them seemed to go cold. Without a word or a look, he slipped off the bed and padded toward the door. No judgment, no protest. *I can't do this to him again.*

"It was my brother, Justin," she said, not looking up. The words came out so quickly, they barely made sense. But somehow that fit.

"Lexie," he said softly.

Slowly, she raised her eyes. Panic began to stir. "He didn't touch me that way. Not like you're thinking."

His expression darkened. He was like a bow before the arrow was drawn, force waiting for purpose. "Whatever happened was enough."

She didn't want to talk about it. It was like an ugly,

twisted scar that deformed the parts of her that should have been lovely. It was proof that she couldn't fix herself, or protect herself. Pride—shame—had made her want to be whole, but that was a lie. And it was costing her Faran's love.

"Justin is dead. He died when I was sixteen. He was three years older." She hauled in a breath and let it go. All at once breathing seemed like a terrible chore. "The police shot him. He was involved in a home invasion. They think he killed a nine-year-old girl." *After all, he'd been practicing on me for a dozen years, bit by bit.* "My parents still don't believe it. Not even with all the evidence in front of them."

The room fell eerily silent, as if the air itself stopped dead. Lexie could almost hear her blood moving through her veins.

"There's a lot more to that story," Faran said.

"Yes."

"You never went home the whole time we were together. I don't think you even called."

"Like I said, my parents didn't believe. Especially not Mom. Not the way Justin died, and not about what he did to me. Not even when he broke my arm." Her hand went to the spot just above her elbow. A feeling of hopeless, helpless rage awakened in her gut, scrabbling like a rat. "They called it sibling rivalry, but that doesn't usually involve repeated trips to the emergency room."

Faran hadn't moved a muscle, but the color drained from his face. "When did it begin?"

"I'd just started school."

Random images spiraled through her mind. Her favorite plaid dress. The chain-link fence around the playground. Her stepdad's car driving away in the bright California sun. Those were okay, but there were others. Finding out her real dad was gone forever. Her brother watching her from an upstairs window like some ghost from a horror film. Her mother taking endless pills. Lexie had been fascinated by the amber plastic bottles that rattled like candy. It was only when she was older she learned the problem was depression.

"Mom was under the weather all the time, and my stepdad traveled a lot. I was just a kid, into everything, making messes. Justin never was. It was like he was already old when he was born. Mom said he looked just like our real dad. Maybe that's why she liked him so much."

"So your brother looked after you when your parents weren't around," Faran guessed.

"Yeah. He looked after me."

Other people would have called it torture, but that conjured images of chains and dungeons. That wasn't it at all. They'd had a nice house with a nice yard, and she'd had swimming and piano lessons. There were never any pets, though. Her parents were that smart, at least. "It went on for ten years."

"Until he died."

She nodded. "It was all about Justin being in charge. He'd set traps just to show he could get me whenever he liked. This—" she pointed from herself to Faran and back "—this doesn't come easily. I don't trust. Not after looking over my shoulder every day for a decade, waiting for the next ambush."

With soft-footed grace, Faran crossed the room and sat down on the edge of the bed. He took her hand, holding it lightly, and kissed her palm. He shut his eyes, saying nothing but just warming her flesh with his.

Lexie's throat ached with remembered pain. "This is the moment people want to tell me Justin is gone and it will all be okay," she said faintly. "Don't ever do that. He's still with me every time I jump at a loud noise."

"I'm not going to tell you what to think or feel." Faran leaned close, the line of his body touching hers. "I just hope it fades over time."

She bit her lips together, refusing to cry. "I want this to work." She kissed his cheek, feeling the roughness of his beard. "I hope I don't drive you crazy first."

"I know it's complicated. Believe me, I know." He slid an arm around her, but he did it gently. Justin had stolen the kind of carefree rough-and-tumble she knew Faran liked—but horseplay set her nerves on edge. It was too much like an attack.

A hot tear rolled from under her lashes. "I'm not much of a girlfriend, am I?"

Faran's head was bowed, but he smiled with a touch of his old mischief. "That's what's great about dogs. They adore you no matter what."

She kissed him. There was nothing else she could do because she thought her heart would break from the sheer weight of her feelings. He responded, easy and sweet and yet with a heat and hunger that let her know he wanted more than just to be her friend. Somewhere in their years apart, Faran had grown wise.

And maybe she had, too. The wolf mattered—it was an essential part of him—but it didn't frighten her nearly so much. Not when she felt the gentle affection in his caress. Faran was right. Her body knew things about him her brain had skipped over.

His teeth tugged at her lip, teasing her, promising her as much as she could handle. Daring her to match his fire. He knew all too well that, for all her uncertainties, she was proud and that spark inside her would give her the strength to be whole.

Her hands slid over his skin, reassuring her that Faran wasn't just a wonderful dream. She wasn't alone, and for the first time ever, the possibility of healing seemed real.

Chapter 11

"I don't know why we're doing this," Lexie said as Faran's car wound up the mountainside the next morning. True, it was a magnificent day for a drive, with a cloudless sky and only the lightest breeze, but their last road trip had ended in the fight with a melting man. She wasn't getting over that in a hurry. "Don't we have bad guys to catch back at the palace?"

"Sure." Faran turned the car onto a narrower path that led to an abrupt stop on a grassy plateau. "But investigation is about more than running around shooting people. I need to think. And I need to get away from the city for a while. Yesterday was a little intense."

As Faran parked, Lexie scanned the scene through the windshield—rolling hills, mountains and a hawk against the flawless sky. Faran had always been a lover of the great outdoors, and now she knew why. Part of him belonged to it. She waited for that reminder of the wolf to rouse her anxiety, but it didn't. "Okay, but this is pretty isolated. What if Gillon's friends show up?"

He turned off the motor and opened the car door. "This isn't a twisty back road like yesterday. No one is going to take us by surprise here. Look around you."

Lexie got out and did as he asked. They were in the middle of a flat meadow, the sheltering side of the hill a hundred yards away. The only break in the rough grass was an irregular ring of gray stones about four feet tall and too narrow for anyone larger than a child to hide behind. He was right; there was no opportunity for an ambush. It should have been reassuring, but there was something odd about the place. "It's awfully warm here. It almost feels like summer."

"They say it's because of the stone circle."

Lexie gave them another look. "Is that an ancient monument of some kind? Like a mini-Stonehenge?"

"Apparently. There are circles like this all over the countryside. Ancient human tribes used them as meeting places, but the fey built them."

"The fey?" she asked curiously. "For real?"

He nodded. "People sensitive to magic say touching the stones gives them pins and needles."

She approached the closest stone, half expecting it to start glowing. Nothing happened. The stone was just gray rock, lumpy and hunched. It leaned to the side like an old gravestone, its base lost in the long grass.

But despite its plain appearance, it felt very much alive—not as if it would move or make a sound, but it was somehow *aware*. She stopped walking. She didn't want to get any closer. "Can't you feel it?" Lexie asked.

"I can tell this was a fey place, but not more than that. I'm just a werewolf. It's not the same thing."

Her thoughts slid sideways a moment, as if they'd lost

their footing on the strange subject matter. "You say it *was* a fey place, like they aren't here anymore."

"They're not. The Light Fey keep to themselves, far away from the Company. The Dark Fey were exiled from the mortal world a thousand years ago."

Lexie stretched a hand toward the stone. She felt tingling, but it might have been no more than the power of suggestion. No, it was more than that. Truth be told, it felt like sticking her finger in a light socket.

I can feel magic? So not what she wanted to know—and yet it made sense. She'd felt that buzzy, unsettled feeling she'd experienced around the stones—and Gillon and Faran—off and on ever since childhood, mostly in times of stress. As her relationship with Faran had stirred up other anxieties—mostly to do with her family—that unsettled sensation had only muddied the waters. The wolf had eventually become the focus of her dread.

Complicated? Yes. There were a bundle of factors at work—misunderstood psychic abilities, deep-seated family trauma and a boyfriend who turned into a raging werewolf. No wonder she was a bit tense. But just now Faran had given her more insight than the past three shrinks and a Reiki master combined.

Yet all this would explain why proximity to Gillon had sent her senses reeling—because he was definitely connected to magic. And it would explain at least one reason why the closer she'd grown to Faran, the more restless she'd become. He might be just a werewolf, but he hit the same radar. She definitely had a sixth sense for the supernatural.

Stuffing her hand into her jacket pocket, she turned back to him. Faran was unloading something from the trunk of the car. "Is that why you brought me here? To see if I could feel the stones?"

He was rummaging in the trunk of his car, his back to her. "Maybe. It was an idea."

"I can feel them."

"Cool."

She felt a brief stab of irritation. She could feel magic! Surely this was big news! "What does that mean?"

"From what you were saying last night, I wondered if you might be a little bit psychic. From what I've heard, understanding that helps when you cross paths with the supernatural." He didn't sound particularly excited by the fact. "It's less freaky if you understand you're picking up energetic backwash."

Backwash? It sounded about as exciting as dishwater. Disappointment edged her mood. "You mean this is just a piece of practical information?"

"For now." He turned around, a bundle in his arms and a sneaky grin on his face. "Maybe you've got a nonhuman ancestor in the family tree. It could happen."

That sounded oddly suggestive. She eyed Faran, wondering what he was up to. "What's that you're holding?"

"We're having a picnic," he said, and shook out a large checked blanket. The wind caught the fabric for an instant, making a huge sail of the red-and-white fabric against the blue sky before it settled on the grass. "You know I always want to eat."

He ducked back into the car and pulled out one of the huge wicker hampers the city's delicatessens rented to tourists for their day trips. "See?" He opened the lid, and even from a distance Lexie could tell it was packed to the brim with food.

Her mind stalled as she tried to deal with magic and Faran at the same time. They were two huge subjects, both loaded with land mines. Suddenly overwhelmed, she approached the blanket with caution.

It felt like stepping into the past. They used to have picnics all the time. She'd forgotten what it was like to be with Faran like this—drowned in sunshine and creature comforts. She didn't need to look to know he would have brought her favorites from the deli. He'd remember what they were.

"Can I help?" she asked.

"Sit," he said. "Relax. I've got it covered."

But she stayed standing, unable to let down her guard. It struck her, perhaps deeper than ever before, how much his revelation of the Night World had changed everything. She was about to have a picnic with a wolf, caught in some bizarre reversal of Red Riding Hood. And she could feel the magic of fairy stones—which was amazing even if he dismissed it as *backwash*. If it was that mundane, why had he even bothered to test her perceptions?

Faran uncorked a bottle of Cabernet, drawing the cork out with practiced ease. He sniffed it appreciatively.

"Do you still cook?" she asked, still standing.

"Not much. I don't have free time."

It was a shame. He really was an artist in the kitchen. "You're too busy saving the world."

With a droll expression, he poured wine into glasses. "No, it's more like I don't make time. Cooking isn't fun unless there is someone there to eat it, and vampires make terrible dinner guests."

Lexie took the hint. She sat and took the glass of wine he handed her. *"Salut,"* she said.

He clinked his glass against hers. "Your health."

They sipped the ruby wine. It was the way she liked it, with a good body but not too heavy. "Answer me this," she said. "What kind of genes make a person sense magic?"

"Recessive ones." He set the glass aside. They were sitting cross-legged, their knees nearly touching. Lexie could see the forest rising a little distance behind him in a curtain of deep green. He pulled a cardboard carton out of the basket and opened it. "There's a nice selection of cheeses here."

"Is there a known DNA factor?" she countered.

"You'd have to ask someone with medical knowledge. I do know there are plenty of people with some sensitivity to magic and it tends to run in families."

The words held a strange echo, like something she'd heard as a little girl. "But you think it's from a mixed marriage somewhere along the line?"

Faran shrugged. "Not necessarily. Humans have their own powers, even if they deny it." He was unpacking the picnic basket, putting out one thing after another: olives, bread, grapes, thinly sliced ham and slivers of dried fruit. "I can't explain why you in particular seem to be sensitive to the presence of magic. I don't know anything about your family history."

She picked up a grape and rolled it between her fingers. "My mother was a schoolteacher. Clive—my stepfather—was a businessman. He was the one with all the money. My brother and I were the only two kids. That's all there is to know, except for my father. I don't remember him very well. I was really little when he left. Justin would remember more."

"Your father left?"

"My mom waited years before she divorced our dad and married again." The grape was mangled. She tossed it into the grass. "How would I know if there was something special in my bloodline?"

"With mixed families—and I'm not saying that's what's going on with you—supernatural skills tend to show up as a person matures, and occasionally not at all. Often it's no more than weird dreams and luck playing the lottery."

"I want…" She trailed off, not sure how to finish the sentence.

He reached over, squeezing her knee. "Tell me."

Lexie was at a loss. What *did* she want? It was an endless list, and a lot of it had nothing to do with Faran or what they were doing there. She wished she could remember her parents before everything went wrong. She wished her brother hadn't become the terror that defined her childhood—and maybe her adulthood, too. *No, I won't let that happen.*

"Lexie?" Faran asked. "What is it?"

"I was just thinking about the past. This conversation is so strange. I remember as a girl I felt like there was nothing special about me. Like I was the most boring creature in the world."

He went still, but it was a solid, quiet stillness. "Where would you get that idea?"

She picked another grape. "I remember walking to school one day and seeing my brother up ahead. I slowed down so he wouldn't notice me. He was standing in front of the corner grocery store talking to some guy who must have been in his fifties. I don't remember his name, but my brother was around him a lot for a while. He was a teacher or a tutor or something."

Faran said nothing, but refilled her wineglass.

"They saw me," Lexie went on. "I remember my brother telling his friend that I wasn't anything special. And then I remember the older guy saying they'd never know until I feared for my life."

Faran looked up. "He said what?"

"At that point I turned and ran. I don't think I've ever stopped. It was bad enough to read the look on that man's face and realize he was serious. He'd kill me to figure out what he wanted to know. Worse, I still wonder what he expected to find out."

Faran set the bottle down and captured her hand in his. This time he didn't try to hold back but squeezed, imparting all the warmth and strength she could ever need.

Lexie desperately wanted to change the subject. She'd spoiled the mood enough, but memories were lurching to life. "I think they tried not that long afterward. When Justin was around thirteen, he stuck me with a meat skewer."

Faran swore, but she barely heard him. Thinking about it brought back the burn along her nerves. What she remembered even more than the agony, though, was the look of trepidation in Justin's eyes. "He was waiting for something to happen, but nothing did, of course."

Justin had been exhilarated and curious, but he'd also been afraid. Of what? *Of not being the special one.* She shied away from the thought as if it had been poison.

But there wasn't room to think anymore because Faran's mouth was on hers. "Hush," he whispered, sliding one hand behind her head to cup it securely. He leaned in for the kiss, tasting her as if she were one of the treats in his picnic basket. Lexie leaned forward to meet him, careful of the glasses. He tasted of wine and fresh grapes, like some ancient god of revelry.

Maybe kissing was a simplistic cure for all that old distress, but it was an effective one. Faran touched her face, lightly brushing it with the backs of his fingers. It was a cherishing gesture, relishing the simple contact of skin on skin. There'd been a time when neither of them had possessed that kind of self-control, and there was a burning deep in her belly that said that restraint wouldn't last forever. She kissed him again, feeling the warmth in his flesh. He was filled with life, rich and vibrant as the sun-warmed vintage.

"I don't want all that garbage following me around anymore," she whispered. "I want to be rid of it and be happy."

"Then that's our plan A," he replied with a wicked smile.

Her fingers ran down his arm, tracing the tight, heavy muscles. He was indeed a male animal, his very presence making her chest ache with wanting. She sucked in a gasp as his hand found her ribs, the stroke of his fingers wildly intimate though they were both fully dressed.

She could feel the tension—the magic—of the place spiraling through her, twining with the coil of her desire. Faran smelled so good, so familiar. Her fingers laced in his hair, loving the rough texture of it.

And yet the ghosts they'd disturbed—those memories she wanted gone—refused to lie still. Too much had come back to life today. The hum of magic clinging to the stones pulsed behind her eyes like a headache about to happen.

Lexie broke the kiss and sat back on her heels. For an instant, Faran seemed surprised but he followed her lead. His blue gaze lingered over her every movement, as if watching for cues. She picked up her wine, ignoring the slight tremor in her fingers that made the red liquid quiver against the glass.

"I think I'm ready for some of that food," she said lightly, praying he'd understand.

"Whatever you're ready for is fine," he said. "This is just the appetizer."

Chapter 12

"Great fuzzy balls," said Faran, surveying the main banquet room of the palace

When royals partied, they did it on a grand scale. The kings had at last returned from the countryside, the final treaty arrangements in hand. After that much negotiation, only a world-class shindig would do. About seven hundred guests were finding their seats now, and it wasn't a quiet process despite the formal wear and good breeding.

"If I ever get married," Faran said to Chloe just loudly enough so that she could hear, "it's going to involve takeout and paper plates."

They stood near one set of huge double doors, watching the guests mill and eddy like colorful fish in a sea of pink marble and white damask cloths. Wheel-shaped crystal chandeliers sparkled above the tables like elegant spaceships. A small chamber orchestra was playing at the far end of the room, but Faran couldn't hear them over the crowd. It was going to take an army of cooks and servers to get five courses out and that didn't include the wines. Just thinking about the organization required made his head hurt.

Almost as much as wondering what plots were being woven beneath the veneer of genteel civility. After everything that had happened—the mayhem at the reception, the theft of the ring and the attack by Gillon—Faran would have called the whole thing off. Sure there was money at stake, but what about lives?

But nobody asked a wolf.

Chloe stuck out her tongue. "If you get married, I'm going to get rich off all the bets I've placed with your co-workers."

"Say what?" Faran tried to remember what they'd been talking about.

She thwacked his arm with the back of her hand. "You put on a good act, but you're the least confirmed bachelor I know."

He winced. The events of last night and this morning had left him feeling raw both for himself and Lexie. After all this time, she had finally opened up about her family, and now he understood why she had issues with trust. It was going to take time to work through her past. "If that's true, then why am I not hitched already?"

"Because only one woman will do for you, and she's right over there." Chloe nodded toward Lexie, who was deep in conversation with the chief of security for the event.

Faran grimaced, but held his tongue. He'd finally begun to understand much of importance, but nothing was going to be solved overnight. He was no psychologist, but Lexie could still cut and run in an instant.

"What's wrong?" Chloe asked, suddenly losing her light tone.

He shoved his hands in the pockets of his perfectly tailored suit. "Nothing."

That earned him a sidelong look from the pretty blonde. "Lexie's my dearest friend. She talks a good line but she needs someone steady. That's why I'm rooting for you."

"You are?" He wondered how much Chloe knew about Justin.

Chloe's gaze slid away. "I'm a romantic. And I've got fifty dollars with Mark Winspear that says you'll have a ring on Lexie's finger by Christmas."

Faran made a derisive noise. Vampires were the worst gossips he knew. "You remember she dumped me, right?"

"Where's your fighting spirit?" Chloe chided. "I thought you were a contender."

Faran shrugged. Chloe's faith pleased him, but he wasn't ready to give anything away. "Let's just say I'm playing a long game."

"Just stay in the game, okay?"

The conversation ended there because Lexie was coming their way. She was wearing a silky pantsuit and had her wealth of fiery hair pinned up. She looked amazing.

"All set?" Chloe asked her.

"Absolutely," Lexie replied, her tone calm and confident. "Mr. Security Maven is very eager to limit what can and can't be photographed. I think he'd rather I wasn't here at all."

"Yeah, well, he's already nixed the videographer," Chloe grumbled.

"Once everyone's seated, I'll start by taking some wide shots. He's not keen on it but it's good to have them for reference."

"I agree. I don't know what the problem is," said Chloe. "You're the best compromise between no coverage of this and full-on press mayhem."

Lexie nodded. "How do you want me to fit in with the event schedule?"

"You need to get the personal shots done by the time the meal is over. I need you set up and in place to photograph the speeches. And get some shots of Amelie wearing the ring on her necklace. It's got a nice romantic touch, like she can't wait to wear it."

"Yes, ma'am," Lexie said.

"Just remember I handpicked you for glory." Chloe kissed Lexie's cheek and left them. "Remember, all personal shots done by the time dinner is over."

Lexie shot Faran a slightly wild-eyed look. "Do you know how many people are on that list? That girl doesn't want much."

"And yet she pretends to be so sweet," Faran said regretfully.

Lexie's hazel eyes looked unusually green, as if her inner fires were burning bright. "I'm glad you're here."

For an instant, he could see how vulnerable their recent conversations had left her. Her protective shell was still in place, but it had cracked and he'd caught a glimpse of the chaos inside. He ran his thumb down her cheek, caressing the curl of hair that escaped her messy bun. His fingers brushed the pulse of her throat, and it was beating fast. There was too much emotion between them for such a public place.

Faran brushed a kiss across her lips. He didn't care what others thought. Lexie was all that mattered. "I'm glad to be here. Tell me what to do."

She cocked an eyebrow. "Just follow me and don't photo bomb King Renault."

His role turned out to be playing fetch and carry with an endless array of awkward, expensive equipment. He listened with half an ear to the surrounding conversations, hoping for useful scraps of information, but the real perk was watching Lexie. Her graceful motions, the bend and flex of her body, were mesmerizing. Yet that was not what transfixed him most. It was the intense concentration she gave every photograph. Lexie hunted her images the way a wolf hunted prey. That much precision and focus was compelling, even sexy.

He'd kept his wolf on a leash, giving her space and coaxing her to trust him again, but the beast inside was growing impatient. A good alpha respected the needs of his pack, doing his best to give each member what they needed to thrive. But Faran wanted Lexie and, as he watched her bend over to get the best shot of a centerpiece, he nearly lost command of human language.

Once Lexie was done with general shots of the event, they moved on to a list of individuals. Given the importance of the occasion, there were a lot of guests who wanted their picture taken that night, either for posterity or in hopes of making the gossip pages. Maurice was one of them. He sat at one end of the high table, next to an elderly duke and duchess. At first Faran thought the musician had worn a traditional black tuxedo, but as Maurice lifted his glass of water, the motion revealed the fabric was shot with a sparkling scarlet thread.

"Don't you know it's bad manners to upstage the bride?" Faran asked under his breath while Lexie took a shot of the older couple.

Maurice set down his glass and looked up. He grinned. "Why, if it isn't my prison buddy. Sit a moment. My date has fluttered off to chat with friends and I'm bereft of companionship. Such is the fleeting reward of fame."

Faran sat as Lexie moved on to her next subject. "At least you get fed. Tonight, I'm the photographer's pack mule."

Maurice laughed. "Ah, you're working while everyone else eats. I've played that gig before."

Faran returned Maurice's smile. "I see Valois let you out unscathed."

"Well, they've found the wretched ring now."

"I heard the princess mislaid it," Faran said casually.

Maurice raised an eyebrow. "I find it hard to believe Princess Amelie would be that careless. Who knows what happened, but hurrah if it keeps Valois happy."

"I'll go along with that," Faran said, noncommittal. "I'm not a fan of guards with guns."

Maurice waved sparkling nails. "There wasn't much Valois could do to me in the first place. They searched my rooms. There was nothing of interest to find."

"You did mention naughty schoolgirls."

Maurice quirked one corner of his mouth. "I plead innocent. Even I know that young lady was too young for me. Maybe she was the one who made the security bloke faint dead away. Valois was very interested in that detail."

A tendril of suspicion wound through Faran's thoughts. He rummaged in Lexie's bag for her cell phone and thumbed open the photo she'd taken of Gillon. "Is this the guard?"

Maurice looked at the picture while Lexie snapped another barrage of shots a few seats away. The flash and whirr of the camera barely made a dent in the noisy, glittering atmosphere. "Gods. That's him all right, but he's not coming back to us, is he?" Maurice returned the phone, his face pale.

"I hope not. Any idea why he passed out?" Faran asked. "Did he eat or drink anything in your room?"

"I'll tell you what I told Valois," Maurice replied, still obviously shaken. "He complained about being thirsty. I was out of bottled water, so I gave him an energy drink. He must have had an allergic reaction to it."

An image of dissolving flesh slithered through Faran's imagination. "Maybe."

Maurice shrugged. "He recovered after a few minutes and the other guards took him away."

"What kind of energy drink?"

"One of those all-natural vegetable ones. Tastes like lawn clippings, but it packs a vitamin wallop. You should try it."

"I'm more of a carnivore."

A server came by with a plate for the fish course. Faran sniffed. His sense of smell and taste was far better than any human's and he'd outstripped every other student in the chef's academy when it came to identifying ingredients in a dish. It didn't take much effort to identify pan-seared scallops with green beans amandine in a light sauce of seasoned oil, lemon and dill.

Maurice waved it away. "Speaking of allergies, I don't eat seafood."

After the server left, Maurice leaned close. "Why are you asking questions?"

Faran considered. Sometimes he had to go with animal instinct. "I'm doing a little undercover security work," he said in a low voice.

"Ah. Does Cousin Kyle know?"

"Yes, he knows," Faran replied, remembering what Lexie had said about the musician being a relation to the royals.

"Okay." Maurice took another sip of water. No wine, Faran noticed. He took his vitamins seriously. "If you need anything else, let me know."

Lexie had worked her way down the table, so Faran said goodbye to Maurice and rose to follow. He glanced at the dish the other guests were eating, idly thinking the sauce too heavy on the lemon. Scallops of that quality shouldn't be bullied on the plate—but he forgot about that the moment he caught up with Lexie. She was trying to take a picture of the Vidonese royals, which should have been easy. The high table only had seating on one side, allowing the public full view of their monarchs and Lexie a clear shot. Unfortunately, not everyone was happy about it.

Faran had never seen King Targon of Vidon in person before. He was a stern, sturdy man with iron-gray hair and the same handsome features as his sons. "I don't understand the need to have our dinner interrupted by photographers," Targon grumped. "This is a serious occasion. Court protocol should be observed."

"It is the new way, Father," said Prince Kyle, who sat between his father and Amelie. His tone said they'd had this conversation many times before. "The public likes their royals accessible."

Lexie took a cautious snap, leaving the flash off. "One more, Your Majesty, if you don't mind."

"I do mind." King Targon waved a dismissive hand. "Laundromats are accessible. I am a crowned head of state and I am eating my dinner. Go away. No one needs to see me chewing."

King Renault of Marcari, younger and quieter than his counterpart, endured the camera with more grace. From time to time, he touched his daughter's hand, as if reassuring himself that she was safe. The king had sent the Company away as a goodwill gesture for the wedding and Faran wondered if he was regretting it now.

"May I take a photo of Your Handsome Highnesses together?" Lexie coaxed Leo and Kyle. "For the ladies?"

Kyle wiped his mouth with his napkin while Leo gave her an assessing look. The younger prince gave a silky smile. "It hardly seems fair that you take our picture and yet I get nothing from you. One sweet deserves another, Ms. Haven."

"Leo," Kyle said in a warning tone.

"Be careful what you ask for, Prince Leopold," Lexie replied. "Cameras always tell the truth."

Leo's eyes narrowed. "You promised to join me for dinner before you took my picture."

Faran bristled but Lexie stepped on his foot. She clearly wanted to handle things her own way. He folded his arms and scowled.

"That's not how I remember the conversation," Lexie replied. "But here I am, at your dinner. Does that please Your Highness?"

"You're being tiresome, Leopold," King Targon said, tearing a dinner roll in two. "Let her take a photograph and move on. This is unseemly."

"Relax, Father, I'm being *accessible*. I'm inviting the lovely media content provider to dine." With a smug expression, Leo snapped his fingers. "A chair for the lady."

"Stop this," said Kyle, clearly irritated.

On alert, Faran caught Renault's eye, and the king of Marcari gave a slight nod, telling him to let the scene play out. That seemed too much to ask, especially after what Faran had learned about Lexie's brother. Faran guessed there were similarities between Prince Leo and her brother—a need to control, a pleasure in watching a victim squirm. Faran's skin crawled with the need to change and sink his fangs into Leo's throat.

Lexie must have heard his thoughts because she gave him another quelling look. Against his better judgment, Faran remained still.

An expressionless server arrived to place a chair across from the princes. Lexie sat, as cool as if this was nothing more than a coffee date. Faran put a hand on the back of her chair, gripping the carved wood. He couldn't exterminate Prince Leo in public, but he could loom.

With a slight, mocking smile, Leo cooperated. Lexie lifted her camera, the shutter whirring half a dozen times while the princes posed. Lexie seemed to understand just how to handle the royal antics. *Good work*, thought Faran.

"I don't suppose your dear husband could take one of us together?" Leo said to Lexie, pushing a glass in front of her. "Some wine?"

But I'm still going to kill him.

"Oh, Leo, don't keep our poor photographers," said Amelie. "They don't get their own dinners until they're done." She frowned as several servers arrived to deposit tiny glass serving bowls on the table. She leaned over to poke the contents with her fork. "What is this? I approved the menu, and I don't recall seeing this."

"It smells spicy," said Kyle.

"I like spicy," Amelie said with a wicked smirk. "It's my favorite."

King Renault cleared his throat.

Faran's nose wrinkled as the serving tray went past. *Lemon, grapefruit, raw scallops, mint, peppers, shallots, a hint of garlic oil.* It was a ceviche, and if the seasonings in the first dish had been badly balanced, by Faran's standards this one qualified as a train wreck. *You'd think a royal court could hire someone better than this.*

"It's scallops done a different way," said Leo in a bored tone. "That's a thing, you know, doing the same food several ways. Though I think the variations are usually presented on the same plate. Would you care for a taste, Ms. Haven?"

Something was off. Catching King Renault's eye once more, Faran picked up one of the little bowls to sniff.

"Or take the whole dish," Leo amended dryly.

"You can have mine," Kyle said, pushing his over, "since you're in such a charming mood tonight."

"That's hardly necessary."

"I insist."

Faran tuned out the princes, still considering the ceviche. The noise level throughout the room inched up as the guests investigated the new treat. Lexie kicked his ankle, but Faran was concentrating. Scents and tastes were a landscape of sensation, forming patterns and colors in his mind. Nuances of earth and ocean lingered in the food. He could smell the soap from the cook's hands, the fact that the grapefruit juice hadn't been fresh squeezed. This wasn't top-quality work. Spicy chilies overpowered the citrus and mint, hiding the fact that the scallops weren't as fresh as the ones in the main dish. And the timing of the service was all wrong. This item should have been an appetizer. Uneasy, Faran set the dish down and looked around for the head server. Someone in charge should have been having a fit.

Then two things happened at once. Amelie reached for the dish of ceviche next to her. The movement of air wafted the chili scent under Faran's nose again. But this time there was a different smell underneath it, like the bottom note of a perfume.

At the same time, Prince Leo leaned forward with a forkful of the fish for Lexie to taste. "Come, Ms. Haven, tell us what you think."

"Don't," Faran said, the word cutting across the table like a scythe. He lunged, grabbing Leo's wrist, but Lexie had already taken the sample from the fork and was chewing.

"Don't swallow it!" Faran ordered. "It's poisoned."

King Renault's hand grabbed the bowl from his daughter. The table fell silent. Lexie's hands went to her mouth as her eyes widened in horror. Faran crouched before her chair, his heart hammering, praying she hadn't swallowed. Sweat rolled down the small of his back. He was going to tear Prince Leo into tiny shreds.

But his first concern was Lexie. Grabbing one of the thick linen napkins, he pressed it into her hand. Her skin had gone clammy, her eyes moist with tears. He kept his voice calm even though he wanted to bellow his rage. "Spit it out. Now."

"What is this nonsense?" demanded King Targon.

A small noise came from the princess as one hand went to her throat. "What do you mean it's poisoned?"

Horror crawled up Faran's limbs as he took a second look. Amelie's portion was half-eaten.

Chapter 13

Faran stormed into the infirmary. This part of the palace was small, but tonight it seemed a nightmarish labyrinth of corridors and identical doors. He'd been separated from Lexie. The medics had brought her here with Amelie and the other poisoned diners while Faran had helped to secure the banquet hall. With so many guests, that had taken a while but they'd been thorough. If the poisoner was in the crowd, he wasn't getting away—but that was Captain Valois's concern now. Faran needed to be there for Lexie.

He barely kept his pace to a walk. As a wolf, he could have covered the distance in seconds, but for now he had to play the human. Distracted, he dodged around a nurse pushing a medical cart and nearly ran into someone in a lab coat. He wheeled around, muttering an apology. *Get yourself under control.*

Faran banged through a set of double doors and skidded to a stop. The full force of the disaster at the banquet flooded home at a glance. Not everyone's ceviche had been poisoned, but there had been enough to cause chaos. Gurneys jammed the hall, each with a patient in evening finery and many with a friend or partner waiting helplessly by. The infirmary had been set up for a handful of patients at a time. There were too many sick and not enough beds—and even fewer answers.

Now that Faran was forced to be still and take stock, he could smell sickness—the putrid, acid stink of sweat and stomachs gone wrong. The animal part of him sensed death waiting for a crack to steal through. His own heart thudding, he examined the faces of the patients one by one, looking for Lexie.

He found her sitting at one end of a padded bench, her back propped against the wall. A young woman barely out of her teens lay with her head in Lexie's lap. The girl's skin was waxy and pale. Lexie didn't look much better, but she was stroking the girl's fair hair, the way a mother would comfort a child.

Faran froze, a complicated mix of anger and yearning closing around his heart. He was at her side in an instant. "Lexie!"

The look on her face was pure relief. His chest easing a little, he went to one knee beside the bench, needing to be close to her. "How are you?"

"Better than the others." Lexie sat up straighter, her brave exterior firmly in place. "Two more doctors have arrived, but it's slow going. So many people got sick."

Faran didn't like the pallor that dulled her features. "Has a doctor seen you yet?" he asked, touching her face. He'd half expected a fever, but she felt unusually cool. He pressed her hand, but it was no better.

"No," Lexie replied.

The girl on the bench stirred and made a faint gasp as

if she was in pain. Lexie looked up, her eyes fearful. "Can you find someone to look at her? She's not doing so well."

"I'm on it." Faran was back on his feet and searching the crowds in an instant. He didn't want just any white coat, but the man in charge. According to the nameplate on the door marked Head Physician that was Dr. Lemieux. He began pushing his way down the hall, reading the badges the staff wore pinned to their lab coats.

Dr. Lemieux was noting something on a clipboard when Faran cornered him. He was small and grizzled, with a receding chin and dark, penetrating gaze.

Faran cut to the chase. "There's a girl over there who's getting worse."

"Young man," said Lemieux testily, handing the clipboard to a nurse. "Look about you. Unless you are the princess with her private physician, everyone must wait their turn and, sadly, everyone is getting worse."

Frustration slammed through Faran. He wanted the Company, with its labs and experts and his vampire friend, Mark, who knew more about medicine than anyone could learn in a mortal lifetime. But rumors were already blaming the Company for the poisoning, saying it was an act of revenge for their dismissal. The most Faran could do was send them a sample, but there wasn't enough time for that. He had to work with the tools at hand.

Faran slid a hand around the doctor's arm. "Let's go."

"I will not be—"

"You will." Faran marched him through the infirmary, taking advantage of his more-than-human strength. "I sincerely apologize, Doctor, but you're needed over here."

The doctor began spluttering.

Faran cut him off. "I'm sorry, but self-control is for people with more time. I don't have any."

"I will not be bullied!" spat the doctor.

"Have you identified the poison?"

"No, and it was food poisoning."

"No, it wasn't. I can tell the difference."

Lemieux stopped struggling and began to walk under his own power. "You're the one who smelled it?"

"I have a keen nose."

The doctor's gaze traveled over Faran's face with new interest. His manner grew speculative. "Are you certain? Shellfish can be tricky, and the distribution of diners who fell ill seems to be random."

That was hard to answer without revealing too much. The doctor was doing a little investigating of his own. "I know the difference between rot and something else," Faran replied, "just like I'm pretty sure you already know that based on symptomology. Random victims are a good way of hiding the real target." He didn't bother to add that the royal couple was almost certainly the mark.

Lemieux nodded, giving him the point. "The palace has a history of security staff with exceptional talents."

Faran wasn't stepping into that one, either. "What's the poison, Doctor?"

"I can't release information to unauthorized persons."

"Rules don't mean much if all your patients are dead."

Lemieux gave in. "I don't know the answer. The toxin is an unstable compound and the acid in the food is complicating its identification. In turn, that makes it hard to find an effective antidote."

They'd reached Lexie. She was leaning against the wall, looking more drawn than she had even a few minutes ago. She hadn't ingested as much of the poison, but she was still feeling the effects. She gave Faran a tired smile, but she didn't speak.

While the doctor examined the girl, Faran bent over Lexie, kissing her temple. A primitive need made him long to take her away to someplace safe, but there was no better help anywhere nearby. This wasn't something strength and speed could help.

Dr. Lemieux straightened, releasing a worried breath. The young girl's lips were bluish.

Anxiety made Faran's voice sharp. "What do you need done, Dr. Lemieux?"

The physician's face grew pinched. "It's up to the doctors now, young man."

That wasn't good enough. Faran stepped close to Lemieux and dropped his voice low so that only the doctor could hear. "That is Lexie Haven. She's mine. There's nothing I won't do for her."

"You have the exceptional nose." The doctor folded his arms. "Identifying the poison would be far less difficult and faster if we had a pure sample uncontaminated by food. Can you find it for me?"

Faran's stomach dropped. Even if the poison was in a bottle marked with skull and crossbones, he would need to search the entire palace. It was looking for a needle in a rambling haystack. But one look at Lexie's pale face—at all the faces in the infirmary—confirmed that he had to try.

"I'll be right back."

Faran started with the scene of the crime, telling himself at least he knew his way around food. The servers and guests had been herded off to the same rooms where Lexie and Maurice had been questioned. He was hoping the banquet room would be quiet.

He should have known better. A royal princess was among the sick, and no effort was being spared. When he arrived, the hall was swarming with green-coated Vidonese guards, some of whom bore the insignia of the

Knights of Vidon. Faran's neck hair prickled, but he kept his expression mild as he skirted the areas cordoned off with yellow tape. The guards had been joined by the local police, and crime-scene technicians were examining the high table, fingerprinting dishes and sealing samples of food into tiny jars. It was painstaking, precise work.

Faran passed through the banquet hall and into the servers' passageway. The stainless steel doors to the kitchen were directly ahead. Yellow tape forbid entry, but Faran didn't slow until he saw Captain Valois lurking in a shadowed corner just outside. *Great fuzzy balls, not now!*

"Mr. Kenyon," said Valois, "what an interesting surprise."

"You're not questioning the staff and guests?"

"Oh, I will be," Valois gave a ghastly smile. "But there are so many things to attend to."

Faran held up his hands in a peacemaking gesture. "I'm here on behalf of Dr. Lemieux. He's the—"

"Yes, I know who he is. What does he want?"

Faran didn't have time for games. "A sample of the poison. He's looking for an antidote."

"And you happen to know where that is?" Valois folded his arms, his lined face somewhere between skeptical and suspicious. "I hear you were the one who—correct me if I'm wrong—*smelled* it."

Two people in the past half hour had remembered that scrap of telltale information. Faran wasn't pleased. "Yeah. That's how I hope to find the source."

"In the kitchen?"

"That makes sense, doesn't it?"

"It's crossed our minds. We've done a search already, although the crew with their brushes and sample bags haven't been through yet." Valois's gaze flicked to the kitchen doors. "It's a mess in there. It's going to take them all night."

Faran opened his mouth to demand entry anyhow, but to his surprise Valois pulled down the yellow tape. Then the police captain drew his weapon with a whisper of metal on leather and fabric. "If it saves the princess, you're welcome to try. I'm going to be at your elbow every step of the way."

Triumph flared in Faran's chest. "I can live with that."

"You don't have a choice." Valois pulled a pair of latex gloves out of his pocket. "Put these on."

Faran took the gloves. He wasn't going to argue with the man as long as he got where he needed to go.

The kitchen bore the marks of an ordered chaos Faran knew well from his brief culinary career. Trays and mixing bowls sat on long steel tables, food half-plated, a dish towel dropped to the floor in Faran's path. The grill was off, but a fortune in choice beef congealed where it had been searing. Cooking stations along the wall were similarly abandoned, knives set down with bits of vegetable still clinging to the blades. The place was beginning to stink as the unrefrigerated food turned rancid.

"We took the staff into custody, or most of them," said Valois. "Two of the servers and three cooks are missing. They all left at different times—for a smoke break or to make a call—and never came back."

"The cooks—where were their stations?" Faran asked.

Valois pointed. "The one on the end belonged to the saucier."

Faran snapped on the gloves. "I'm going to look around at everything first. I'd guess at least one of the cooks was working with the missing servers. Poisoning a dish wouldn't be as easy as it sounds. There are a lot of people in a kitchen. A lot of potential witnesses. For a job like this one, you need someone to add the poison to the food, maybe another person to plate it and someone to get the dishes to the right victims. Probably both servers, to be sure the distribution looked random."

"You're saying it would take a whole crew. What about one server with an eyedropper?"

Faran shook his head. "It would be hard to pull off in a barn of a kitchen like this. There's no privacy. I would bet you all five of your missing staff were in on it."

"We'll see." Valois made an "after you" gesture. "Your theory sounds complicated."

Faran started with the tables closest to the doors. Plates had been arranged on the stainless steel surface for prep. Garnishes were already on about half. The scene revealed nothing.

Faran moved on to a sink heaped with a drift of arugula. Valois stayed a step behind, weapon in hand.

"Do I make you that nervous?" Faran asked. "You trust me enough to let me in here."

"No human can pick out a trace amount of poison like that."

So he knows what I am. Faran didn't answer, but pointedly looked at the gun. Valois paled, a sheen of sweat glistening at his receding hairline, but he stood his ground. "I've been with the Marcari police for twenty years and know all about the vampires and werewolves. Not much surprises me anymore."

"So?"

Valois licked his lips. "I don't like your kind, but solve this and nothing else matters."

"Fair enough." For an instant, Faran thought about telling him everything he knew. But then again, Valois might have hired Gillon—if one actually hired such a creature. No, he had little reason to trust the captain, especially since the man was holding him at gunpoint.

Keeping his movements as calm as possible, Faran moved to the next cook's station. "This is where they made the ceviche."

The captain's nose wrinkled. Scraps of raw seafood lingered on the counter. Faran felt his mouth sour with revulsion, but beneath the fishy stink he caught a faint, foul whiff. He stopped, sniffing again.

Valois watched, his brow furrowed. "Is it here?"

"It *was* here," Faran replied. He made a quick survey of the work area. There wasn't much to see—knives, dirty dishes, stray vegetables and a dish of salt.

"Let me play devil's advocate," said the police captain.

"Aren't you on the side of the prosecution? I thought thumbscrews were more your style."

"Wouldn't the culprit want to take the evidence with him?" Valois asked, ignoring his gibe.

Faran scanned the surrounding area. "Or perhaps he wouldn't want it anywhere near him if he was taken for questioning. My guess is our poison is hidden in plain sight."

A rack of spices and flavorings stood at the far end of the room, next to an enormous pantry. Beyond that was a walk-in refrigerator large enough to park an SUV and leave room for a bike. Faran strode to the rack and began scanning jars and bottles labeled in a variety of languages.

Valois watched him, eyes narrowed. "You mean it's in disguise as another ingredient."

"Or mixed with one. Something strong enough to mask the flavor and close enough to the taste of the dish that it wouldn't stand out. At least, that's what I would do."

"Oh, really? Remind me not to eat at your house."

Faran's hand skipped over the dried herbs and spices. A foreign substance would probably be too visible or else settle to the bottom. He reached instead for the bottles of flavored oils and thick, dark vinegars. And then, almost without thought, he moved on to the sauces and picked up a small, dark bottle. He unscrewed the top and smelled the concoction, and knew he was right. "This is it."

Valois wrinkled his nose. "What is that?"

"Garum. It's made from fermented fish." But the salty, pungent smell was only clinging to the scum around the cap. The liquid in the bottle bore the bitter scent he recognized as the toxin. "I'd say our evil cook emptied out the sauce and put the poison in the bottle. Garum isn't an everyday ingredient. He could have easily hidden this here for a few days."

With a grim smile, Valois finally holstered his weapon and produced a plastic bag, holding it open. "Drop it in there before you smudge the prints."

Faran did. It hit the bag with a satisfying plop. "I need to get that to Dr. Lemieux."

Before Valois could reply, Faran felt a waft of air. He spun to see the pantry door swing open on silent hinges. He ducked on instinct, dragging Valois with him. A knife went crashing into the rack. A bottle of balsamic vinegar crashed to the tiles, releasing a nose-puckering scent. Valois stuffed the evidence in the pocket of his coat and drew his weapon.

"I think we found one of your missing suspects," Faran said grimly. "His knife skills need work."

Chapter 14

The door to the pantry slammed shut.

"Idiot," Faran muttered.

"Crooks usually are." Valois rose from his crouch and approached the door, gun at the ready. Cautiously he reached out and tried the handle. The lock was a dead bolt, the kind with a safety latch on the inside that prevented anyone from getting trapped.

Unfortunately, that meant their adversary could lock himself in and it would take a key to get him out. Or a werewolf. Valois nodded at Faran. "I'll cover you."

Faran took a firm grip on the handle and twisted. The mechanism was good quality steel, so Faran had to lean into it. He braced his feet, muscles straining. He took another breath and tried again before he heard metal tear. The door flew open once more, the sudden release sending him reeling back.

Valois was there, scanning the opening and ready to

shoot. Faran half expected to be pelted with food, but nothing came. They cautiously stepped inside. The place was ringed with shelves with deep bins beneath, but there was no one there.

Valois swore, lowering his gun. "Where is he?"

Faran finished his visual sweep of the room and began a second, looking higher. Still nothing. Was someone hiding in the bins? Unlikely. Still, they were on heavy casters so he pulled one out to look.

"What are you doing?" Valois asked.

"Looking for villains."

"In the potatoes?"

Faran moved a second bin. "There. Look at that."

There was a small door in the wall about three feet square. Valois crouched for a better view. "I heard stories of secret passages in the palace when I was a boy."

"More likely a ventilation shaft." Faran got down on all fours and tried the door. It wasn't even latched. An intriguing passageway beckoned. His first thought was to investigate, but he paused. Catching the poisoner was vital, but so was saving his victims. "I need to get back to the infirmary with the poison bottle."

"Understood," said Valois. "Just poke your head in and tell me what you see."

Faran hesitated. It was hard to trust a man who'd been holding him at gunpoint.

Valois seemed to read his thoughts. "If you believe nothing else about me, believe I'm a cop. I want to see justice done. If you're not back in one minute, I will take the sample to Lemieux myself. You have my word."

Still reluctant, Faran stuck his head through the opening. Then his curiosity caught. While the door was small and hidden, the passage behind it was man-size. Faran squeezed through and got to his feet. The space was only about four feet wide and a little higher than his head. The walls were made from the same stone as the rest of the palace, but roughly finished. He let his fingertips graze the cool surface, feeling a film of ancient grit. He had great night vision, but it was truly dark here, with only the light from the pantry creeping along the floor. Nevertheless, Faran suspected someone might have used this as an escape route. He pulled out his phone and switched on the flashlight app.

"I'm going in," he said. "Start counting your one minute."

"Go."

Faran moved silently, his feet barely scraping on the sandy floor. The air here was musty. Whoever had passed before had left a trail of perspiration and food smells. About twenty seconds along, the passage branched, but he turned right with confidence, using his nose as a guide.

He could see the tunnel ended abruptly a stone's throw ahead. He stopped, scanning the walls with his flashlight for another door. Nothing. It was narrower here, with barely enough room to walk without hunching.

A noise made him flick off the light to hide his presence. He remained frozen for a long moment, the sudden close darkness making him twitch. Such thick walls muffled and distorted sound and he searched his memory, unsure if the scrape he'd heard was a footfall or the scurry of a mouse. He could smell rodents, too. Eventually, skin prickling with apprehension, he turned the light back on.

It fell on an object at the end of the passage. Faran approached, unsure what he was looking at until he got close enough to see it was a bundle of pale cloth. He shone the light straight at it. A cook's white jacket lay crumpled into a corner. It was the source of the scent he'd been following. Faran kicked it in disgust and immediately doubled back, cursing himself for wasting time.

The door to the pantry was still open, but Valois was nowhere in sight. Had he left for the infirmary to deliver the bottle of poison? Undoubtedly. The police captain wasn't the type to lose interest and wander off. Faran left the pantry for the kitchen and stopped. There was nothing more to keep him here but he didn't want to leave. His instincts were waving a red flag. *There's something I should be paying attention to.*

The cook's jacket in the dead-end tunnel bothered him. It was as if someone had wanted to confuse Faran's sense of smell. To lead Faran down one tunnel while he went somewhere else? Had the knife-throwing perp been listening the whole time he'd been talking to Valois? *In that case, the noise I heard was a person, not a mouse.* Someone had used the opportunity to give him the slip.

A muffled crash made him spin around. He couldn't see anything, but another thump drew him to the walk-in fridge. Faran picked up one of the chef's knives from the counter and pulled open the fridge door. A gust of cold air turned to fog.

A figure in black had the captain trapped against the shelves. Valois's face resembled the raw meat on those shelves. In the brief time he'd been out of Faran's sight, he'd taken a beating, maybe broken his nose.

Faran lunged forward, nearly tripping on a frozen chicken that skittered aside like a bowling ball. He grabbed the back of the man's hooded jacket, hauling him off Valois. But as the man wheeled, he grabbed Valois's gun and shoved it into Faran's face. Faran sliced upward with the knife, slashing the gun hand. Recoiling, the man dropped the weapon but ducked under Faran's upraised arm, darting away from both him and Valois. In a flash, he was out the refrigerator door.

The police captain scooped up the gun, eyes flashing with rage. "He came out of the tunnel before you got back. You have to catch him. He took the evidence."

Faran bolted for the kitchen. The man was heading for the back door but spun at the sound of Faran's running feet. For the first time, Faran saw his face. He was wearing the same type of flesh-colored balaclava as the man who had tried to scale the wall to Lexie's window. In a flash, the man had turned and was running again. Anger shot through Faran. This time he wasn't going to worry about witnesses. Using his inhuman agility, he sprang to the top of the table, scattering plates and bowls, and then leaped for the culprit, a snarl ripping from his throat.

The man slammed against the door in his panic. Faran grabbed him, letting the tiniest bit of claw rake the man's shoulders as he dragged him to the tiles. The man fell with a scream of protest and kicked out, slamming one foot into a mop bucket that toppled over, spewing dirty water over them both. Faran grabbed him more tightly and they rolled, crashing into the work table and raining more plates on the floor. Broken china stabbed into Faran's back, and then his knees, but he finally trapped the man facedown on the floor.

He heard the clink of Valois's handcuffs. Faran held the man down as the police captain cuffed him. Then Faran ripped off the balaclava. The face looked vaguely familiar, but he couldn't place it.

Apparently, neither could Valois. "And who are you?"

The young, dark-haired man snarled and spit but would not speak. Even so, Valois sat back on his heels with a look of satisfaction despite the blood streaming from his nose. He reached into the young man's jacket pocket and pulled out the evidence bag. The bottle was mercifully intact. Valois held it out to Faran. "Take this and go. I've got this, werewolf."

Faran didn't need to be asked twice. He sprinted for the infirmary at wolf speed.

The next morning, Lexie perched on the examination table, her arms folded across her chest. It was the only place in the infirmary where she'd been able to stretch out for a bit of sleep, and that had only been a few hours ago. Her silk jacket and slacks were too thin for the air conditioning and the cold made her light-headed.

At least, she hoped that was all that was making her dizzy. Her mind grappled with the fact that she had nearly been fatally poisoned, but it was hard to grasp. Nevertheless, the place smelled of the tongue-shriveling medication—antidote, she supposed—that left her saliva the flavor of bleach and rotten orange peel. Nothing was going to taste right for days. She desperately wanted something ice-cold to drink and could almost see a frosty glass of iced tea.

Lexie closed her eyes, fighting a headache. Her nerves were jangled until she could barely sit still. She was alone for the moment and grateful for the chance to pull herself together. She'd been dreaming of her birth father. She could barely remember his face, but she did remember the time she'd been sick in bed and he'd sat by her side all day, telling her stories. But in the dream, her father's face had kept changing from the doctor to Faran to King Renault.

She jumped when she heard a footfall outside the flimsy door. The knob rattled and she opened her eyes, ashamed of being so jittery. Her visitor was probably the nurse, and she could ask for something to ease her headache.

She had a feeling she was going to need her wits sharp for the next while.

"Lexie?"

"Faran!" Lexie slid from the table to greet him. He was holding—joy of joys—a glass bottle of iced tea. He always seemed to know what she wanted.

He set the bottle down and folded her in his arms, all his worry present in the fierce hug he gave her before he eased his grip. He hadn't forgotten her dislike of being held too tight. "Are you sure you're supposed to be up?"

She relaxed a moment, the sense of security washing back from her dream, if only for a moment. She knew Faran had found the poison, which had made it possible to administer the correct antidote. They all owed him their lives, including Princess Amelie and the young girl Lexie had been with on the bench in the infirmary waiting room. Her name was Mireille, and she was only fifteen.

Lexie had gotten off easy. Most were still very ill, and more than a few lives hung in the balance. They'd been transferring patients to the hospital all night, including Mireille, who would recover but was badly dehydrated. Lexie silently thanked her stars one more time. Another few seconds, and she'd have swallowed the poisoned fish.

"I hope they discharge me soon. My bed is just in another part of the palace. I want to be there, not here." She kissed his cheek and then murmured a protest when he kissed her lips. She probably tasted like medicine.

Faran didn't seem to care, but shifted his arms so that she could lean against his chest. It felt so much better that she realized he was the only thing keeping her on her feet. Maybe she wasn't as recovered as she thought.

He was still dressed in the suit he'd been in all night, although he looked as if he'd been someplace dirty—and he'd clearly not slept. Haggard lines etched his face, making him look older. He'd spent much of the night at her side, but she knew from time to time he'd left to help Valois investigate. She wouldn't have wanted it any other way—it would be selfish to keep him entirely for herself at a time like this.

"Any news of Princess Amelie?" Lexie asked quietly.

"She ate more of the fish than you did, so she's in worse shape. But they think she'll recover in about a week."

Lexie could hear worry behind the words. "I'm glad to hear she'll get better."

"So am I." Faran took a quick breath, as if commanding himself to the task at hand. "Are you sure you want to stick around after this? You'd be a lot safer if you went home."

Lexie blinked, confusion adding to her pounding head. "Does that mean the wedding is canceled?"

"No," he gave a wan smile. "At least, not yet. The more someone tries to stop this match, the more the royal families refuse to cave. Barring further misfortunes, the marriage will go ahead. But no one expects you to stick around. Prince Leo fed you rotten fish."

She nearly laughed. The universe was mocking her. She was good at running and Faran was holding the door open for her, but she wasn't having any of it.

I'm fearless. I'm the one who lives without a care. It had been her mantra for years, and now she knew how utterly false it was. Carelessness didn't breed courage—it bred, well, nothing much at all. "I, for one, don't want to give anyone the satisfaction of spoiling the wedding."

"Your welfare comes first. Bravery doesn't count if you're dead."

"I'm only brave because I care what happens. I can't leave now." Chloe was counting on her—and so, in their own ways, were Kyle and Amelie. And Faran deserved her loyalty most of all. He was alone on this mission without

Sam or the other Company agents. She owed it to him to watch his back as best she could.

He was hers to watch over, just as he'd spent the last night watching over her. This time when she straightened her spine, she felt the burn of conviction deep in her gut. "No, I'll stick around. After all this, Princess Amelie deserves the best wedding pictures ever, and frankly, that's what I deliver. You're not rid of me yet."

Faran hugged her again and kissed the top of her head. "I'm glad."

With her face hidden against his shoulder, Lexie let down her guard. It was one thing to be brave, but she knew they were far from safe.

Chapter 15

Faran left around midmorning. A few hours after that Lexie was released and she returned to her room. Faran jumped up from the couch the moment she opened the door, looking scruffy and red-eyed.

"You should have called me to come get you," he said, taking her hands.

"It was a five-minute walk." She gave him a kiss, but halfway through she became uncomfortably aware that they weren't alone.

"Forgive my intrusion," said Prince Kyle, rising to give her a polite bow. He looked just as tired and rumpled as Faran, and it made him look younger. "Amelie is deep asleep, and there is nowhere else I can go to speak freely about any of this."

Lexie shoved a hand through the rat's nest of her hair. Kyle was reported to have plenty of friends, but he was right. Who else knew about vampires, melting spies or any of the other truly bizarre pieces of royal family history? More to the point, who could he trust?

"Please," he said with a sheepish smile. "Be comfortable."

Lexie didn't need a second invitation. She kicked off her shoes and padded across the carpet. A pot of coffee sat on the table, and it smelled like heaven. "I need some of that."

Faran poured a cup and handed it to Lexie. "Black and thick the way you like it."

"Thank you." Lexie took the cup, letting her knuckles brush his. As always, his skin was warm. She settled into a chair, feeling infinitely grateful to be back in her own quarters.

"I should go and leave you in peace," said Prince Kyle, rubbing his eyes. "But first I must apologize. I'm very sorry that you were put at risk, Ms. Haven. My brother was being difficult."

"But it was a fortunate incident," said Lexie.

Kyle's eyes widened in surprise. "Pardon me?"

While she'd been sitting idle in the infirmary, she'd reconstructed everything that happened at the table. Faran had picked up Leo's dish to inspect. Leo—snide little toad—had been trying to feed her Kyle's. "That was your portion that nearly got me."

The prince's surprise turned to anger. "What?"

Lexie took a deep swallow of the coffee. It was bitter, but it thankfully drowned out the lingering taste of the medicine. "The only two people at the head table who got bad fish were the bride and groom. Coincidence? Not likely."

"What about everybody else who got sick?"

"Smoke screen," Faran replied.

"You cannot be serious!"

"You'll have to start using food tasters."

Kyle swore. "That's medieval. Who uses tasters anymore?"

"Apparently you do," said Faran, his expression serious for once. "The poison wasn't quite a lethal dose, but that was just luck."

"But you caught the poisoner?" Lexie asked.

Faran summarized what had happened in the kitchen. "It was a sophisticated plan with a lot of players. The prisoner hasn't said a word beyond claiming that the order for the ceviche came from the royal housekeeper. I checked his personnel file. He was a brand-new employee and should never have been hired. His qualifications weren't up to the usual standard. Obviously a plant."

"What about the fact that he was hiding in the kitchen?" Lexie asked. "How did he avoid getting arrested before you found him?"

"He probably hid in the secret passage. My guess is that he was sneaking back to retrieve his poison bottle from where he'd hidden it."

"I'll find someone who knows where those passages lead," said Kyle. "Many old palaces have them, but they're a security nightmare."

Lexie pondered that. "If this was the same man who was trying to crawl up to our window, then I don't think this room has a secret door. I mean, why go to the trouble of climbing a wall if you can just walk in?" That was something to be thankful for.

"But what's the point of getting in here? Or the poisoning? At least the theft of the ring made sense." Kyle rose and paced the tiny room.

"Do we know anything more about the theft of the ring?" she asked.

"Only one thing. Gillon was one of the men who searched Maurice's rooms," said Faran.

"Why?" asked Lexie. "By the next day he was in possession of the ring. However he got it, at least part of that time he was just carrying it around. That seems like an unnecessary risk."

"Not really," Faran replied. "Who would search the guards searching your room for the very item that was taken? He was the perfect person to hold it."

Kyle pressed the heels of his hands against his brow, as if staving off a headache even worse than Lexie's. "But what has this to do with the other crimes?"

Lexie was wondering the same thing. She couldn't see a common thread.

"If we forget about money," Faran mused, sitting back on the sofa and bracing his ankle across his knee, "what does the ring get someone?"

"It holds Vidon's blood rubies," Kyle said immediately. "Those are of great value to us as a national treasure. The ring itself is a symbol of unity between our countries."

Lexie thought about the two kings and their secret negotiations. Neither looked happy at the dinner. "What does Vidon lose through the union?"

Kyle's mouth pressed into a flat line. "There is a great deal of resistance to the idea of uniting with a nation that fosters an intimate relationship with nonhumans."

"I thought the Night World was secret knowledge," said Lexie.

"There are enough among the noble families and the Knights who know about the nonhumans in very general terms. Those dignitaries will not come to Marcari to witness the marriage as long as the Company is present. That is why they were asked to leave. A political union will never work if the most important Vidonese houses refuse to witness the wedding."

Faran glowered into his glass. "That doesn't bode well for the future."

Kyle sighed heavily. "It might take time, but Amelie and I *will* change the attitudes of those that fear your people."

His firm and earnest words stirred Lexie's sympathy, but they also pointed out his vulnerabilities. Kyle might be a reformer, but his father absolutely wasn't. Could King Targon be fighting the future Kyle and Amelie promised? Family didn't always fight fair.

Lexie knew that well enough. She swallowed the rest of the coffee, feeling the heat as it slid down her throat to her stomach. *I nearly died last night.* Justin would have laughed.

Her musing was interrupted by a knock on the door to the hallway. All three of them stood, clearly tense. Faran moved to answer the knock, but not before he picked up his weapon from the side table. Kyle stood to one side. It suddenly occurred to Lexie that he was on his own with no bodyguards.

Faran opened the door a crack, but then relaxed and stood back. It was Chloe. She rushed in, a sick look on her face. "I think something new has happened."

"Is it Amelie?" Kyle demanded.

"Your Royal Highness!" Chloe exclaimed softly. "I didn't expect to see you here."

"Answer me," Kyle said, anguish beneath his hard expression.

"No," Chloe replied. "The princess's health is no worse. But while she was asleep, someone crept into her room. No one can figure out how."

No one said a word for a moment. *Secret passage.* In all likelihood, the Company would have known the entrances and guarded against them, but they were gone.

Lexie broke the silence. "What happened?"

Chloe heaved a weary sigh. "The ring is gone again. Someone took it from the chain around the princess's neck."

Hours later, Lexie woke up with a jolt. Darkness closed in around her like a muffling pillow. Scrambling to free herself from the covers, she sat up, pushing her hair out of her eyes. She blinked, heart pounding, air cool against her sleep-flushed skin. The room resolved itself into her bedroom at the palace. A known landscape. She released her breath in a rush. She'd been having a nightmare.

The details of the dream receded from her mind, but her body still ached with remembered fear. She took another deep breath, hunching and releasing stiff shoulders. She must have been curled into a knot while she slept. She felt as bruised as if she'd lost a battle with a two-by-four.

The flavor of the dream came back, an elusive wisp that nagged like a forgotten name. Something she'd known once but eluded her now. Lexie slipped out of the bed, pushing her feet into slippers. She'd showered and changed before finally giving in to sleep around two in the afternoon. Faran had left with Kyle to investigate Amelie's missing ring. She'd wanted to go with them, but a sleepless night coping with poison in her system had finally caught up. She'd barely been able to keep her eyes open.

Lexie picked up her phone and checked the time. It was a little after eight. Dark. Night. She pushed the curtain open, feeling a flicker of apprehension as she thought about someone crawling up the outside wall. She looked down just in case, knowing it was stupid.

And yet that's what the dream was about. Justin had crept into her room at night, once to destroy her stuffed walrus, once to cut off half her hair. Once he'd woken her by sticking a meat skewer into her leg. After that, she'd stuck a chair under the doorknob at night.

And now someone had tried to get in this window. And someone *had* got to Amelie. The theme was simple—sleep wasn't safe. The traditional refuge of bed was a place where something bad could happen and in ways she just couldn't anticipate. There was no way to brace for what was coming. No way to deal with it.

Lexie stared at the fairy lights of the palace grounds. Justin was gone, but there was someone behind her present troubles. Who? Why? She'd tried to look at it analytically, the way Valois might, but she got nowhere. This time, the devil wasn't in the details. It was in the wide-angle view, the pattern of light and shadow.

Actions mattered, but so did effects. Justin would have loved all this chaos and panic.

Her thoughts dissolved as the door rattled. Lexie froze, listening, and then relaxed, muscle after muscle letting go, her heart gradually slowing back to normal. It was Faran—no one else moved quite that way. The bedroom door opened quietly.

"Hi," he said. "You're up."

Lexie leaned against the window frame, liking his long perusal of her bare legs. "Yeah. Find anything new?"

He lifted a book. "No joy finding out who took the ring. Valois is going out of his mind, but he's got plenty of men on the routine stuff. So I got some reading material instead."

"Reading material?"

"History of the rubies. There's got to be more reasons that ring is so important."

Lexie switched the bedside lamp on low, casting a comfortable glow over the room. "More reasons than a fortune in cash and the pride of a sovereign nation?"

Faran flopped onto the bed, a pleased expression on his face. The old book was bound in faded red leather and he'd marked the pages with half a dozen scraps of torn paper. "There's a reason Vidon had those particular stones, but the average Joe has to go digging to find out. And the average Joe doesn't have access to an old, moldy private library stashed in the back room of the Dowager Queen's apartments."

"What made you look there?" Dowager Queen Sophia, King Renault's mother, was on a goodwill visit to Vidon, charming those who couldn't or wouldn't come to Marcari for the wedding. Lexie was glad the grand old queen had been safe from all the troubles.

"Queen Sophia arranged to have the Marcari diamonds sewn onto Amelie's wedding dress. Jack told me once that she knows every stone of the Marcari crown jewels. It stood to reason she might know about Vidon's collection, since once upon a time they belonged to the same treasure hoard brought back from the Crusades. The jewels are what first started the war between Marcari and Vidon."

Lexie pushed a hand through her hair, wishing for coffee. Her brain wasn't quite keeping up. "And that book was in her library? You helped yourself?"

"It was and I did." He held the volume out for her to see.

Lexie opened the pages. They were old, the letters dented where the type had pressed against the paper. "You read Latin?"

He grinned. "I'm not just a pretty face. Ancient lore tends to show up in ancient languages, although I still think *Demonology for Dunderheads* is a surefire best-seller with the DIY crowd."

"I think we're getting off topic. What useful tidbits does this book hold?" She flipped the pages, but there were no pictures. She returned the book to him.

"I'm not sure about useful. I'll go with suggestive. The rubies in Amelie's ring are the same ones that were used in the ceremony that sealed the gates of the Dark Fey kingdom a thousand years ago. Presumably they could unseal them the same way."

"Whoa. Slow down. The ring could let all the Dark Fey out?"

"Basically. And nobody wants that. The Dark Fey aren't nice."

She sat down next to where he had flopped. She really needed that coffee. "This isn't just more anti-supernatural propaganda put out there by the Vidonese?"

"No, they called this one right." He gave a huge yawn. As far as she knew, he hadn't slept since before the banquet. "Light Fey are unpredictable. Dark Fey make vampires look like bunny rabbits. But it is logical that grumpy old Vidon had a magical implement that could shut the doors on an entire supernatural kingdom."

"Which is why someone wants the ring," she said softly. "They want to unlock those doors."

"Bingo. And fey magic would explain Gillon. I'm no expert, but I'd bet you a steak dinner he was a fetch—someone created by magic. They run on salt and water. Remember all those snack wrappers in his pockets? Maurice said Gillon was thirsty when he went to search his rooms. He took an energy drink from the party and passed out."

She was lost again. "How is that significant?"

Faran closed the book and tossed it onto the coverlet. "What's the one thing energy drinks have that fey are allergic to?"

Lexie searched her memory of fairy stories. "Iron."

"Bingo again. A fey fetch after a ring that would loose the dark fey kingdom. This is starting to add up."

She digested this a moment, studying his face. Fatigue

had etched lines around his eyes, but he looked pleased with himself. And so he should. "You really are a detective, aren't you?"

"Working on it." He gave her that grin again, half surfer boy and half devil.

Then he sobered. "But the fey connection—and the ring—is only one piece of the puzzle. There's all the other stuff, like the poisoned ceviche. I might have found a corner, but this jigsaw puzzle has a thousand pieces. The only thing Valois has gotten out of our rogue cook is that the dose was never meant to be fatal. He didn't mean to actually kill anyone and so far, thankfully, he hasn't."

Lexie's dream pressed against her thoughts. "Still, the mass poisoning of innocents takes a certain kind of crazy. It's like something Justin would do."

Faran frowned. "What are you saying?" He sounded worried.

She waved a hand. "I'm not saying he's risen from the grave—he was cremated, for starters—but we're looking for someone who thinks the same way."

"Such as?"

"Someone who understands how power and chaos work."

Faran propped himself up on a pillow, getting comfortable. "Yeah, but that profiles half the people in the palace. Royal courts are hotbeds for schemers."

"But what's the *effect* of what he or she is doing? What does making a bunch of random people sick do? It creates an uproar. What happens during an uproar? People get distracted. Amelie is sick in bed, an attendant turns her back and the ring goes missing again. It's still about the ring. The only reason the poisoning happened is because you and I caught up with Gillon and got it back." Lexie finished, feeling exhilarated. The connections between one fact and another shimmered in her imagination like a blade ready to slice through to a solution.

"If that's the case," said Faran, "how did they put the poisoning in motion so quickly? They couldn't know we'd find out Gillon was the thief."

"This was probably their back-up plan in case the theft at the reception failed. Any good villain has a plan B," she said with confidence, although her first-hand knowledge was admittedly small.

And then she noticed Faran was quiet. His eyes had drifted shut, his breathing growing slower and more even. After working for almost two days solid, he'd fallen asleep. Lexie lightly brushed his fair hair. It was thick as a wolf's pelt and almost as rough to the touch. She bent, kissing him lightly. Faran had always slept with utter abandon, as boneless as a child, but could be alert and on his feet in the blink of an eye. She didn't want to wake him now.

She turned off the lamp and lay down, careful not to disturb him, and pulled a blanket over them both. Sleep wouldn't come to her so soon after waking, but she wanted the time to think. She slid an arm over his chest and tucked her chin into the crook of his shoulder, just as she'd done so many times in the past. It felt right.

Lexie meant to think about the case, but that wasn't the thought that flitted through her head. *I wonder if he still might want to marry me?*

Her eyes snapped open, the dark pulsing with new questions. She hadn't meant to go there at all. Faran's wide shoulder rose and fell with his breath, solid and comfortable and—part of a werewolf. Mortal, like herself. Occasionally fuzzier. Sometimes deadly ferocious.

However kind he'd been, however wonderful, there was still part of her that went cold when it came to what that wolf could do. That it had done. But that corner of her heart was forgetting to be afraid.

I wonder if someday I would say yes? For a second she let herself drift with that dream, thinking only of the happiness she felt in that moment. And, perhaps because Faran's quirky sense of humor was infecting her, she saw herself in a bridal gown standing next to a wolf in a top hat. She had to bite her lip to keep from laughing out loud. What a wedding portrait that would make.

And then she saw the piece of the case she'd completely missed.

Chapter 16

Faran stumbled from the bedroom like a cave bear in spring: sleep-addled, hungry and sorely in need of grooming. He squinted in the brightness. Someone had turned on the sun.

Lexie was sitting cross-legged on the couch, her laptop balanced on her knees and her hair piled up and skewered with a pencil. "Hey there," she said with a bright smile that made everything seem better. "It's morning, in case you're wondering."

He wandered behind the couch, pausing to kiss the creamy skin where the collar of her pullover dipped at the nape of her neck. She smelled of shampoo. "It's a good morning."

She quirked a grin. "Is it?"

"Sure." After all, they were smiling at each other like total goofs, happy to be in the same room. It had been a while since that had happened.

There was a paper bag on the table that showed telltale

signs of grease. He picked it up and looked inside. A waft of chocolate and butter made his mouth water. "Brioche?"

She continued clicking keys. "I found a bakery open. I was starving. Help yourself."

He bit into it greedily. "What are you working on?"

"I'm sorting through the pictures I took at the banquet."

Faran looked over her shoulder. Maurice was twinkling back from the screen with a Cheshire cat smile. A bit much for first thing in the morning. "He didn't have the scallops or the ceviche. I wonder if he's really allergic to seafood."

"Hmm," Lexie replied, hitting a key that cropped part of the background. "Kyle didn't have the ceviche. He gave his to Leo."

Because he'd been sniffing Leo's. Faran frowned. "I wonder what ordinary people talk about before breakfast."

Lexie kept tapping. "We'll never know."

Faran's mind rambled on. The only royal who had eaten the poisoned food was Amelie, who was unlikely to steal her own ring. "Can you make a folder of all the photos that show the servers? I'd like to verify who served what table."

"Sure. I'm going to check the reception photos, too. See if there are any common faces that raise alarm bells."

She said it confidently, not as a question. She had the end of an investigative thread and was following it with a vengeance. *You go, girl*, Faran thought.

"That's why someone was trying to get in through the window," Lexie said. "They want the photos. When I was taken for questioning, my cameras were searched, but I had the memory cards. But when my cameras came up empty, Gillon tried to run us off the road."

"Because they figured out you had the cards with you." Faran was wide-awake now, and glad he'd had a full measure of sleep. "Our mastermind thinks you took a picture of something incriminating."

She tapped the screen, poking Maurice in the nose. "That's why I need to spend some time going over these. That and the fact Chloe needs to keep the palace media crew happy or we'll both be fired."

"I'll leave you to it, then," said Faran. He didn't like the idea of Lexie on anyone's radar, but she had a point. "I'm taking a shower."

Once he had dressed, he went out in search of steaming hot protein—something Lexie was never interested in until much later in the day. There was a reason he was the Horseman named Famine. Shape-shifters of all kinds had a faster metabolism than humans, which was half the reason he had learned to cook.

On his way, he phoned Valois and requested a guard—a trusted officer not in any way connected to Vidon—be put on Lexie's door. After the struggle to retrieve the poison from the kitchen, he was certain Valois wasn't on the side of the bad guys. The police captain might not love the Company, but he wouldn't do anything to endanger an innocent woman.

And if they were right about the photos, Faran didn't want Lexie left alone. Just as important, he wanted her to *feel* safe. Getting a few things out in the open—like the business with her brother—had seemed to turn things around. There was a long way to go, but he was beginning to hope that their relationship would eventually get back on track. He would personally shred anyone who messed that up.

Faran found a café that offered a hot breakfast and refueled with oatmeal, eggs and spiced sausages while he read the coverage of the poisoning in the paper. The palace was blaming it on bad fish, which was close enough to the truth that the press believed the story. He paid the bill and left, deciding to check in with Valois one last time before contacting Sam and filling him in. The Company was going to be highly interested in the fey connection, especially the older vampires who still remembered when the Dark Fey walked free.

He decided to make his first stop Valois's interrogation rooms at the palace. On his way, Faran walked past the maze and crossed the croquet lawn where he'd chased the would-be intruder. A game was in progress, the players surrounded by a crowd of onlookers with cameras. It looked as if Prince Leo had just beaten Maurice. Today, the musician was wearing something that looked like a zombie version of the Great Gatsby, but with powder-pink fingernails.

Faran stuck to the path, not wanting to get sidetracked from his mission, but it was too late. Leo had spotted him. The prince handed his mallet to one of his flunkies and strolled toward Faran. Forced to be polite, Faran left the path and went to join him near the wickets.

"Mr. Kenyon," said the prince. For once, his tone was friendly. "I want to take the opportunity to thank you for your timely intervention at the banquet."

Faran was mildly surprised by the polite opening. "It was my pleasure and duty, Your Highness."

"We will, of course, be taking better precautions as we lead up to my brother's wedding. My father, despite his old-fashioned ideas, is right about one thing. Royalty has remained aloof in part for its own safety. The closer we get to the people, the more we put ourselves at risk. Mingling with the commoners is a necessary step, but not one that should be taken lightly."

Faran smiled but changed the subject. "How fares the princess?"

"Amelie's health is better, but she is upset at being the victim of theft, especially as she slept." Leo gave a weary smile. "Princesses are not accustomed to such treatment, and she's letting everyone know it."

Faran couldn't stop a chuckle. Amelie had a temper when roused. "I'm relieved to hear that she is feeling well enough to make her opinions heard."

"And Ms. Haven? I am ashamed of the role I played in putting her at risk."

Decking the prince would have been unwise in front of witnesses, so Faran merely nodded. "She is also recovering."

"Good. I will be sure to extend my apologies in person."

As they spoke, the prince's smooth manner began to grate. Faran could have accepted that Prince Leo was a jerk who had been shocked back to civility by a close call, except Faran's nose was telling another story. He recognized the prince's scent from another night in the garden.

"You're quite the sportsman, my lord," Faran said. "I saw you with your friends coming in from the tennis courts, and now you're playing croquet. Do you have other sporting pastimes?"

The prince's smile deepened. Clearly he enjoyed talking about himself. "Many."

"Did I read about you in an expedition up Kilimanjaro?" Faran hadn't, but the lie got him where he needed to go.

"No, Everest."

"Definitely a skilled climber, then."

"Definitely," Leo said. "I've made twice the ascents Kyle has."

The fact that he made that point to a relative stranger said everything about his relationship with his brother. It also said that Faran's nose was right. It had been Leo who had tried to climb Lexie's wall, wearing almost exactly the same gear as the cook who'd poisoned the ceviche.

At first glance, Faran had thought the two balaclava-wearing baddies were the same man. Both were the same height and build, but now he knew the truth. The climber and Leo smelled the same. Unfortunately, Faran had no proof a human could verify, and without it he was useless.

Useless. Faran wanted to howl. His essential need to protect and keep order rebelled. The wolf in him saw no reason why this princeling deserved to continue breathing, much less to be shown respect. The wolf pushed so near the surface of his skin that it prickled.

He took just one step toward the prince—no raised fist or bared teeth—but it was enough to send a coward running. Leo took a wavering step backward, but the heel of his supple leather boot caught on one of the wickets and he went sprawling with a cry of rage.

A bevy of aids dove to help Leo, which only made things more embarrassing. Faran didn't care, but watched the fawning lackeys hinder more than they helped. He was suddenly struck by the memory of these same young men coming in from the tennis court. He had taken note of their faces and a few were missing.

And then two memories clicked together like puzzle pieces. One of the missing lackeys was the evil cook. Faran hadn't made the connection until that instant, but the man had been there in the Queen's Gallery the day Leo had salivated all over Lexie. That meant the poisoner—now in police custody—was Leo's employee. No wonder the princeling had forced Lexie to eat the fish instead of dining on it himself.

Faran nearly lunged for the prince, for one moment eager to simply rip out Leo's throat and damn the torpedoes. It was the way a wolf would handle it. Direct. Honest.

Maurice grabbed his arm. He was unexpectedly strong, his voice low and serious. "Whatever you're thinking, don't."

Faran swore. Leo was up now, being dusted off by his lackeys. The question was what happened next. Company training said to back off and get his ducks in a row, but letting Leo go was a risk. At the same time, he couldn't bring someone to Valois on suspicion of body odor. That sort of thing didn't hold up in court.

The musician leaned close enough to murmur. "Leopold is a brat and deserves whatever you could dream up, but he's also very powerful."

He was. And a prince and his minions would know exactly how a palace worked—how people got hired, how to find out the security routines, how to locate any secret doors or passages. It all made sense.

"You should probably make yourself scarce," Maurice added.

"Great fuzzy balls," Faran growled. "I didn't do anything. Yet."

"You saw Leo embarrass himself. That's crime enough." Maurice's face—eyeliner and all—was grave. "You can nail him properly if you bide your time."

"I don't want to admit it, but you're right," Faran said with great reluctance.

Maurice released Faran's arm and made a shooing motion. "Don't dawdle."

Faran vanished before Leo could gather his wits. But Faran's mind was already galloping ahead. Prince Leo's lackey was in the palace lockup. Faran wondered what it would take to get the man to roll on his prince.

Lexie shoved the computer off her lap. She'd been working long enough her joints felt permanently frozen and her eyeballs fried. So far she'd cleaned up and emailed Chloe images from both the reception and the banquet and sorted the rest for potential sleuthing. She then copied everything to a couple of private clouds just in case something happened. Normally she was paranoid about hackers and avoided storing sensitive work online, but in this instance the more copies there were, the better chance there would be that evidence would survive. Nevertheless, nothing in the zillion photos she'd taken had jumped out at her as remarkable. Maybe she didn't know what she was looking for.

Lexie got up to stretch, walking around the tiny room just to get the blood moving. Her bare foot stepped on something metallic. "Ow."

Bending slowly because she was still stiff from sitting, she picked up the object and rolled it between finger and thumb. Disbelief stunned her thoughts to silence, but her hand went to her thigh anyhow. Her body, if not her brain, understood the thing's significance in those first seconds. And then came a molten anger that ran as slow as honey distilled from the deadliest blooms.

It was a meat skewer, just like the one her brother had used to stab her in the middle of the night. Someone was playing games.

Rage cleared her head, giving her mind speed and logic. The thing hadn't been there last night. It had to have shown up this morning, when she went out to get something to eat. Faran had been in the bedroom, but he was a quiet sleeper—no snoring—and had been keeping odd hours. It was possible no one knew he was there. Nothing had been disturbed, but she'd taken the laptop and memory cards with her to keep working over breakfast, so there had been nothing to steal.

But why leave this? It was clearly a personal attack. Very personal. Intimate, even, and made directly against her.

Her first instinct was to hurl the skewer from the window, but she needed it for proof. She would get the malevolent creep who had left it for her to find.

Lexie slammed it down on the coffee table and scrambled for her phone. In the aftermath of the poisoning, Valois had given her his private line, and she dialed it now.

"You did a background check on me when I was hired. You had a lot of detail," she said once the preliminary greetings were over.

"Yes," Valois replied. "We did so for everyone who was to be close to the prince and princess."

"Who has access to those files?" She stared balefully at the skewer.

"I assure you, we treat those with the utmost confidence."

"Who, Valois?" she pressed. "It's important."

"Me, my two deputies and the head of Vidonese security," he answered defensively—and probably only because of her connection with Faran. "What's this about?"

Vidonese security. The green-coats who had chased Faran with hounds. "Is that Captain Gregori?"

"Yes."

"Who does he answer to?"

"His royal sovereign, of course. Again, Ms. Haven, why do you ask?"

King Targon. Lexie chewed her lip. Outside of the fact that the king didn't like getting his picture taken, she couldn't imagine why he would terrorize a photographer. "Was there anything in the file about my brother?"

She heard the pause. It didn't last long, but it was there. "Yes."

"How much?"

That was the wrong question. She heard the alarm in Valois's tone. "Ms. Haven, I insist you tell me what has prompted these questions."

She ended the call, her face going numb with horror. *I can't relive this again.* It had been hard enough talking about her experience to Faran. She couldn't discuss it with the police captain, who had held her and grilled her in that tiny, oppressive room. Some things were too private to share.

But right now, she couldn't afford privacy, could she?

Lexie began pacing, looking everywhere for other details that said her childhood terrors had returned to haunt her. Few people knew about the skewer incident besides her immediate family. Her stepfather had abdicated responsibility for Justin by then, working out of town as much as he could. Her mother insisted Lexie's injury had been self-harm, that a twelve-year-old girl could and did stab her own thigh for no reason but to get her brother in trouble.

There had been a doctor. Years later, a therapist. The doctor had tried to involve the police, but it had ended up a case of one child's word against her family.

If nobody believes you long enough, eventually you stop talking. And it also meant very few people knew the story. There were even fewer who would want to taunt her with the details.

The room began to grow close, the walls pressing in as if they would crush her to paste. Lexie scrambled into the bedroom and hauled up the sash window, breathing in the cool, sunny air. *I need to get out of here.*

The room began to spin. Panic was shutting off her air. *I have to think logically. What is the effect of all this?*

Someone had come into the room while Faran was alone and asleep. When her back was turned. That was what was most frightening: there was no way to anticipate who would invade their privacy, or when. No place was safe.

Such ambushes had been one of Justin's favorite tactics. The message was fear. *What does that achieve?*

Distraction. Lexie hated herself even as the thought formed in her mind. While she and Faran were gingerly nursing the spark of their relationship back to life, she was the weak link in Faran's defense. If someone got to her, they threw him off his game—and by all evidence he was giving their adversaries a run for their money. *I will not be a liability.*

Lexie couldn't stay in the room a moment longer—not after it had been invaded. She slipped her laptop in her backpack and pulled on a coat. Grabbing her keys, she unlocked the door to the corridor. But as she turned the knob, a weight against it pushed her inward. Caught by surprise, she didn't have a choice but to stagger backward, fright skittering up her spine as the body of a man collapsed into the room. He lolled at her feet, arms splayed, blood trickling into his eyes from a gash on the scalp. He wore one of the gray-and-red jackets of the Marcari palace guard.

With a cry, Lexie instantly dropped to her knees, checking for signs of life. Thank heavens he was human-warm, a faint pulse fluttering at his neck. He wasn't a *thing* like Gillon.

Only then did she think of her own danger. If someone had attacked a guard, that someone was probably still around. The attack must have happened while she was in the bedroom where she wouldn't have heard any noise. She grabbed her phone, hitting redial to call Valois again.

"I wouldn't do that if I were you," said Prince Kyle, stepping over the man to get into the room. He was dressed for the road, in a tight-fitting zippered jacket and driving gloves, sunglasses clipped to his breast pocket. "I don't like it when people ignore me while I'm talking."

He kicked the downed man's feet aside so that he could close the door. The casual contempt of the gesture tore a curse from her. She was flabbergasted. *Prince Kyle?*

Kyle—handsome, suave, the darling of every tabloid—flashed her a look that said he cared no more for her than the wounded guard.

Chapter 17

"I don't believe this!" Rage and fear tore at Lexie, leaving her breathing ragged. Sweat dampened her skin, sticking her clothes to her body.

"That's the whole point. Put away the phone, lovely Lexie," the prince repeated in a warning tone. "It's time to talk."

The Kyle she'd always known would be calling an ambulance. He'd be bandaging cuts and scrapes himself. "This man's wounded," Lexie protested. "He needs help."

"Color me astonished, since I'm the one who wounded him. Put the phone away."

Her hands shook as she pretended to end the call. But living with Justin had given her an ability to cope with insane situations. Instead of ending the call, she turned down the volume and put the live phone in her pocket. If Valois picked up, he'd be able to hear the conversation. She met Kyle's eyes, careful to look submissive even as disbelief and disappointment tore her in two. "What can I do for you, my lord?"

"My lord," he mocked. "You're a good little groveler, aren't you?"

He sounds just like my brother. Tears stung her eyes, but she wasn't sure how much was fear and how much was for Amelie, who had no idea how deceived she'd been.

As they all had been. Hadn't the prince sat here last night, listening to every detail of the case? They'd handed their enemy far too much information. She had to warn Faran, but first she had to get through this. "Yes, my lord, I'll do whatever you like, my lord."

"Will you?"

The guard groaned, his eyelids fluttering. He was coming around. Kyle looked at the man with distaste before flicking his dark gaze back to her. "You have something I want."

"My lord?"

"I want your photos."

No surprise there.

The guard flailed and started to roll over. Kyle kicked him again, and the guard stopped moving.

Taking her time, praying for the cavalry, Lexie reached into her pocket, pulling out the memory cards. She set them on the coffee table. Kyle scooped them up with a smug look that made her want to do serious damage to the crown jewels of Vidon.

"Where are the rest?" he demanded.

"The rest?"

"You downloaded the images somewhere."

She slid the backpack across the floor. "My computer is in there."

As he bent to pick it up, her hand snaked to the top of

the coffee table, snatching up the skewer and holding it so that her sleeve hid the glint of metal.

"Is that it?" he asked, dropping the memory cards into the front pocket of the pack. "Every copy? No more disks or flash drives or tablets?"

"No. Of course not," she lied.

Kyle gave her a condescending smile. "I'll have my people trace your internet accounts just in case."

Lexie ground her teeth.

"Keep in mind, Ms. Haven, that this gives me a record of which photos are yours. If I see any of them in the media, I'll know you have another set. I'll leave it to your imagination how I'll react to that."

"What's in those photos that matters so much?" Speaking up wasn't smart, but Lexie couldn't help herself.

He grabbed her jaw, the light leather gloves he wore cool against her burning skin. He pinched until it hurt. "I didn't give you leave to question me."

His slap made Lexie's head ring. She fell to the carpet, tasting dust. The room wheeled, a rushing sound drowning out every thought. Her stomach rolled dangerously.

As he reached for the door, she shook her head to clear it. Then she silently rose, palming the skewer. She'd first been faced with Justin when she was little more than a baby. Now she was no longer a helpless child. She didn't have to take the same crap.

As Kyle opened the door, she readied herself to strike. He wouldn't be expecting her to do anything but cower.

She heard the scrabbling of claws an instant before Kyle turned the door handle. Relief leaped in her chest, but she caught herself before she made a peep. Kyle wasn't looking at her—he'd smacked her down and was waltzing out in triumph. The handle clicked and the door began to swing.

The wolf—Faran—burst through the door with a snarl.

Lexie stabbed upward with the skewer just as Kyle fell backward in surprise. She felt the point sink into flesh as Kyle, the wolf and Lexie tumbled in a heap. Faran rolled away, vibrating with a low grumble, every line of his body curled with surprise and confusion.

"It's Kyle!" Lexie cried. "He's the one!"

Her word was enough. The wolf sprang, snarling. Ivory fangs snapped like scythes, huge paws reaching for the prince. But Kyle was quick, dodging neatly behind the couch despite the skewer stabbed into his rear. It hadn't gone in far, but it had to hurt like blazes.

Except he wasn't bleeding. He should have been bleeding at least a little.

Faran landed, immediately crouching low, ears flat to his head. Then he began to creep forward, fangs bared. He was slowly driving the prince into the corner where he could be controlled. But Kyle was reaching behind him, groping for something at the small of his back. It was a small, sleek gun—Lexie had felt it dig into her ribs as they'd fallen to the floor.

"He's armed!" she cried, but a warning wouldn't be enough. She knew Faran wouldn't let Kyle go, even to save himself.

The guard had crawled to his hands and knees, wiping the blood from his eyes. Lexie snatched the gun from the guard's holster and trained it on Kyle. "Stop right there! Hands where I can see them!"

Valois pounded through the door with a handful of police. He skidded to a stop, pure astonishment on his face. "Your Royal Highness?"

Kyle's expression was one of pure horror. Lexie looked from him to Faran to the doorway. Prince Kyle—another Prince Kyle—was standing there, too, looking equally astonished. Lexie's brain froze. *What in the blazes?*

Faran's confused growl rumbled low as he looked at the prince in the doorway. Nasty Kyle seized the moment and dove for the bedroom, slamming the door shut and locking it just as the wolf smashed into the panels.

"Stop him!" Valois and the rest dashed toward the bedroom door, ready to break it down. But Faran had already wheeled and bolted for the corridor, disappearing from sight in a streak of gray fur.

Lexie stared at Nice Kyle, utterly shell-shocked. "Since when did you have a double?"

He shook his head, his dark eyes wide. "I don't. I didn't."

Valois's boot crashed the bedroom door open, but the sash was up and the room was empty. Nasty Kyle had jumped or climbed or flown.

Valois holstered his gun and hitched up his belt, his expression one of profound disgust. "If I didn't see him myself, I'd say he was a ghost."

"He's not a ghost," said Lexie. "I skewered him in the butt. He was solid."

Kyle's expression was scandalized. "You skewered him?"

She set the gun on the coffee table and picked up her backpack, clutching it close like a security blanket. "I don't think he was human."

"You think he was like the man who called himself Gillon?" asked the prince.

Valois looked very interested. "Gillon was one of the green-coats. Pardon my saying so, Your Royal Highness, but while most of the Vidonese guard are solid men, there are a few who could do with a second look."

"You have my permission to look as long and hard as you like, Captain," said Kyle.

The prince helped the security guard from the floor

to the couch while Valois called the infirmary for a doctor. The guard was holding a towel to the cut on his head.

Lexie sat down next to the man. "Is there anything I can get you?"

The guard shot her a pained look. "I thought the palace would be an easy position, but no. Wolves? Doppelgängers? Poisonings? I'm putting in my retirement papers first thing in the morning."

Lexie sank to the bed slowly, as if it might explode beneath her. It was hours after her visit from the anti-Kyle, as she was starting to think of the creature, and she could feel her mind thrumming like an overtaxed hard drive. Faran had hunted for the fetch but couldn't find a scent to track him. Technically, the enemy had fled, but there had been a victory of sorts. Now it was clear the enemy was after Lexie's photos, and she had to admit striking back with the skewer had felt liberating.

She didn't want to be in the position where it was hurt or be hurt—so desperate that she'd choose to drive a weapon into flesh. But underneath the prettiness and protocol of the Marcari court, there was war. If she was going to stick around, she had to accept the fight.

And she had to stay—running would cost her far too much. Top of that list was Faran. Once again he'd come when she needed him. That was simply who he was.

He was irreplaceable.

The wolf was standing in the bedroom doorway, yellow eyes watching her. He'd approached so quietly, she hadn't heard. Now that she knew he was there, she could feel his scrutiny, sense him testing her response. Wondering if seeing him chase a villain had brought back memories of that blood-soaked alley in Paris. It did, but she understood so much more now.

"I'm not going to scream and run," she said quietly. "Unless I jump out the window, there's nowhere to go. But you never know. Kyle's double tried it."

He padded forward a step, then paused. Lexie's heart skipped a beat, but she didn't move. Apparently encouraged, Faran drew near and put his chin on her knee, eyebrows lifting. Werewolves didn't normally fall in the cute and cuddly department, but he was giving it a good try. Gingerly, she touched the rough coat of his ruff and he whined in pleasure, ears cupping forward. Encouraged, she dug her fingers in deeper, feeling the solid warmth of him.

"This is kind of weird," she said. "Should I be throwing a ball for you? Taking you for walks? Filling a water dish?"

Faran backed away, giving an enormous yawn that showed the long, razor-sharp teeth. Lexie hid her shudder as best she could, but it was impossible not to feel like Red Riding Hood when she saw those fangs. The wolf bounded onto the bed, making the entire frame skid with his weight.

"Hey," said Lexie, jumping up. "Get off the furniture!"

But when she spun around, Faran was back in human form, and entirely naked. He folded his hands behind his head and grinned. "Do you really want me to leave?"

Lexie's cheeks heated. "That's the thing with dogs. They let it all hang out."

Faran's lips twitched. "At least I don't claw the couch."

He raised himself up on one elbow and held out his other hand, beckoning when she didn't move right away. Still balanced on the edge of her mental precipice, Lexie took his hand, letting him pull her forward until her knees bumped the edge of the bed.

"What's wrong?" he asked. He had that animal way of knowing when she was unhappy. It would have been perfect timing if he weren't so utterly, gorgeously distracting.

"I'm not used to stabbing people, even when they're not actually people."

"Do you want to talk about it?"

She could have, but the mood was too good and both of them needed a break. She bent forward, kissing him lightly. "We'll talk, but not now."

He ran his fingertips down her throat and into the hollow of her collarbone. Her nerves sparked wherever he touched, leaving tingles of fire and ice. "I want you," he said.

Her breath caught. This had been coming for days.

They hadn't made love since he'd told her what he was. They had slept together for a year, but the strangeness of his revelation had made her slam that door tight. And now she could see the wolf stir just beneath the surface of his smile. It wanted her, too, and that was the problem. She ducked her head, not able to meet his gaze.

"Don't hide from me," he whispered. It was a plea, plain and clear. "You don't have to be brave in front of me."

"You wear a mask just as much as I do," she said softly.

"I took mine off," he said, a hint of tension in the words. *And you ran.*

Lexie wanted to back away, but every instinct told her the wolf was relentless. It had patience and stamina she could only dream of. Wherever she ran, Faran would follow, if only as a ghost in her heart.

In Paris, things had been very clear. She had lived as prey for too many years to accept the ultimate predator as her partner. They might have been worlds apart, but they both understood jungle law. She had refused to put herself in that position again.

Faran frowned, as if the same thoughts were going through his mind. "I never knew what was going on with you until now. Still, I'm sorry I handled everything so badly."

"I wasn't exactly sharing." But her words were lost as he pulled her onto the bed. "Faran!"

"Relax," he said. "You have the upper hand between us."

He rolled onto his back, carrying her along with the motion so that she was on top of him. Her legs straddled his narrow waist, her skirt hitching up so her bare thighs felt the play of his muscles. Old habit brought her hands to his shoulders and chest—she'd always loved the feel of his warm, smooth skin—and she realized why some habits should never be shaken. Heat rippled through her as his hands gripped her waist. His eyes were drowsy with lust.

Faran's gaze slowly focused. It held hope and trepidation and just a pinch of mischief. "I get that I have to earn your trust, after what's happened to you. But I need you to give me the chance."

Lexie's words scattered. She could only find one. "Why?"

He slid a hand beneath hers, lacing their fingers together. "I love the way you see the world in ways no one thinks to look. You push yourself to ridiculous lengths before you even begin to think you measure up. I'm fascinated and appalled that you can live on Gummy Bears and coffee for days. You're astonishingly beautiful. I could go on forever, but I'm no poet. All I can say is that I think you and I deserve some happiness, and I think we can give it to one another."

Lexie's throat ached with longing. She could feel Faran's pulse pound, steady and strong. He was an anchor, a safe harbor, and yet the shadowy memories of her childhood whispered that safety was a treacherous illusion. "It may take some time."

"I have time."

His hands slid under the hem of her skirt, one finger teasing the strap of her thong. She squirmed, feeling his interest alive and well. Her slight movement made him catch his breath. Lexie raised an eyebrow. "Maybe you're not as patient as you think."

He closed his eyes. "That's the part of me that doesn't think all that much."

Parts of her weren't doing all that much meditating, either. A warm, liquid heat was slowly eroding all caution. "What if I lose the ability to form words?"

"Pick a safe word. See if you can manage that."

Lexie leaned forward and whispered in his ear. *"Crispy shrimp."*

Faran rumbled a laugh. "And here I thought it would be *gummy bear.*"

Since she was already there, she nipped his ear. "You're elevating my tastes."

"You're enjoying this far too much."

She was. It felt as if she was remembering how to breathe.

He was still stroking the skin beneath her skirt, tracing her hip bone, teasing the elastic of her lingerie until the strap of her thong broke. With a slow, deliberate movement he drew it from beneath her. The lingering friction sent a jolt of sensation from her sensitized flesh all the way up her spine, her nipples peaking beneath the fabric of her pullover. The thong hit the floor with a faint whisper of silk.

All at once the fabric of her clothes felt unbearably coarse and heavy. Lexie took her pullover off, letting the long, thick curtain of her hair fall bare against her skin. It felt wildly sensual, as if a rich palette of colors had been translated to touch. He reached up to twine it in his fingers, his eyes going dark with interest. His nostrils flared, clearly scenting her. Lexie's skin pebbled, aroused and a little fearful at once.

She wriggled her skirt off, and then Faran's strong fingers were stroking up her sides, coaxing her without confining, leaving her free to bend and kiss the rough stubble of his jaw.

His mouth found hers, hot and demanding. They kissed urgently, with an insistence that spoke of long denial. They nipped and sucked, fencing with their tongues and drawing out that first hot contact as if it was the whole of their lovemaking. Lexie moved with the ebb and flow of the tension, still straddling Faran's waist and bracing herself against his broad chest. His hands found the straps of her bra, working them loose until his fingers found a path beneath the lace. She gasped at his touch, the sweet pleasure of it sparking in her belly. The bra fell, joining the thong on the floor.

For all her resistance it had taken no time at all to find herself naked in Faran's arms again. Fire raged in her. She had wanted this without admitting it—and not any touch but his. It was as if she had somehow become addicted to him. She needed his touch to truly live.

She leaned forward, giving him access to her breasts. He squeezed and teased them, tonguing the nipples until they throbbed and her core was on fire. She arched against him, pressing her mound into the hard length of his sex until they both were gasping. When he at last slid on the condom, she was truly ready. He filled her utterly, stretching her hot, greedy core until she thought she would burst.

She could hold still no longer. Lexie rocked her hips forward, glorying in the feel of fullness within. Her hair brushed against her shoulders with each motion, a counterpoint of soft against hard as Faran thrust with her. For the first time, she was fully conscious of setting the pace, of being in control. The sense of power increased her plea-sure, but also the sense of giving pleasure. For the first time, she was fully there and not trying to hide.

And then the coil of tension inside her began to unwind, like a spring losing integrity. Her muscles clenched around Faran, pleasuring him as she rocked. He made noises that might have been encouragement, but she couldn't under-stand words anymore. Their rhythm began to break, as if her muscles no longer obeyed her brain.

Faran growled, and the low, shuddering vibration in his chest undid her. Lexie's mind blanked, losing the signal of the world around her. The thrust of his release filled her as she cried out and melted into a pulsing, aching ecstasy. Faran gripped her tight, anchoring her so that she could abandon herself.

Lexie released a wordless gasp of surrender. Sex be-tween them had always been good, but it had never been like this. She slid down, curling against him. She felt his muscles uncoiling as he tucked her close, gathering her into his warmth.

Tears blurred Lexie's vision—not from sadness, but from release and relief. For once in her life, she felt a mo-ment of certainty. She belonged here, at Faran's side. She wasn't giving this up for anything.

If staying meant she had to fight, then she would fight.

Chapter 18

King Targon raised his eyebrows. "You are telling me that someone is impersonating my son to obtain photographs taken by this woman?"

He pointed at Lexie, who was standing next to Faran in the small private study King Renault used as his personal refuge from the pressures of public life. From the paintings and knickknacks, it seemed Amelie's father had a passion for sailing. She couldn't imagine what Targon put up on his walls. Maybe genealogies to prove he was as extra special as his attitude claimed.

The two kings sat in identical armchairs, framing tall windows with an ocean view. Kyle stood next to his father. Only the five of them were present. Amelie was still resting, and Leo was sleeping off a late night.

"I saw it with my own eyes, Your Majesty," Kyle said, using his father's formal title. They didn't seem to be a warm and fuzzy family. "The intruder was perfect in every detail, although it is still not clear why the photos are important."

"Perfect in every detail? How is that possible?" Targon shot back. "I know there are witnesses, but surely there was some kind of trickery involved."

Lexie tried to listen, but her imagination kept conjuring the night before. She cast a sidelong look at Faran, admiring his straight nose, the firm set of his jaw and the easy way he stood in the presence of these kings. He was utterly comfortable in his own body, sure of his own worth.

Making love to Faran had been very good, and by letting her take the lead, he had known exactly how to keep it within her comfort zone. The fact that he hadn't broken his word and pushed her boundaries before she was ready meant more than she could say. His presence beside her now, warm and vibrant, was enough to make her dream of a repeat performance right there on the rich Oriental carpet.

"Your Majesty," said Faran. "I believe Prince Kyle's double was a fetch."

"A fetch?" Targon asked. To Lexie's surprise, he'd seemed perfectly aware of Faran's role in the Company. It seemed the two kings were working together in ways she hadn't expected.

King Renault shifted uneasily in his chair. "Are you saying that we are dealing with fey magic?"

"Dark Fey magic. Lexie and I destroyed one already. The man named Gillon."

"Can you explain how those work?" Kyle asked. "I thought you had attributed your melting man to fringe science."

"I did," said Faran. "But then I considered fey involvement. The point is that a fetch of an individual can be made using hair, blood, nails or any other part of their body. It's a dark ritual, often involving blood sacrifice. The more blood, the more real the fetch, and they need to keep ingesting it to stay functioning. That's why they're always craving salt and water."

Lexie thought of Gillon and his snack food, and then wished she hadn't. Recalling the melting episode totally dampened her mood.

Faran went on, sounding very much as if he had been doing his homework. "Fetches can walk, talk and function like a living person until they're damaged beyond repair. The main difference is they're cold to the touch."

Everyone looked at Lexie. Her face had bruised where the anti-Kyle had hit her. "He wore gloves, but I noticed when I skewered the fetch, there was no blood. Gillon didn't bleed, either, until he was fatally wounded."

"I don't understand one thing," said Kyle, looking acutely uncomfortable. "Why was my double's personality so different?"

"Because he was made by the Dark Fey, my lord," said Faran. "They don't think like we do. Our understanding of thought and emotion do not apply."

"We might view their way of thinking as a pathology, maybe psychopathy," said King Renault. "But to them it's utterly logical."

This led to a discussion of the ring and the link Faran had discovered between the rubies and the gates to the Dark Fey kingdom. Faran explained it all well, but in his typical no-frills manner. It seemed to be the right choice because everyone listened intently, even Targon. When it came to matters of the Night World, Faran was the expert and the alpha in the room. *He's more confident than he used to be*, Lexie realized.

Kyle was the first to speak when Faran was done. "But why would anyone wish to release the Dark Fey?"

"Allies," said King Renault. "The fey have great power, and the Dark would promise anything to be free of their bonds. They are the one force that could possibly destroy the Company."

A strained silence filled the room. Lexie's mind drifted back to the stone circle and the magic she'd sensed there. She tried to imagine what fey would be like, but kept coming up with the winged creatures of her childhood books. *Probably not.*

Then Targon cleared his throat. "As you are no doubt aware, there are elements in Vidon opposed to the wedding, particularly when it comes to the Company. However, I have chosen to move forward, and I will not tolerate dissent on the matter. It is clear that somewhere in the two courts hides a traitor."

"A traitor?" Prince Kyle exclaimed. "Why have I not heard of this?"

"To be frank," said King Renault, exchanging a look with Targon, "while we've been aware of a plot ever since the wedding plans were finalized, it was a difficult thread to pursue. Does the plot originate in Marcari or Vidon? We don't know. The impulse was for each of us to blame the other. We had to go carefully."

Targon picked up the story. "That was another reason to send the Company away—to see what mice came out to play when the cat was missing."

"I'd say the mice have been working overtime, my lord," Kyle said dryly.

"Your Majesty," said Faran, "is the aim of the traitor to stop unification of the two countries?"

"More likely it is to take both kingdoms for himself or herself," Targon replied. "The Company would not stand for that, nor would those of my loyal guard. There is a third player involved. This lends credence to your theory that fey might be in the mix, probably in return for the release of their kin. They have the resources such a plot would require. Of course, they would find a way to turn on their masters. Fey always do."

None of this was comforting news. As if sensing her mood, Faran squeezed Lexie's hand as Renault gave the order for Captain Valois to be summoned. A few minutes later, he arrived with two guards escorting a prisoner in chains. A chair was placed in the middle of the floor, and the man shoved into it. The guards fastened his chains to the chair and left. The man sat sullenly, hanging his head.

Discomfort tightened Lexie's skin. The chains bothered her, but the man's identity bothered her more. Valois said the prisoner's name was Poitier, and he was the cook who had poisoned the ceviche.

King Renault stood, clasping his hands behind his back. His calm, almost mild manner didn't waver, but Lexie could feel the steel beneath his refined persona. He walked around the prisoner slowly, viewing him from all angles, before he said a word.

"This wretch does not look like much," he said quietly. "And yet he hurt my child. He insulted me. He endangered my guests. Under Marcari law, there is no reason for me to let him live. And yet knowing all that, he will say nothing to help himself. Have I got that right, Capitaine Valois?"

"You do, sire. Poitier here has refused to give us anything."

Faran folded his arms. "I would suggest turning him over to the Company, Your Majesty. They have ways and means of making the most stubborn prisoner talk."

At that, Poitier lifted his head. He looked straight at Lexie, his eyes red-rimmed and haunted. Part of him clearly wanted to confess. But his dark, stubbled jaw worked as if he was chewing whatever he might have said to bits. Lexie knew that look. It was the face of someone who had been terrorized. It went straight through her, sharp as an arrow.

"Wait," she said. "He's obviously *more* afraid of someone else."

"Very astute, Ms. Haven," said Valois, who sounded unhappy about that fact. "Obviously we need to establish the fact we're the ones he really needs to fear."

"Maybe you need to convince him you'll keep him safe," Lexie shot back.

Valois wasn't buying it. "Perhaps you care to leave, Ms. Haven?"

"Lexie," Faran began, but he was interrupted.

"No," said the prisoner, his voice rusty with disuse. "It's not that, miss, but thank you."

Valois gave him a withering look.

"I saw you with Prince Leo," Faran said. "Of course you were using a different name."

Lexie caught her breath. So had she, the same day they'd met Leo in the gallery. It seemed ages ago, but it had only been a few days.

Faran continued. "Not too many of the prince's other school friends decide to get a job in the royal kitchens, not even when they have gambling debts mysteriously paid off."

Lexie heard Targon mutter a curse. She doubted the king liked many of Leo's friends.

"What can I say," Poitier replied, stretching cracked lips into a false smile. "Food service pays better than anyone thought."

Faran snorted at that. "I don't think so."

"Haven't you asked Prince Leo for protection?" Lexie asked.

At that, the prisoner laughed. "Oh, miss, you know nothing about this place."

"Why would my son protect a traitor?" King Targon demanded.

That made Poitier laugh even harder.

Valois shook the man's shoulder. "Silence!"

Faran moved suddenly, approaching the prisoner in the chair. At first Lexie thought he was going to shake Poitier to silence his laughter, and she caught her breath, ready to interfere. But instead Faran nudged Valois aside and stood over Poitier, arms folded.

Faran radiated authority, but it was of an earthier kind than Renault's. "Short of torture, we've tried all the usual means with you. I'm sure you realize how unusual it is for a prisoner to be personally questioned by Their Majesties. In fact, I doubt it's been done for a hundred years. You're being given a last chance to clear your name that many would plead for."

Poitier just looked up at him.

"Tell me one thing, yes or no. We think Gillon was holding something for safekeeping when he died. Am I right?"

To Lexie's surprise, Poitier answered in a firm voice. "Yes."

Faran nodded. "Good. Did Gillon take that object in the first place?"

"No."

"Was the person who took that object the same person who told you to apply for a job in the kitchen?"

"Yes."

"Why do you keep saying *the object*?" asked Kyle. "It's Amelie's wedding ring."

The prisoner made a noise deep in his throat.

"Because I just realized that he can't," said Faran. "And I bet you can't talk about Prince Leo, either."

Poitier made the same noise again. Lexie's curiosity rose to a white heat.

"What is the meaning of this?" King Targon demanded. "What has Prince Leopold to do with any of this?"

Faran stepped back, his face dark with worry. "Sire, Poitier literally cannot speak of it. He's under a compulsion. It's like hypnosis."

"What?" Lexie cried, appalled.

"That is a vampire trick," King Targon snapped. "And I understand you, Mr. Kenyon, are an employee of the Company. Is this an honest interrogation?"

"Compulsion is also a fey trick, Your Majesty," Faran replied. "The Company has no hand in this, I assure you."

"The fey again," muttered King Renault.

"But you suspect my brother of something," said Prince Kyle in a tight voice.

Faran shook his head. By his expression, Lexie guessed he was treading with extreme care. "I have no evidence that would stand up in a court of law."

"But?" Kyle prompted.

Faran's shoulders tensed. "Forgive me, Your Highness, but he does seem to be connected to these events."

"This is ridiculous," snapped Kyle. He stormed to the door and put his head out, barking orders at someone Lexie couldn't see. "Bring my brother here at once! In his bathrobe if need be. We have questions for him."

Poitier began thrashing and howling in the chair. For a moment, all Lexie could do was stare. She'd never seen a grown man do such a thing. "What on earth is the matter?"

"I'd say he doesn't want to see the prince." Valois shook the prisoner again. Poitier stopped howling, and sobbed a long, hollow moan that froze Lexie's blood.

King Targon had gone pale. "Well, if there is such a thing as compulsion and he is suffering under it, then perhaps the best course is to take the prisoner back to his cell and ask him questions he can answer. I don't see what else we can accomplish here."

Except to question Leo, Lexie thought. That was a door Targon was clearly reluctant to open. Her mind flashed back to the banquet, the prince forcing her to eat the poisoned fish. Guilty? Hell, yes. But of conspiracy?

Urgent footsteps pounded outside the door. A breathless footman presented himself and bowed. "Your Majesties, Your Highness, I regret to say that I am unable to summon Prince Leopold."

"Why not?" Kyle asked.

"My lord, he has left the palace."

"Then tell him I want to see him when he's back."

"I'm afraid I did not explain myself perfectly, Your Royal Highness. The prince is gone. His belongings are no longer in his guest room, and his car has left the garage."

Lexie couldn't see the footman's face, but his whole body was ramrod-straight with tension.

"Thank you," said Prince Kyle, his voice tinged with shock. "You may go."

The door closed behind the footman. Everyone looked around the room, as if the others had answers. If nothing else made Leo look guilty, this certainly did.

Lexie's mind flicked to her phone call with Valois about her personnel files. She'd wondered if Captain Gregori and the Knights of Vidon had accessed her information, looking for details about Justin. But if King Targon also had access, did that mean Prince Leo could have snooped, as well?

King Renault finally spoke. "Captain Valois, please return the prisoner to his cell. Ms. Haven, Mr. Kenyon, thank you for your account of Prince Kyle's double. Those of us who count Prince Leopold as family should remain to discuss this latest development."

Lexie nodded, relieved to be dismissed. Faran put a possessive hand at her back, guiding her toward the door. Their path took them past the prisoner.

Just then, Poitier turned his head to get a better view of Lexie. "You're Ms. Haven?"

"Yes."

"I thought I remembered you from the Queen's Gallery." His face twisted. It wasn't a pleasant expression in the least. "I was given a message for you. I was told I had to say it when I met you. I guess they knew this was going to happen."

"What message?" Faran asked darkly.

"Justin says hi."

Chapter 19

It was time for explanations, Lexie realized.

"A skewer?" exclaimed Faran. "So that's what you stuck into him?"

The visceral memory of the point driving into flesh made Lexie shudder. "You were going for his throat. My work was on the reverse side. I wonder if I'd pulled it out if he'd have started to leak that yellow ooze."

Faran jammed his hands through his thick hair, making it stand on end. "And you didn't tell me about finding the skewer till now because?"

"Last night was too good. I didn't want to spoil it with stories of my sick brother."

They were sitting on the couch in their rooms, Lexie on one end and Faran on the other. He looked oddly helpless, as if the cushions between them stretched for miles. Lexie bridged the distance, putting her hand on his knee.

He huffed a sigh. "I was getting my Barry White on

while you were wondering why some psycho is stalking you. I always had the best timing."

She winced. "True, but you managed to take my mind off it. That's saying something."

"Next time tell me right away." He put a hand over hers. "You realize that your life could depend on it?"

She hitched herself toward him, so she could lean against his shoulder. "Sure."

His fingers tightened. "You're not alone."

No, because Justin says hi.

"I know," she said. "And I also know that whoever is behind this is trying to reduce me to a mass of quivering goo to throw us—you—off your game."

Faran looked dubious. "There are many more superheroes where I came from. I doubt this is all about me."

"Don't sell yourself short." She leaned close, giving him a kiss.

His eyes seemed to flash wolf-yellow, although it might have been a trick of the light. "Let me put the Company on this. It's the kind of thing they're good at, and they're gnashing their fangs at being kept out of the game."

"Now there's a pretty image."

"It's better to keep them busy, trust me."

She had a mental vision of Count Dracula doing background checks. By the end of it, they'd know every sordid detail. Every time she had to stay after school. And the time the child welfare people had come to the house after she'd started cutting herself in the school bathroom. As if she needed that dredged up.

She loathed the invasion of a past she wished she could obliterate, but somewhere in this mess she'd lost her privacy. Everyone had chips on the table. That were hers. "Okay."

Justin says hi, but we'll say hi right back at you.

Faran kissed her temple, but she twisted around, giving him her mouth. She couldn't live in the past without shriveling up. Relief was the only thing that mattered right then, and Faran was exactly what she needed.

He tasted faintly of chocolate from the mocha he'd been drinking, and beneath that was the wild, unique taste of him. His beard was already rough, but she liked it that way. She spent more than enough time with the pretty men of the fashion world. Faran was like whisky after ice wine.

His hands slid around her waist as she crawled into his lap, lacing her arms about his neck. He was still wearing the dress shirt he'd had on to visit royalty, but the tie and cufflinks had gone missing. He cleaned up well, but it wasn't his default setting. She began working on the buttons, unwrapping him with the same anticipation as when she lifted the puffy white paper that covered the top layer of a box of chocolates. Anticipation. Reveal. Then heaven. Her lips found the spot right below the notch of his collarbone. He made a thrumming noise in his chest that went straight to her belly. Heat suddenly pooled there and every other idea fled from between her ears.

"I need you. Now."

She pushed against him, her breasts aching to be touched. She slid her hands beneath his shirt, his smooth, taut skin quivering to life beneath her fingertips. She pulled the shirt loose and he threw it aside. Their lips met again in an ecstasy of heat. She could feel the evidence of his arousal and fumbled for his buckle.

"I'm not so certain of my control right now," he said hoarsely. "This might not be the best idea."

His face was nearly blank, as if he was holding back. But she was too far gone to care. "Bring it."

"Are you sure?" The buckle gave, and he moaned.

"Do you want me to sign a waiver?" she asked wryly.

He stood, lifting her with him as if she was no more than a doll. Lexie's insides felt electric, pulsing with the need to have him then and there. Her legs wrapped around his waist—an interesting position but the *wrong* position for what she really wanted. "Bed. Now."

"Yes, ma'am."

They left a litter of clothes behind them and somehow picked up a bottle of wine and two glasses Lexie had got when she first arrived at the palace. Not that Lexie really wanted wine now, but there was something decadent about sex and Cabernet in the afternoon.

But they never got to it. They had barely pulled the cork out before Faran set the bottle aside, losing interest. He prowled across the coverlet, bending to kiss the soft part of her stomach. His lips and beard made an entrancing combination of scratchy and silk. Her muscles tensed, laughter bubbling as his tongue found her navel.

"You taste good," he said. "Sweet."

And then he nipped her. It was soft, hardly painful, but the sting of it rippled through her, subtly arousing. Instinctively, her knees flexed, giving access lower down. His teeth and tongue found more flesh, teasing her in ways both familiar and new. He'd learned a few tricks she didn't expect, though any surprise she felt immediately melted in a puddle of sensation.

He applied a condom and eased into her, filling her deliciously, driving out every unhappy thought from her head. It felt different with him on top. She was less in control, but it didn't seem important. She wanted him. Lexie moved to meet his thrust, welcoming the strength and desire that seemed to flow from his massive body into hers. She reveled in his sculpted form, enjoying him as much as an artist as a woman.

And then the pressure inside her began to build, unraveling thoughts and images into a kaleidoscope of color and sensations. Need coiled up her spine, urgent for relief, bringing cries to her lips that only seemed to spur Faran on. He drove her to the brink and backed away again, teasing her with caresses, suckling her breasts and driving her mad with a game of delay and retreat.

Until eventually, he could take it no longer. His rhythm changed, quickening and deepening. She grabbed hold of his arms, planted like oaks to keep her free of his weight. They felt utterly masculine, roped and corded and moist with the strain of his exertions. Control slipped, all tethers to reason flying apart. Desire thundered through her. She cried out, not sure if she was falling or flying. She felt his answering response, a triumphant cry that deepened to a growl.

Time stretched out a delicious, incalculable length. At last, she fell back, wrung out and with no more will than a leaf circling on a summer pond. Pleasant sensations wafted through her like the pure notes of a scale. She was relaxed. Utterly. Entirely at peace.

"Faran," she whispered, touching his hair.

He rose up from where he lay beside her, straddling her again. While she had not minded his limbs caging her a moment ago, it felt confining now and she tried to squirm to a position that gave her more room. Something in the way he moved was different. It was and was not the body language of a human lover. At least a little of it belonged to the wolf.

Her bliss evaporated as apprehension prickled her scalp. "Faran?"

He eased down as if to kiss her, but he went to her throat instead of her lips. She felt the scrape of whiskers, the soft hot press of his mouth, and then suddenly she felt teeth.

Not human teeth, but long, fierce fangs denting her skin. One snap and her flesh would be gone.

Lexie's heart hammered so hard she felt dizzy. The feeling in her limbs deserted her, as if every nerve ending was focused on her vulnerable throat. Lexie made a high, keening sound she didn't even know she possessed.

Then the fangs pressed in. It hurt—not like his love nips but a real knife of hot agony. Her breath sawed in like a dying woman's, squeezed by terror. A warm trickle of blood coursed down her neck. Lexie tried to summon a breath to scream, but then the pain was gone, replaced by the velvet of his tongue licking up the blood. "No one touches you but me," he murmured, his voice more rumble than speech.

Lexie's brain froze, fury and horror struggling for mastery. She lashed out, the thump of her fist laughable against the enormous plane of his hard muscles. He didn't laugh or try to stop her. Instead he rolled, pulling her on top of him.

She moved to strike him again, but jerked to a stop. The room was dim, the curtains drawn, but she could see the wolf in him now, naked though his features were the same, familiar Faran. A dual response flared in her. Unexpectedly, the raw wildness was jaw-dropping, burning hot sexy off the charts. Her inner core ached with possessive heat. She'd seen hints of this side of him before, but now it raked her with claws bared—and she wanted it. But more than that, she knew without a need for words that the bite was the wolf's response to the threat against her. He had marked her for his own.

At the same time…there were the teeth. On her throat. Biting. That was exactly the nightmare that had made her hop a plane out of Paris.

Her neck throbbed with every beat of her heart. Tension had set her trembling, but she stiffened her joints. Somewhere in the back of her mind, she knew running would make her look like prey.

"You should warn a girl before you bite her like that," she said, keeping her tone light.

His eyes narrowed, as if language took extra focus. "I didn't know I would. I just needed to."

Surging up from the mattress, he pressed his mouth to hers. The coppery tang of her own blood teased her tongue. He laced his fingers through her hair, holding her while he claimed her mouth again and again. A wildness rose up, a sudden white flame of heat. Where it came from, she didn't know. It was just there, boiling over, all but bringing a snarl to her own lips. She gave him a taste of his own medicine, catching his lip in her teeth.

With a stomach-dropping lurch, Lexie's world came into balance. With a violent, terrifying need, she ached to pull him into her, his blood, his heat, his seed—all that was Faran. She wanted to devour him and be devoured by him at once. She hooked a leg over him, pushing him back to the pillow.

An inner beast of her own had suddenly awakened. It had stirred when she'd skewered the anti-Kyle, but now it was fully awake. Primitive, fierce, it didn't need coddling or caution—all it wanted was to be in charge.

"Oh, yes," Faran said with a soft laugh. "There you are."

Chapter 20

Faran opened his eyes. The wolf was satisfied, but his human half felt incredibly sheepish. He didn't normally think of himself as two separate beings, but there were times instinct and higher functions weren't on the same page. This was definitely one of them.

He'd promised to give Lexie full control of the bedroom. The wolf had gone for the classic dominance mating. Lexie had more than come along for the ride—he certainly didn't remember *that* much fire in Paris because the city would have burned down for sure—but the morning after was always the acid test.

It was early, but the bed was empty. Deep inside Faran, the wolf was curled up in a blissful, sated slumber leaving the rest of him to face the music. *Flaming fuzzy furballs.*

He slid out of bed, muscles burning with overuse. Right around three in the morning, he'd started to lose track of everything he and Lexie were doing. It was as if they'd been trying to catch up on all the romance they'd missed during their time apart. With interest. He grinned but then lost his smile when he looked at the empty sheets again. They were cold.

He pulled on sweatpants and shuffled out of the bedroom. Thank the gods Lexie was still there. She'd resumed her station on the couch, computer drawn onto her lap. She looked clean and groomed and good enough to eat with ice cream. And then he noticed she was wearing a turtleneck to hide what had to be ungodly bruises down her neck.

Faran experienced a moment of utter trepidation. She had that pencil in her hair again. Lately she'd proven handy with pointy objects. But that was only a metaphor for what she'd done to his heart once, and had every right to do all over again. All the caution he'd used to buffer himself from torment had been swept away by a possessive need last night. He'd laid himself bare, and this was going to hurt.

"Hi," he croaked.

She twisted around to watch him as he circled the couch to stand in front of her. Her hazel eyes were wary. "Hi. I'm afraid I didn't go out and get anything to eat yet."

The last time she had, someone had crept into the room. "Smart call."

Words died on his lips. A cowardly part of him wanted to dive for the shower. Surely anything he had to say would go better when he was shaved and dressed. But stalling was just prolonging the agony.

"About last night," he ventured.

Her lips thinned. "I don't know what to think."

Here it comes. "I know, I know." He jammed his hands into his hair.

Lexie dumped the computer off her lap and reached forward, grabbing the ties of his pants. She dragged him onto the couch beside her. "Listen. I'm not an idiot. We're trying to control something here that can't be tidied up and served on a paper doily. Rules and restrictions don't go with wolves."

His heart crashed to his feet. She'd given up on him. "Normally I keep good control. It's kind of all werewolves think about. When to let it out. When not to. I lost my pack young, maybe I didn't learn all I needed to, but I've kept working on it."

He stopped talking right there. That babble was so not what he'd meant to say.

Her mouth turned down, but he couldn't tell what her expression meant. He could smell the stress in her, but not the exact cause. "I'm not blaming you. In case you hadn't figured it out with all the moaning and screaming, I had an amazing time. I mean, amazing with underscores and about a hundred exclamation points."

"Only a hundred?" he said, reaching for a quip to hide behind.

At that her mouth curled up into a lopsided and very wicked grin. "You should come with a dosage limit just so I remember to take too much."

"You mean *not* to take too much."

"I meant what I said."

Faran's whole body eased. It was like the sun coming out from behind a cloud. "Okay."

"But here's the thing." She sat back with the heel of her hand pressed against her forehead. "I completely responded to your wolf."

"Why is that a problem?"

"It's not. Or shouldn't be. But I liked it." She covered her face. "I'm not saying this right."

But Faran knew all about a person's shadow side. "You shocked yourself."

She pulled her hands away, almost panting. "I was totally into it. What does that make me?"

He took her hand and kissed her palm, reveling in the taste and scent of her. "It makes *me* very lucky."

"I stabbed someone yesterday. In self-defense, but still. What's going on? It's like I'm—I don't know, not acting like me."

"Now I'm confused." He released her hand, his stomach going tight with nerves.

"Oh, please. I'm not equating having sex with you with stalker psychos."

"Thanks for that."

She squeezed her eyes shut, clearly struggling to find the right words.

"Are you okay with what you've done?" he asked quietly.

"I'm pushing down every protective wall I've ever built around myself and it's scary."

He heard the bald honesty in her words and was grateful. He could work with honesty. "Think of it this way, Lex. You've spent a long time healing. We connected before, but I don't think either of us was ready. I had an idealized view of what would happen when I found someone to love, and I didn't realize it wasn't going to happen according to the script in my head."

She opened her mouth to speak, but he held up his hand. "Let me finish. We're both more experienced now. I've rattled around the world, seeing what matters and what really doesn't. You've come out from behind your walls. You're fighting to be who you were supposed to be when you first landed on this planet, before your brother's horror show."

Faran took a deep breath. He really hated it when people gave him advice, so he hoped his little speech didn't suck. "You took the skewer and turned it into a weapon.

You met my wolf head-on and made his head spin. And you're using your photos to help people you care about with the investigation. You're doing okay."

Lexie swallowed. "You make it sound so natural."

"It is. So is a touch of self-doubt. A little bit makes us check to make sure we're not fooling ourselves."

She leaned her forehead against his shoulder. "Since when did you get so wise?"

He lifted Lexie's chin and kissed her long and slow and full of everything he wanted for her, from her, for them both. "Hey, I'm brilliant until it comes to my own stuff. That's when I'll need you."

Having someone like Faran in her corner meant the world to Lexie. Having that person tell her she was on the right path rated an entire star system.

Accordingly, Lexie felt far steadier than she had before they'd talked. Filled with fresh determination, she tapped the computer back to life to get some work done while Faran showered and dressed. The screen filled with an image from the reception. It wasn't a great one, just a general reference shot she'd taken to show the mass of glittering humanity who'd shown up to celebrate. Sometimes it helped to remember who had been sitting with whom.

Her gaze caught on a pair of men talking in the background. She zoomed in on them, folding her legs to boost the screen to a better angle. One figure was Prince Leo, champagne flute in hand, the other was Gillon. They were chatting, heads bent together. A conspiratorial pose if ever she saw one, but a prince talking to a security guard in a public place was hardly a hanging offense.

Except—Gillon's eyes were reflecting like a dog's. She'd passed over it before, not picking out the odd effect among the glitter of jewels and crystal chandeliers.

It was creepy enough to raise Lexie's skin to gooseflesh. She began flipping through the crowd shots, looking for that one tiny detail. In every one, there were a few people with glowing yellow eyes. She clicked on the folder of the banquet photos. She saw the same inhuman faces, and this time one of them was serving the royal table. There was only one possible conclusion: those were the fetches.

That's why they wanted the photos. She'd heard stories about supernatural creatures that couldn't be photographed. The truth was, they showed up all too well. There were details that couldn't be hidden on film. *I wish I'd taken some photos during the showdown at the reception.* It would have been interesting to see how many of the Vidonese guards weren't human.

The bathroom door opened releasing a cloud of steam and a soapy smell. Faran's feet padded from the tiles to the carpet. He wore nothing but a towel, his wet hair plastered down and dark with moisture.

"Look at this," Lexie said, trying to keep her mind on the computer and not on his water-flecked skin.

He bent over the back of the couch, his freshly shaven cheek touching hers. "What am I looking at?"

"The people standing around Leo. Look at their eyes."

She began clicking through a series of pictures. In every shot of Leo, there were always one or two fetches nearby, often right at his elbow. One photograph could be explained away, dozens could not.

A random memory bumped her consciousness. "Leo came up to me the night of the reception. It was when everyone was leaving the hall."

Faran's breath fanned her cheek. "What did he do?"

The prince had handed her the coiled electrical cord and she'd thought nothing of it. "He stood right next to the ring case. It would have been too easy to take the ring and give it to Gillon for safekeeping."

"In other words, means and opportunity were right there."

"But what about motive?" Lexie countered. "Why would he be at the middle of the conspiracy? He's already a prince. What more does he want? If he's working with the fey, it can't be because he hates nonhumans."

"All we know is that he's not afraid to use the fey to get what he wants."

"To be king of both Marcari and Vidon?"

"And to get back at his brother? In case you hadn't noticed, there's a sibling rivalry there the size of the Mediterranean. The fact that the fetch who attacked you looked like Kyle—that had to be a royal *up yours.*"

"But how…" Lexie floundered, beset by a vision of Prince Leo in wizard robes, bringing a fetch of his brother to life. "How is he doing all this?"

Faran's face darkened. "Well, he's not working alone. That much is certain."

Chapter 21

Too much sex definitely impacted productivity.

Lexie's phone chimed, dragging her back from sleep just as her eyes drifted shut. "Go away."

The nubby fabric of the couch pillow dug into her cheek, making her itch. Last night had caught up with her and she'd stretched out on the couch for just a moment, but she guessed more time than that had passed. Faran had left to show Prince Kyle what they'd found in the photos after Lexie had uploaded a slide show of evidence to his phone.

She sat up with a groggy yawn, her phone chiming again. She picked it up see a text had come in. She swiped the screen, thinking it might be from Faran.

Hi, Lexie. It's been a while since you hugged your brother. XXOO.

"That's a three out of ten." She threw the phone down on the couch in disgust and slid back into a sleeping position. She might have said it a bit too loudly but, seriously, that wasn't her persecutors' best work. As intimidation tactics went, the skewer was way better.

She leaned her head back against the cushions, but now her eyes were wide open. She fervently wished Faran was back. The room was quiet, the only noise the rattle of the palace's ancient water pipes. But her mind was hooked like a fish on a line, unable to shake free of the text message. Surely Valois's people could figure out where the message had come from? No, catching her stalker—for that's what this was—couldn't be that easy. Poitier had supposedly delivered a message from Justin, so she already knew his masters were in on it. It was all the same bunch of bad guys, out to drive her crazy so Faran wasted too much time looking after her.

She was beginning to think that last bit of her theory might need a bit more work. It seemed like an awful lot of effort just to distract one agent, even if Faran was the only Company man at the palace.

Gradually, Lexie became aware of the sound of breathing. At first she thought it was her own, but she silenced herself and listened. The sound continued. Someone was there with her. Her scalp prickled with alarm.

Although by now she was fully awake, she didn't move. She didn't want to tip her hand. Instead, she tried to guess where her visitor was standing. The noise seemed to be all around her, growing steadily louder. *This is where the kick-ass heroine would have a gun. Why don't I have a gun?*

Because she had always been a runner, not a fighter. Inwardly, Lexie swore. Stone-still and cramped with tension, she was growing colder and colder as she listened. She had to move. She had to do *something*. But she had never really learned how to fight. Not like Faran.

Lexie looked from side to side as far as she could without moving her head. There was no one in front of her. Whoever it was had to be in the bedroom—standing there, watching her and planning who knew what. The sheer creepiness of it made her stomach lurch.

She was supposed to be safe. Faran had put some sort of super locking gizmo on the window sash so it couldn't be jimmied open, and yet somehow her stalker had gotten in. This was far, far too much like the endless nights of her childhood, when she'd huddled in bed, frozen and trembling. Her neck was starting to cramp—there was no way she wanted to remain like this until Faran returned. Maybe she could make it to the door. They'd posted more security guards in the corridor—several of them this time.

Inch by inch, Lexie sat up and looked around. There was no one. Stiff with tension, she stumbled off the couch, her shoulders hunching as she looked around. It was only then that she realized the sound of the breathing was coming from her phone. It had landed right behind the cushion she was using for a pillow. She snatched it up. The phone wheezed at her like Darth Vader in miniature. "Oh, come on."

Embarrassed, she flipped the phone over and popped out the battery. The noise instantly stopped. Frustration hummed along every nerve, making her squeeze the phone until her fingers ached. *What makes you think you can do this to me?* Worse, she'd fallen for it. Lexie dropped the phone to the cushions as if it had burned her, but then her fingers curled into fists.

A knock came at the door. Lexie stiffened. "Who is it?"

"It's Maurice, love," came the familiar voice.

Maurice? She'd met him a few times, but there was no reason he would be seeking her out. She hurried to open the door. Sure enough, the tall musician stood in the hallway, wearing what appeared to be an electric-blue leisure suit from the '70s. She hadn't seen lapels that wide in her lifetime.

"Come in," she said, still slightly mystified.

"What do you think?" He gave a feline smile and twirled as he followed her inside her rooms. "Resplendent?"

She nodded. "It, um, well, the color pops."

"Yes, I know. I'm a lounge lizard waiting for the right sunny rock."

They exchanged a few pleasantries while he strolled aimlessly about the room like an exotic butterfly unwilling to settle.

"What's the occasion for the fashion statement?" she asked.

"Rehearsal. Then a concert in town for the right kind of charity donors. Invitation only. Amelie is all about the children's hospital." He gave another sly smile. "I don't mind. I've been very fortunate and don't mind spreading a bit of that luck around. After the concert, I'll be doing the fireworks event at the palace, not to mention the celebrity croquet tournament for those of us who can't manage polo."

"That's quite the schedule."

"Let's just say I'll be earning my keep the next few days." Maurice raised an eyebrow. "I don't get to be idle rich, just look like it. Anyhow, I was hoping to find the inestimable Mr. Kenyon. I have a tidbit of news to share before I head off to town. He seems to be a man in need of the right gossip."

"Okay," she said, part of her mind still on the invasion of her phone. "Faran's out for a few minutes."

Maurice looked at the huge cartoon character wristwatch he wore. "Too bad. I need to toddle. I may be mad, bad and dangerous to know, but the contract says I must also be punctual."

But he didn't stir, instead studied Lexie intently. "Are you all right, love?"

There was so much she could have said, but she didn't know Maurice well enough. "It's been a strange few days, with the bad fish and everything."

He gave her an assessing look that said he probably knew more than he was letting on. "Point taken."

She was spared a reply. Just then Faran walked in, clearly surprised to see Maurice there. "Hi."

"Is Leopold still missing?" Maurice asked unexpectedly.

Faran frowned. "Yeah, why?"

"Gossip has it that yesterday our younger prince was seen madly hunting for a dropped *something* on the lawn— apparently lost after he tripped over a wicket and fell."

"Really?" Faran said slowly. "He didn't happen to say what?"

"No, but I have it on good authority from one of the part-time gardeners that this afternoon some tourists found a ring in the bushes. Honesty would compel most to return it to the lost and found but, alas, not everyone is so high-minded. My trusty garden gnome believes they came on the shuttle bus from the Hôtel de la Plage."

The ring. Lexie wanted to blurt it out, but she wasn't sure how far Maurice was in Faran's confidence. But the words rang like an insistent chime in her head as they said goodbye and Maurice strode off in a swirl of electric blue.

"Is he your informant?" Lexie asked.

"No, although in this instance, he seems to have appointed himself one."

"I don't get why he's involved," said Lexie. "He's insanely rich and famous and some kind of relation to the Vidonese royal family. He probably played with Kyle and Leopold when they were kids." Then Lexie stopped herself. She'd just answered her own question. Maurice was sticking his nose into Faran's investigation because Kyle and Leo were family. One way or the other, he cared about the outcome.

"At the moment he's being useful. I was there when Leo tripped," Faran said. "It never crossed my mind that he would have been carrying the ring."

"Well, giving it to a flunky didn't work out so well."

"And now he's lost it and is on the run." Faran rubbed the bridge of his nose, as if a headache threatened. "Does that seem odd to you? Wouldn't he stick around and try to find it?"

Lexie went to the couch, pushed her laptop and camera into her leather backpack and zipped it up. "I think if he hears someone found the ring, he'll go after it. Or send someone. Those people might be in danger."

"What are you doing?" Faran asked.

"Aren't you going to go after them? To the hotel?"

"Yes," he said.

"I'm going, too."

"It could be dangerous."

She stuck her chin out mutinously. "What are you saying? Weren't you glad I was there to beat up Gillon with a tire iron? Besides, it's just a hotel."

Faran held up both hands. "Okay. I get that you need to go. This is about you and your right to control your destiny, and I'm all about making sure you get what you need. But if I say duck, you do it. No arguments."

"Agreed," she said. "But we're taking your car. We broke mine already."

He held up a set of keys. "Prince Kyle gave us a loaner Jaguar."

"Nice."

"Not bad. But I'm serious—if you want to bail at any point, just say so."

"I won't bail."

"You don't have anything to prove," he said.

"I know. But I mean it. I'm really tired of these nut jobs getting their Norman Bates on." *You, my heavy-breathing friend, just made my ass-kicking bucket list.*

It wasn't how she was used to thinking, but getting to know Faran's wolf last night had taught her a thing or two. The wolf had shown its strength to challenge and dominate, because that was in its nature. But so was a fiercely protective love. Strength, even force, didn't have to be abusive. Intent was everything. Fighting back didn't mean joining the dark side.

She intercepted Faran on the way to the door and caught an arm around his waist, pulling him closer for a kiss. He responded instantly, deepening it until she rose up on her toes to get more, and more. She wasn't going to be left behind, and she wasn't going to let anyone get between them.

Faran was right. Lexie had to be the person she was born to become.

Chapter 22

The Hôtel de la Plage was the kind of place married couples went when they wanted a vacation but were still paying for their kids' tuition. Decent, but no one was calling Condé Nast.

Faran pulled the Jaguar into the parking lot, which had a view of some scruffy palms and a collection of concrete pillars meant to imitate a Roman ruin. Kitsch, apparently, was an international phenomenon. The hotel was long and low, set around an apathetic garden with a swimming pool.

Lexie pulled a camera from her backpack and slid out of the car, the wind catching her long, fiery hair. She pulled it back, knotting it with graceful hands and sticking it with her pencil.

Despite his speech back at the palace, Faran was apprehensive about her presence. He'd seen enough of these innocent-seeming excursions turn bad. Then again, the past few days had been dire enough he didn't want to let her out of arm's reach. He needed to pick one anxiety and stick with it, but where Lexie was concerned all he wanted to do was put her in his cave and guard the door. A natural urge for his kind but not very useful, and she'd probably kick him in the fuzzy dice if he tried it.

"Stick close," he said, heading for the administration office.

She matched her stride to his. "What makes you think the manager will tell us anything? We're not police."

"We could lie. That's kind of what undercover agents do. Or, we could use this." Faran pulled out a laminated identification card. "Prince Kyle gave me a palace security card. It's the keys to the kingdom, at least for this kind of job."

"I want one," she said plaintively.

"I'm in charge."

"That's not fair. You're supposed to be *my* assistant."

"No way," Faran said, falling into the spirit of the argument. "We have to take turns."

"I'm telling Chloe."

When they got to the manager's office, it didn't take long to figure out which room their targets had rented. It was the one that had been burgled just an hour ago when the unlucky couple had gone to the lobby for an early drink.

"A crime like that's to be expected," said the hotel manager, wearing a golf shirt at least one size too small. "The royal wedding is announced, and every pickpocket and petty thief in the land descends to prey on the crowds of idiot tourists."

"Did they report anything stolen?"

"Jewelry and electronics. They've gone to the police station to fill out a report. So why are you here?"

"Your guests were at the palace today. The royal guard

is interested in thieves targeting visitors to the palace precinct." Faran flashed the security card and the manager let them into the room without argument.

"What are we looking for?" Lexie asked once the manager had left them alone.

She was doing a methodical sweep of the room, snapping photos while Faran looked around. He didn't interfere, because it was exactly what he would have done. But when he tried to concentrate, she acted on him like a magnet, pulling his attention with her as she moved. The lingering heat of desire flared as she drew near, scattering his thoughts.

His gaze drifted to the bed—big and comfy-looking, with fresh sheets judging by the scent of laundry soap in the air. He could see Lexie reclining on a stack of snowy pillows, her flame-colored hair spread out like a banner against the white. The mere thought threatened to short-circuit his reason. Unfortunately, there was the chance the couple might come back from the police station and turn his fantasy into a nightmare. Maybe there was an empty room somewhere nearby?

Get your head in the game. If he was going to romance Lexie, he'd pick somewhere nicer than this. He sniffed the air again, detecting the usual mix of industrial deodorizer and mildew, as well as the parasitic wildlife that settled in urban settings. "I'd keep an eye out for rats, but I don't think anyone we know has been here lately."

She tapped the tip of her nose. "You were hoping for an ID?"

"Yeah, or maybe Prince Leo tied to a chair with a note addressed to the mayor of Gotham City."

Lexie picked up a flyer from the dresser. "This is for Maurice's concert tonight."

"And?"

"Maurice said it was invitation only. Why pass out flyers to something most people can't get into?"

Faran gave her a sharp look. Good thing someone was using their head. "Because most people wouldn't catch a detail like that. But passing those around would give someone a chance to try a few doors."

She dropped it back on the dresser. "Should we fingerprint it? Did I smudge something?"

"Probably not, but it's best not to touch stuff even if we are wearing gloves." He picked up the flyer with tweezers. "And everyone treats you with more respect if you're holding an evidence bag. It just looks better."

They finished searching the room and went back to the office to find out if the manager had approved the flyers for posting. He had, but he didn't have a working security camera covering the desk, or anywhere else for that matter.

"I approve everything," the manager declared. "No one wanders around here without my permission."

"Did you get a look at the guy?" Faran asked.

"He was shorter than you. Wearing sunglasses and a cap. Oh, and he had a red windbreaker stenciled with a logo. Other than that he looked like all the young men, like we owe them something."

Faran couldn't exactly put out an APB on *Entitled Young Dude, approach with caution.* The guy had, however, left the plate number of his van on the clipboard at the desk so that his ride wouldn't get towed.

As Faran and Lexie walked back to their own car, he phoned Valois to run the plates. Valois checked while Faran was still on the phone. The plates turned out to belong to a stolen vehicle belonging to a beachfront florist's shop. Valois gave him the address. Faran hung up, despondent. "I think it's a dead end."

"Should we visit the flower shop?" she asked, getting into the Jaguar.

"What for?"

"Don't criminals work in a comfort zone?" she asked, twisting in her seat to face him. "They stick to areas they know, right?"

"Yeah," he said, "depending on the kind of criminals, that is."

His old gang had gone where the goods were, but not every thief was so specialized. It was hard to tell with this bunch. Nevertheless, Lexie might be on to something. He reread the address. "That florist is near the site of Maurice's concert. The thief printed flyers for the concert. I'd bet you anything the copy shop where the flyers came from is in the same neighborhood. Maybe they used a credit."

"Okay, now we're talking." Lexie was getting excited, talking with her hands. "That neighborhood is away from the palace but not so far that it would be hard to get there in a hurry. That's got to be their home base. See, it's not a dead end."

Faran was more cautious. He'd had his fair share of disappointments during an investigation. "Maybe. We can go look around," he said, and started the Jaguar.

The waterfront area was a mixed bag. One end was big casinos, high-end hotels and glitter. This was the beating heart of Marcari's economy. The other end, where Faran and Lexie got out and started down the cobbled paths, was small-scale and in his opinion far more interesting. If you wanted handmade glass, authentic cuisine or a rare book, this was where you went. Lots of other people must have thought so, too, because it was crowded.

The afternoon was fading and the tall, ornate streetlights were coming on. Street vendors lined the main walkway, many of them with open-air grills. He smelled lamb, rubbed with the unique spice blends he'd never found anywhere else. Faran's mouth started to water. He hadn't eaten for hours. "Hungry?"

Lexie gave him a smile, mouth quirked. She knew all about his frequent feeding times. "I could eat."

He bought two of the lamb concoctions, the spiced meat wrapped in greens and served on flatbread drizzled in spicy cream. Traditional Marcari cuisine was in the same family as French, but had elements of Moroccan and Greek, as well. They sat on a bench under olive trees and ate. It was messy and Lexie was soon licking her fingers.

"Sticky, but food always tastes better outside. Even the burgers from the fair back home," Faran said.

It was out of his mouth before he thought about it. He didn't have a lot of memories of his pack, but he did remember the traveling fair that visited a nearby town once every summer. His home was no more than a hamlet way up in the mountains where a few dozen werewolf households kept themselves to themselves, but they came down for the fair.

"What was your home like?" she asked, wiping juice from her chin.

It was all he could do not to lick her clean himself. "Small. Insular. It was a logging settlement and really cold in winter. We only got two TV channels and then only if the weather was right."

"Sounds very back to the land."

"It was, but it was a great place to be a kid. Lots of room to run around. We played in the woods all the time."

He'd belonged, and been loved. He'd come across other packs as an adult, but by then he would only ever be the outsider looking in. It was easier to go it alone. Except now he wanted a pack of his own, starting with a mate. *Slow down. Don't screw it up this time.*

"Do you ever go back home?" she asked.

"It's not there anymore. People started building out that way and it wasn't a good place for wolves." He looked away, unable to keep his thoughts off his face.

"Everyone moved?"

"Not exactly." More humans in the area had meant more incentive to get rid of the wolves. Hunters called it wild-life management. For him, it had meant walking out of the mountains with his entire pack dead in the snow behind him. He'd been the only survivor because he'd been too young to go roaming with his parents.

Unnerved by the memory, he picked up their garbage, looking around for a recycling bin. "It's a long story."

She touched his arm. "I want to hear it someday."

He stopped, letting her hand keep him in place. He wasn't sure he could tell it. Not all at once. He tried to smile. "Maybe a bit at a time. That was my first deposit."

"It's a deal." And then Lexie let him go.

He took a steadying breath. If they'd been any other couple, all this would have been part of the getting-to-know-you phase when they'd first met. But they weren't average, and even the little he'd just said hadn't been possible before now.

She helped him clean up and they started looking for the florist. "I don't remember fairs, outside of one," she said. "My stepdad took us. It was the only time I remember us doing anything as a family."

"What about your real dad?" Faran asked. He couldn't imagine having a family and not doing things with them. They weren't something to take for granted.

"I don't remember him all that well," she said, her voice filled with regret.

It was almost full dark, and shop windows glowed like beacons up and down the waterfront. They'd reached the front of the flower shop. Faran regretted letting the threads of the conversation slip, but his eye caught the sign before a large building in the next block. "There's the concert hall. The flower shop is almost next door."

The hall was where the action was. A knot of people milled on the front steps—concertgoers, security and fans wearing pale imitations of Maurice's outlandish outfits. No doubt the guy kept the world stocks in eyeliner afloat. A couple of random blasts of fuzzy guitar stabbed the air. Inside, the band was doing a sound check.

Faran considered the options. Usually once the sound check was over, the venue would open the doors and start letting people in. And wouldn't the dark, crowded crush of a rock concert, dazzled by flashing light, explosions and Maurice himself, be the perfect place to hand off a stolen ring? Absolutely no one would notice.

Then again, there were a hundred other ways the thief could connect with his employer. This could be a complete waste of time. But Lexie was watching him expectantly, waiting for direction. "Let's look around," he said. "Maybe one of the fetches from the photographs will show up."

They went to the left, toward the back of the concert hall. The surrounding area was set out like a plaza, with benches and trees lit by strings of sparkling lights. The whole place was packed.

Lexie grabbed his arm, turning as if to murmur in his ear. "Is that our guy from the hotel over by the stage door?"

The figure was standing at the edge of the light and wearing a red windbreaker and a baseball cap pulled low over his dark hair. Just like the hotel manager said, the figure was unremarkable, his posture sullen. He was talking to a tall man with close-cropped hair, possibly in his late fifties. It looked like the older guy was chewing him out about something.

Faran steered Lexie along the plaza, passing them downwind. The tall man smelled like French cigarettes, the young man like nothing at all. It was the most damning evidence possible. No scent was why he'd never noticed it in the hotel room. Fetches—until they were self-destructing into stinking slime puddles—were invisible to his nose.

The man took off his hat just long enough to brush his hair back. It was the anti-Kyle.

Inside, Faran howled with triumph.

Faster than Lexie's eyes could follow, Faran pulled out his gun. The move drew exclamations from bystanders. Someone screamed.

"Freeze!" he ordered. Everyone within earshot obeyed, except the anti-Kyle. He took off at a sprint.

Faran whirled to Lexie. He was in full-on Company mode, his teasing smile vanished into hard lines. "Go to the concert security desk and stay there till I come get you."

Lexie barely had time to nod before Faran bolted after the fetch, leaping a wrought-iron bench in a long-legged bound before they disappeared into the darkness.

"Whoa!" someone exclaimed in astonishment. Lexie had to agree.

"Your friend has exceptional talents," said a voice from behind her.

She turned, the hair along her neck prickling. It was the tall man, his hands folded behind his back. He wore a pale trench coat unbuttoned over a tweed jacket and gray slacks. Something about the ensemble screamed professor. His face was the same: worn, a little baggy, more of a thinker than a man of action. What struck her the most, though, was the shiver that suddenly coated her skin. Not a ripple or a wave, but as if she was suddenly stuck in an envelope of electricity. She'd never felt the full force of magic before—not that she knew of—but this was how she'd always imagined it.

Lexie backed away. Faran had told her to go to security, and it sounded like the best idea in the world. But the man matched her step for step, lagging behind just enough that it felt as if he was stalking her. "Ms. Haven. Alexis."

He knew her name!

"Alexis!"

She quickened her step, refusing to answer. Only her parents ever used her full name. Even professionally, she used Lexie.

But as she sped up, so did he. He grabbed her wrist. "Stop."

The encircling fingers gripped like manacles. "Let me go!" She twisted her arm, trying to pull free.

"I wouldn't do that. You've already broken that arm."

She froze. He released her, a look of satisfaction on his face.

"How did you know that?" she snapped. "Who are you?"

"My name is Ambrose." He didn't specify if it was the first or last name. "I've been in touch lately."

This is the one who is tormenting me. "What the blazes do you want?"

"To talk, for now." He held out a hand to the glimmering streetlights. "Come with me?"

"No."

He reached for her again, but this time she was on her guard. She dodged, but the electric prickling grew stronger, weighting down her limbs. It seemed that if physical strength didn't stop her, he'd try other means. Lexie walked backward a few steps, afraid to take her eyes off him, but knowing her window of escape might be small. Her head began to pound, the buzz of the magic almost cracking her skull. "How do you know who I am?"

"Why, my dear, I'm a friend of your father's."

"Why should I believe you? I never met any of his golfing buddies. They wouldn't know me."

"Not your stepfather, Alexis. Your true father."

That nearly caught her. Longing and curiosity welled up, searing the tender places inside where the loss of her father still ached. He'd walked away without explanation— no phone calls, nothing.

Her true father didn't deserve friends. And if this was a real friend, why would he be here, in Marcari, hanging out with a fetch? She spun on her heel and made for the stage door at a run. It was propped open to make way for a pair of enormous roadies lugging a huge silver box that looked like part of the set. They would just be clearing the door by the time Lexie made it there, but another man was stepping into place to block the path of any crazed fans.

She probably looked crazed, but escaping Ambrose was her new goal in life. She just had to get past the big, bearded guy who looked as if he folded sheet metal into origami cranes for a hobby. *Please, please, please let me through.*

The prickling on her skin began to burn as if some strange form of friction was at work. All at once she felt hot and raw, as if she was burning from the inside out. But there was no time to worry about that. Ambrose was close enough that she heard the pounding of his long legs. Fast, for someone who looked more versed in physics than the physical. His fingers grazed her back.

Lexie was no athlete, but she found energy in pure terror. *Please let me through! Please!* She bounded forward, a cry on her lips. The roadie at the door frowned, massive eyebrows scrunching together into one bushy caterpillar.

He unfolded his arms and took a step forward, looking around as if to see the source of the noise.

Lexie zipped past him and through the door to the inky vault of the backstage area. The sound check was over, but the noise of the crew still setting up was all but deafening. The pounding of her feet disappeared in the clamor. She veered right, toward a stack of amplifiers. There was just enough room to wedge herself between them and curl up into a gap between the largest cube and the wall. If the band started to play, she'd be deaf for life, but it was the perfect sanctuary to catch her sawing breath.

She couldn't begin to guess how she'd made it past the guard, but she was glad she did. The air-conditioning was icy on her hot skin, but the magic—and her headache—was gone at last. When she finally stopped puffing, she straightened herself and started to edge around the speaker.

There was a man with his back to her, blocking her way. She silently swore. Now what?

"I know you're there," he said in a quiet tone. "Don't move. He's still here."

Lexie froze. "You mean Ambrose?"

"Yes."

She studied the back of the man's head. Dark hair. Tall and well-built, shoulders sloping to narrow hips in a tautly muscled V. It was the kind of physique had that underwear advertisers waving contracts. "Who are you?"

"A friend," said the stranger.

"You need to do better than that," she snapped.

Silence. "Fair enough. I'm connected with the Company."

"Did Faran send you?" She remembered him saying that he'd get them to look into who might have been asking questions about her past.

"I'm here on his behalf." The man spoke English and

sounded American. Vampire? Maybe. It was impossible to tell from behind. "You're lucky I saw you. I was following Ambrose from his headquarters near here."

So the bad guys did hang out in this neighborhood. "What do you know about Ambrose?"

"Justin knew him from the time he was a boy."

Her attention flipped from the speaker to his words. Maybe Ambrose really was a friend of her father's—but why should she believe this man anymore than her pursuer? Anxiety clawed her, but so did a rising fit of temper. "What does Justin have to do with any of this? Where is my father?"

The last came out on a choked sob. She pressed her back against the huge speaker, steadying herself. *Where is Faran?* She needed to find him.

"Your father had enemies. He left you to draw them away and for a time, it worked. But then they discovered he had left a family behind and Justin became the focus for Ambrose's attentions."

"Ambrose's attentions?" Lexie demanded in a low, hard voice. "What does that mean?"

The man didn't answer, but Lexie caught a glimpse of a trench coat passing by. *Ambrose.* And then she realized who Ambrose was. Justin's older friend from long ago. The one who thought she might do something interesting if she was threatened with death.

Her stomach seized dangerously, fear and disgust bringing bile to her throat. Ambrose was just beyond the speakers, the top of his head moving as he looked from side to side. Looking for her. The Company man didn't flinch. He just blocked the sight of her with his body, making a wall of protection. Eventually, Ambrose moved off to the right. Lexie started to shake.

At last, the Company man spoke again, his voice quiet

and carefully neutral. "Ambrose was grooming Justin, teaching him about his father's heritage. Gaining his trust from the start. It's what every fatherless boy wants to hear—how special he is, how someday he'll have gifts that his friends can only dream of. How he is better than those around him."

"What gifts?"

"Surely you felt Ambrose's magic. He's fey."

Fey. The ring. The gates. There's the connection. What was it the king had said? The fey thought differently enough that they might be psychopaths by human standards. *Did Justin start out like that, or was he twisted by Ambrose?* Tears coursed down her face as she huddled in the dark cave of sound equipment. "What did he do to Justin?"

"He was trying to awaken magic in Justin's blood. I don't know the precise methods he used."

"They didn't work. I never saw any evidence of magic." Just horrible cruelty. "And why would Ambrose think he could do that?"

"Because your father was fey. But it's tricky with half bloods."

"What?" She struggled to keep her voice quiet. Alarm and disbelief kicked her heart into a gallop. And yet she'd guessed it ever since Faran had taken her to the stone circle—she just wasn't ready to accept the facts. "That can't be true. I've been to the hospital plenty of times. I check out as human."

"Fey physiology is indistinguishable from human, unless you're looking for it."

My poor mother! She'd been in love with something more than human. No wonder she'd had such a hard time getting over her first husband. "But I've never... Who are you anyway? Why do I feel like I should know you from somewhere?"

He cut her off, speaking quickly as if he was running out of time. "Strong emotion is a common tool for awakening magic. Ambrose has been playing on your fears to bring your strengths into play."

Which sort of explained the skewer and the idiotic phone message—and maybe even some of Justin's behavior long ago. She remembered the fear on his face when he'd stabbed her with the skewer—had he been afraid she'd display a talent for magic that he lacked, no matter what rosy future Ambrose promised? "But what does Ambrose want?"

"A replacement for Justin, and that means you, with your power awakened. As far as anyone knows, you're the last of your father's bloodline. His family's lifeblood was used to seal the gates to the Dark Fey kingdom, along with the rubies of Vidon. Ambrose and his confederates need both you and the ring to get them open again. Having you here for the wedding might be pure luck, or a coincidence he manufactured."

Lexie tried to gather her spinning thoughts. "This can't be about me. I'm as magical as a loaf of bread."

The man's voice was amused. "Surely you noticed turning invisible when you rushed past the security guy at the door?"

Her mouth dropped open. Was that what the sunburn feeling had been about? "Seriously?"

The man tensed. "I have to go."

"Just one more question!"

He stilled, every line of his body quivering like an arrow about to fly.

"Why did Ambrose wait till now to contact me? Why not do it long ago?"

"I can't be sure," he said, voice tight. "After his failure with your brother, perhaps Ambrose left you in the wild, so to speak, until he absolutely needed your blood. Mixed-blood humans can be unstable once their power wakes. Ambrose would have been stuck if you went off the rails and got yourself killed just like your brother."

And then he was gone.

Grief hammered into Lexie. It stole the air from her hiding place, making the midnight walls of the speakers close in on her with coffin blackness. There was too much to think about—magic, blood ritual, plots. But she wept for something far more simple, pain welling up like a razor-clawed beast.

Justin. If not for Ambrose, who might he have been?

Chapter 23

Faran chased the fetch away from the concert hall, back toward the winding streets of the city. The thing was fast—faster than any human and every bit as fast as Faran himself. After the first two blocks, he knew this takedown was going to be a challenge. After eight, he was growing annoyed and there were too many people around to risk shifting.

The fetch angled its path toward a maze of brick town houses dotted with tiny knot gardens and playgrounds. This was the last place Faran wanted to start shooting. He poured on the speed, heading the anti-Kyle away from the tidy homes. The fetch looped around a row of parked cars and bolted for an alley. Faran leaped to the roof of a Citroen and ran along the cars, ignoring the outraged cries of onlookers. When he saw the narrow alley, ending in a dock, he nearly laughed.

Faran sprang from the cars and landed in a crouch a

dozen feet away, gun still in his hand. The fetch had halted in confusion. The alley was plain and empty of people, but it ended in a modest pier. The tiny inlet had long been used for loading supplies bound for the great sailing ships of past centuries, but that was of no use to a creature of the fey. They might crave salt and water, but running water was poison to their kind.

"Give it up," Faran said. "I'm sure even your kind doesn't like getting shot."

"My kind," said the fetch. "I'm sure you've heard those words before."

He had. He was pretty sure his dead parents had, too, but he would never be able to ask them. A burn of anger flared, but it was an old, familiar one. "It's never right to kill someone just because of what they are."

The fetch pulled off his sunglasses. He had Kyle's face, every detail. But where the prince was magnetic, this thing had none of his charisma. It was like the cheap reproduction of a masterpiece, robbed of everything that made it special. "Then don't kill me. Let me go."

"Gee. No. You're still working for the bad guys."

"I don't have a choice."

"Then tell me who made you."

The fetch gave a slow smile, obviously proud of his creator. "The Five. My master is First."

"Name?"

"He is known as Ambrose."

"Prince Leopold?"

The smile warped to a sneer. "He is one of them also, but he is the least. They need his connections."

That was no surprise. "Come with me. Explain everything and clear your name."

"No." The fetch shook his head. "I am ordered to fight to the death before allowing myself to be arrested."

"Funny how people who never do the fighting come up with these orders."

The fetch shrugged. "I have never expected to live out the week."

Faran winced. "Fun times. Your move."

The fetch turned and ran to the wall, scuttling up it like a spider. Faran cursed, holstering his gun and dashing for the nearest fire escape. If he'd been a werecat, this would have been easier.

The fetch was a faster climber, appearing at the top of the ladder before Faran made it onto the roof. His boot stomped toward Faran's head. Faran jerked aside just in time, grabbing for the ankle. He missed, but it made the fetch stumble, giving him just enough seconds to make it onto the flat roof.

But not enough to avoid getting tackled. Faran went to his knees, skidding with the impact of the anti-Kyle's weight. It wouldn't do to fall backward—not with a two-story drop *right there*.

Faran somersaulted over the fetch and then they were both on their feet. Faran lashed out with his fist, testing the fetch's reflexes. A rain of kicks and blows followed, proving that the anti-Kyle had the original prince's expertise in martial arts.

It was a good fight, but it had to end. Faran made a textbook grapple, but the fetch bounced back up, drawing a blade from inside his jacket. It flashed with an unmistakable gleam. *Silver.*

The blade lashed through the air. Faran grabbed for his weapon but fire flared in the muscle of his arm as the knife struck home, and his weapon dropped from nerveless fingers. Quick as a cat, the fetch's boot snaked out, kicking the gun out of reach.

"Worried yet?" the thing sneered.

"You have my attention."

"Good."

It sprang, just as Gillon had, with all limbs extended toward its prey. Faran spun and kicked, planting a boot heel in the thing's solar plexus. He heard a crack of bone, but still the fetch came on, all but crawling up his leg to drive the knife home. Faran twisted, using the motion to lever the fetch into the air. With a mighty heave, he tossed him off the roof to the cobbled alley below.

Then he snatched up his gun left-handed, aimed with care and shot the thing in the head for good measure. Even at that distance, his shot was true. Matter exploded into the air.

All the same, Faran didn't take any chances. There wasn't time to bother with the ladder, so he jumped, landing gracefully a few yards away from his quarry. Faran rose, checking himself over. His wounds weren't deep, just annoying and painful.

Faran strode to where the fetch lay. It had fallen badly, limbs splayed in ways that nature never meant. Nausea roiled in Faran's gut. Without a face, it looked even more like Kyle sprawled dead on the ground. And then it started to melt with that same eerie, gelatinous slide of flesh. The clothing began to hiss as it burned.

Faran bent and stirred the charring fabric with the point of the silver knife, then drew back as a shiver of power snaked up his arm. It felt like sticking his finger in a light socket. He reached out and quickly searched the fetch's pockets before they self-destructed. A moment's riffling through the contents of its wallet—concert tickets, brochures, a map of the palace maze—told him what he wanted to know. He rose and walked away to avoid the smell of the decomposing body.

Faran pulled out his phone and dialed. "Sam? I know

when and where this is all supposed to come together. And have you ever heard of something called the Five?"

Lexie felt a gentle touch on her shoulder. She opened her eyes and almost squeaked. A glittery apparition was kneeling at the entrance to her hiding place, a bemused look on his face.

"If you wanted a backstage pass, you just had to ask," said Maurice. "But if you stay here, the sound will rattle the teeth right out of your head."

"I'm sorry, I was trying to avoid someone," she said.

"Looks like they already have you rattled."

"They do."

"Come on," he said, extending a hand. "A friend told me to keep an eye out for you. I have some very large fellows on my payroll who will take very good care of you until Faran returns."

Lexie inched out from between the speakers. She had no sense of how long she'd been there, but she'd cried herself into exhaustion. It might not have been the best timing, but mourning for the brother she'd lost—whenever it was she truly lost him—had been years in coming. She felt oddly calm.

But now that she had left her cave, she could hear the rushing surf of the audience chanting, *Mau-rice! Mau-rice!* Feet stomped in rhythm to the words, vibrating through the building.

"Would you like to watch from the wings?" he asked with an amused expression. "I can guarantee a good show." He was vibrating with energy, and whether it was the glitter or something more, he almost seemed to move in a halo of sparkling light.

She nodded. With so much backstage security, it was

probably the safest place in the building. "Can I take pictures?"

"Be my guest." And then he ran ahead, grabbing his sleek black guitar from one of the stagehands. She could hear the moment he hit the spotlight from the ecstatic wail of the crowd.

The relentless, headbanging furor of the opening number was exactly what Lexie needed to counteract her mood. The conversation with the nameless stranger had lasted no more than two minutes, and he'd barely spoken—but he'd blown her entire history to pieces. Everything she'd known about herself was based on half-truths.

Digesting all that wasn't going to be quick or easy. Lexie propped herself against a speaker stand in the wings, applied the earplugs somebody gave her and began shooting pictures. Out of morbid curiosity, she kept checking the images for reflective eyes. The drummer, the keyboard player and the bassist were all human. So were the guys on the soundboards, the roadies and the tough-looking woman who seemed to be in charge of flash pots and other exploding items. Feeling better about her immediate surroundings, Lexie began shooting pictures of the crowd.

That was a different story. It made sense that the palace would have sent over a bunch of security to help with the charity concert, but every other one of the green-coats guarding the stage was a fetch. Lexie's skin crawled. And then she saw Ambrose moving through the audience like a shark, speaking a word to one of them, then the next. Each one nodded as if they understood an order. It was hard to say what it might be. Maybe to capture her, but why stop there? The cream of society—at least the part that liked loud music—was there. Prince Kyle and his entourage were in the best of the gallery seats above.

Maurice went into one of his famous guitar solos. It

started sweet, an intricate dance of two melodies that chased each other in twining counterpoint. Lexie loved it when he played this way, because it showed the talent and years of training that hid behind Maurice's showmanship. But the tune grew angrier, the two voices no longer in harmony but in argument, striving louder and sharper to shout each other down. Then they gave way to a screaming ecstasy of pain—not just physical pain, but the soul-agony of the middle of the night, of every regret and loss that rose like wraiths in the mind. Maurice swayed and stumbled across the stage, his glittering costume dark with sweat. The audience swayed with him, charmed into a trance.

Lexie would have been lost in the music, but her gaze was trained on the fetches in the crowd. They clearly didn't like the howling guitar. Every one of them was squirming and twitching—and no wonder. Lexie could see bones through the flesh of their faces, as if they were… *They're melting!*

The gelatinous ooze that made them was sensitive to sound vibration. She turned to the roadie next to her, shouting in his ear. "I'm with palace security. I saw terrorists in the audience. Don't panic anyone, but lock the doors."

He gave her a look that clearly said she was crazy. But then Lexie held up the camera, zooming in on a row of security guards with eyes glowing in hellish shades of yellow and orange. His brows shot up. He looked at the audience, grabbed his own camera from his jacket pocket, and took a series of shots. Then he carefully examined the evidence on the digital screen. A moment later, he vanished.

Ambrose watched from the opposite side of the auditorium. Lexie saw him there and used her zoom lens to get a closer look. As if he knew she was watching, he gave a slow nod, eyes turned directly her way. A crawling thrill of horror covered her whole body. She looked up from the camera, unnerved. She mentally cursed him, thinking again what he'd done to her family. For that, if nothing else, she was going to ensure he didn't win this battle.

And he wouldn't. Maurice's solo wound on, sobbing and moaning like a heartbroken siren. The pitch of the guitar climbed higher and higher, stabbing knives right through Lexie's earplugs. Ambrose pushed through the audience toward his creatures, but they were already streaming for the door. A monitor popped a mountain of sparks, fountaining white light into the air—but the band played on.

Oblivious, Maurice threw back his head and screamed, his instrument coughing a snarl of distortion as the rest of the musicians jumped in, bringing the song home with a pumping, caveman bass. It might have been the bass that did it, because one by one the fetches shuddered and drooped, like candles melting into puddles of wax. Then, they each popped in a wet, sloppy shower of goo. The audience members shrank away, disgusted, outraged and horrifically delighted.

The newspapers trumpeted the event as the dawn of a new era of interactive special effects. The sales of Maurice's album tripled overnight.

Chapter 24

"So, you're telling me that while I ran around rooftops chasing one lousy fetch, risking my life and getting hacked with a silver blade, you just shut the doors to the concert hall and let Maurice reduce the fey army to quivering jelly?" Faran grumbled.

"Pretty much," she said.

That was unreasonably smug in his opinion. "What did this Ambrose guy do?"

"Vanished in the aftermath."

Faran huffed. "Probably wanted his ticket refunded, too."

He pulled out the piece of paper he'd taken from the anti-Kyle's wallet. The palace grounds were dark, but werewolves could see fine on a clear night like this.

"I suppose there are more fetches around, but at least it stopped whatever they were doing this afternoon. What do you think that was?" Lexie asked.

He studied the sketch and shook his head. Fetches were amazing replicas of human originals, all things considered, but they were also kind of dumb when it came to carrying supersecret plans in their pockets.

"Faran?" Lexie asked again.

He didn't answer. According to Valois, there had been an additional request for added security at the concert made around the same time Lexie and Ambrose had disappeared into the building. It was likely that one reason the fetches were there was to make sure she never left. But without knowing for certain, he wasn't going to put that thought in her head. The fetches were dead and she was safe by his side.

Even more curious, no one in the Company seemed to know the identity of Lexie's mysterious stranger. That was worrisome, too, but again he wasn't going to add to Lexie's anxieties.

Instead, he turned to the papers in his hand. "Exhibit A, a map of the palace maze, complete with little red dots indicating the points of the compass. Exhibit B, a token to tomorrow's fireworks display. Exhibit C, a brochure with a map of the palace."

Lexie fell for his dodge. "Sounds like a treasure hunt. All you need is a few old rusty keys and a list of items to find."

"Kyle's double was going to be at tomorrow's event, and something will be happening in the maze." He looked at the curving walls of tall hedges. "I just have no idea what."

They wandered between the hedges, only the half-moon above for illumination. The white gravel paths looked ghostly, but the air was instantly warmer. Some of it was the fact that it was sheltered, but there was something unusual about the place. It had been built on the site of an old stone circle much like the one where he and Lexie had gone for a picnic. And just like there, the temperature here was always warmer than in the surrounding landscape.

That should have encouraged visitors, but the patrol never entered the maze at night, citing a host of spirit sightings and strange events. Perhaps it was an ancient spell, or a haunting, or nothing at all, but Faran thought it was worth investigating.

Or, at least it was a good excuse for a late-night ramble in the one truly sheltered spot on the palace grounds. It was the first night that was even close to warm, and his wolf needed some outdoors time. Faran spread out the blanket they had brought.

"So what do you think," he said. "A good place for a fey ritual?"

"I wouldn't know." Lexie gave him a haunted look.

She hadn't taken the news about her family's connection to the fey all that well, and nothing could be proved until her blood was tested by the Company labs. Still, Faran wished he'd described the fey in a more positive light. To be honest, he hadn't really examined his own feelings about her father's heritage.

"Do you want to talk about the fey thing right now?" he asked.

"Not really."

"Okay."

He caught her and pushed her against the broad trunk of the tree. Rough bark teased the palms of his hands as his lips met her cool, smooth mouth. Wind rushed in the trees above them, fingering their hair and clothes and bathing them in the sound of wild places. The scent of the sea teased his nose, winding through the rich scent of woman.

It made sense to him that Lexie was part fey. It was not just her cream-and-fire coloring or her love of beauty, but her whole being had always carried the glow of wild magic.

And yet she was also wholly human. Her heart and mind had none of the remote strangeness of the fairy people. She had been formed of the best of both.

She kissed him back, igniting the rage of hunger in his blood. Not a hunger for food, but for her. He drank in the sweetness of her mouth, the delicate taste of her tongue and the sharp contrast of teeth. She nipped at his lips, teasing lightly, inviting him to explore.

His hands slid around her ribs, all but encircling her waist. Her snug white blouse—praise the stars—was fastened with a zipper instead of buttons, and it was a moment's work to undo it. And then there was silken skin to contrast with the cool air and ancient bark. He bent to kiss the curve of breast resting in the lace cups of her bra, like a feast in delicate serving ware. Her nipple hardened, and he sucked it through the silk. She tasted of a floral perfume. Gods help him, he was lost in a symphony of textures and tastes.

And then her hands were on him, spurred by his encouragement. His clothes came off quickly—shape-shifters had lots of practice getting naked. She raked her nails through his hair, tracing his beard and the line of his lips. Her lips were on his throat and then his on her other breast while he kneaded them, teasing the nipples to hard, ecstatic points. Slowly, his tongue and lips traveled the long line of her slender body, following the valley between her breasts down to the cleft of her ribs, and across the planes of her belly to her navel. He slid her jeans and panties down her hips, easing them off as he nibbled the delicate flesh on the inside of her thigh. She smelled of musk and peach, summer and desire, and as he worked she grew damp with anticipation, shifting skittishly as she laced her fingers in his hair.

He worked until she shuddered, cursing softly to the night. He ran his hands up her body, bringing fresh trembling to her limbs. She pressed into him, stealing his warmth and raising it at once as sensation crowded low in his belly. He nuzzled her neck, burying his face in the sweetly scented cascades of her hair. There were private places he loved—the nest of silky flesh below her ear, the hollow of her collarbone, the lean architecture just below her jaw. By the time he'd visited half of them, he was hard as adamant.

And then it was her turn to slide down his body, her red hair like a separate living thing sliding over his skin. It made him think of blood, or rose petals, or a blanket of fire, but always Lexie. Her fingers were soft but strong, the way tender plants will eventually crumble stone. He was a wall, a monument, and yet she brought him to dust every time.

Her mouth on his belly brought a sound to his lips somewhere between a prayer and a curse. Then she was tasting him, teasing and probing with her tongue. She could always find the spot... Faran cursed as he nearly lost it, barely holding on through the onslaught of torture. He had fallen against the tree, letting it hold him up as she worked her magic. Anyone who doubted the existence of the supernatural hadn't spent time with Lexie Haven at the top of her game.

When she'd brought him to the brink of madness she backed away, her eyes shining with wickedness. She spun with her arms overhead, faint moonlight sketching her limbs as she collapsed in a graceful heap on the blanket.

Faran's mind grew suddenly clear and still, as if she was the only thing in the universe worth watching. People thought of wolves as savage. No, they were simply certain. No fuss, no muss, just a single, nonnegotiable target. With pure, mindful intent, he prowled to the blanket. She was his.

He let her slip on the condom, her touch just adding to his urgency. Then he drove into her, the sensation nearly more than he could endure. She was tight and hot, her slender pale body arching beneath him with every thrust.

And then he felt the magic of the maze coursing beneath them, a serpent coiling and rolling like a beast. He'd never felt magic the way fey experienced it, but this was strong. It coursed through his body with an electric, dazzling pulse, as if he was part of the place itself. He drove into Lexie, feeling the answering surge of her power. She was a white-hot fire of need, of pride and untapped potential. The maze felt her power, knew it for kin. Their sensitized skin tingled, the buzz of magic adding to the myriad sensations of lovemaking. Lexie cried out as his thrusts quickened. The air around them crackled with energy. Power bit his skin like hungry teeth, the skin of his shoulders and back burned with it.

He slowed his pace a moment, holding on to his control with all his will, and bent to suckle Lexie's breasts. The power surged, swirling through her. She writhed beneath him, scoring his back in her madness. The pain sang through him, joining the needling power on the edge between pleasure and discomfort.

And then his mind blanked, his focus narrowed to the one task at hand. Lexie's pleasure pulsed around him, hot and thick and urgent. She cried his name, possibly the only word he'd recognize right then and he thrust deep again, and spilled his desire deep into her.

Reason was slow to come back to him, but it came with the delicious scent of grass and green and Lexie. She was cuddled next to him, the edge of the blanket drawn over her. He folded her in his arms, thankful that the rough-and-tumble of love play was no longer a source of anxiety for her. She trusted him enough to let him hold her tight.

He let the gift soak through him for a moment, a delight and a balm.

With his wolf's sight, he could see a faint light clinging to her, as if a dusting of energy had stuck. "You feel this place?" he asked.

"Mmm," she replied. "It's like I've had one of those energy drinks. I'm all buzzy." She rolled over with a feline stretch. It did interesting things to her breasts, and his hand wandered to investigate. She swatted it aside and rolled into him, propping herself on his chest. "Is that why no one comes in here at night?"

"People feel things, they don't recognize it, and they find reasons to keep out. It's sensible from a survival standpoint." There was something to be harnessed here, if the mythical Five wanted a ritual. Not that they would get one—he'd see to that.

She rested her cheek on his shoulder, her eyes drifting shut. "It feels amazing, like the earth is talking."

He stroked her arm, a little in awe of that. "What's it saying?"

Her hand slid down his hip, and let the earth's thoughts be known.

Chapter 25

"How do you deal with it?" Lexie asked Faran the next day.

"What do you mean?" he asked, looking up from studying the map of the maze he'd taken from the anti-Kyle's wallet. He was sprawled on the sunlit bed wearing nothing but blue jeans, his bare feet crossed at the ankles. An unreasoning fondness washed through her. As well as all the explosive sex, she just plain liked his company.

Lexie looked down at her camera, chewing her lip. She was sitting on the end of the bed and fiddling with her lenses, not actually doing anything useful except keeping her hands busy. Her nerves prickled from lack of sleep and too much coffee. "Not being human."

A veil dropped over his expression so quickly, she knew she'd hit a nerve and regretted it. "I've never been anything but a werewolf," he muttered. "I don't know any different."

"I don't know what to think about being half fey. It's not something I even wondered about before now."

He set the paper aside, giving her his full attention. "So you're convinced it's true?"

Lexie hadn't had much time to think about it since their picnic in the mountains. They'd been in a state of nonstop emergency. Still, some part of her subconscious had been dealing with it, because she'd woken up today convinced it was fact. "I'll get a blood test, like you say, but I felt something again last night."

"Well, that's a relief."

"Besides you." She grinned. "Although you were definitely front and center of my thoughts at the time."

Faran crawled across the bed and sat beside her, shoulder to shoulder. The warmth of his bare skin touched her through the light fabric of her blouse. "Good to know."

He was trying to distract her, to put her in a better frame of mind, but she was on a train of thought she didn't want to lose. "The fey thing makes me wonder about my family. However much I tried to tell myself I was over my past, I was a victim back then right up until the moment I walked away. But they might have been victims, too. It doesn't change what happened, but I might be able to forgive a lot more now." She set the camera down. "I should visit my mom. Maybe she'll talk to me if I know some of the story already."

"That would probably make it easier for her to talk about your father."

She met Faran's eyes. His were troubled. She knew going home wouldn't be easy, and no doubt he guessed that, too. "What do you think happened to my dad after he ran off?"

He sighed, leaning back on his elbows. "Hard to say. If his bloodline closed the gates on the Dark Fey, then he's their enemy."

Which meant this plot they'd uncovered was probably

the culmination of something that had been going on for a long time. She imagined her dad, a young father, faced with a huge, implacable, magical enemy. He'd made sacrifices she couldn't fathom. "So Ambrose wasn't my dad's friend at all. Not that I ever thought he was. He's just too creepy."

"Is Haven your father's name or your stepfather's?"

"Dad's. His name was Therriel Haven." The name felt odd on her lips. It had been years since she'd said it.

"It sounds like a Light Fey name, though I'm not an expert."

Lexie's hands moved restlessly in her lap. "So far no one has said he's dead. I want to find him."

"Lexie." Faran sat forward, taking her hand. "I know this is hard to hear, but he may not want to be found."

"I'm his daughter!" she protested. "I finally understand he's in trouble. He shouldn't be alone."

"I think he left, just like your stranger at the concert said, to draw the enemy away from his family. Not just that, but to prevent the gates from being unlocked. Ambrose is trying to work around his absence, but by disappearing your father has managed to delay the process by years. Until this is over, don't look for him. You could lead Ambrose straight to him." Faran leaned his forehead against hers. "Trust me when I say no father would willingly stay away from a daughter like you, so his reasons must be very, very good."

Lexie knew he was trying to comfort her, but for once it wasn't working. "Leaving him out there alone doesn't feel right."

He slid an arm around her. "It won't be long. With Kyle and Amelie working together on behalf of the two kingdoms, it's not going to be a case of the Company versus the Knights any longer."

"How does that matter?"

"Nobody wants the Dark Fey out of the box. They're a big enough threat that vampires and slayers will be on the same team against them, and that's going to be a brick wall not even the Dark Court can crack. We can beat them."

"And how is the wedding connected with this?"

Faran rubbed his eyes, as if fighting weariness. He was more than human, but it had been a hard week. "If I'm right, the fey have been leveraging the Company's war with the Knights of Vidon, stirring up enough trouble to distract us from their own activities. Those efforts have stepped up since Marcari and Vidon have been working toward unification by marriage. The other Horsemen have some stories to tell."

Lexie frowned. "But the wedding itself is just a ceremony."

"A ceremony is a ritual. Magic is all about rituals. Don't underestimate the power of vows when the scions of ancient houses are on board. It's not all corsages and champagne."

Lexie leaned against Faran. "And so you think they're going to make one last stab at opening the gates before the wedding?"

"Exactly. The fireworks ceremony, if this stuff I got out of the fetch's wallet is right." He pulled her close, kissing the top of her head. "Stay close, okay? Ambrose wants to use your blood as a substitute for your father's. Remember that Dark Fey can compel, but they're also the ultimate con artists. Don't believe anything he says."

"I'm not stupid." Irritably, she pulled away. He kept talking about the fey as if they were inherently evil, and that was adding to her sense of simmering panic.

He released her, then took her hands in his, fixing her with his gaze. "Chances are Ambrose is really old and really tricky. Full-blood fey can be thousands of years old. They live as long as vampires."

Slowly his words soaked in. Her father might be that old, with dozens of families scattered through the centuries. She could be just one of many daughters. Maybe he'd already forgotten her. Disappointment—and a touch of anger—rolled through her. "This fey stuff is going to take a long time to process."

"I know." He looked apologetic. "Are you going to be okay?"

"Sure," she said, but the word wasn't convincing even to her. "I think I just need to think for a while."

He squeezed her hands, but she pulled away, folding her arms over her chest. She didn't want magic powers, or to be hunted for a blood ritual. Right now, she didn't want to be anything but human—she'd had enough of the supernatural to last her three lifetimes. Unfortunately, that wasn't something she could say to a werewolf, especially not to one she loved. Lexie bowed her head, her hair shadowing her face.

"I need to go meet Sam," he said, breaking the silence. "The Company is still banned from the city, but whether they'll obey or not depends on what intel we put together. They aren't content to hang back anymore."

She picked up the conversational ball, glad of the distraction. "They found all that information on my father quickly."

Faran was pulling on a sweatshirt. He paused, a considering look crossing his face before he finished tugging it down. "Are you sure you never got your informant's name or saw his face?"

"No, but he said he was connected to the Company."

"The thing is, no one I've talked to knows who he was. And I don't know if the Company could have dug all that up on your dad so fast. Or that they would have known exactly where you were. I mean, down to your exact hiding spot?"

"What do you mean?" she asked uneasily. Maurice had found her hiding place as well and she didn't think he was a vampire. "My guy said he was following Ambrose."

"We didn't know about Ambrose," Faran said quietly. "If your guy's with the Company, he's been working on a highly classified file."

My father's file. "Are you saying I shouldn't trust my mystery man?"

Faran shook his head. "I really don't want to add to your worries, but I had to say something. Just be careful. You're on the radar now. Stay inside and don't use your phone. I'll pick you up a new one while I'm gone."

Lexie shrugged. "They can't scare me with Justin messages now that I know what's going on."

"But they can track your signal." He gave her a kiss on the cheek, as he picked up the car keys. "Embrace paranoia. It's good for you."

She stiffened, tired of fear and plots and feeling like a pawn in a game. "I've spent too much of my life being afraid."

Faran's mouth flattened. Clearly, he sensed her resistance. His eyes flashed amber, a sure sign his wolf was near the surface. "When I let you stay in this investigation, you promised to obey if I said duck."

"Careful how you use the word obey." Driven by fear, her tone came out sharper than she'd intended. "I'll be smart, but I'm not your dog and I won't be your prisoner."

Faran inhaled as if she'd cut him. "That's not what I'm asking for."

But her words hung between them, festering in the air. Without moving a muscle, he seemed to inflate, going from standing to looming in moments. He reached out a hand, but his fingers flexed to a fist and he took a step away from her, as if he couldn't guarantee what he might do. "You're not a prisoner. You're at risk. Yes, I want to lock you away and guard the door," he said, his voice coming from somewhere deep in his chest. "I want to rip out the throat of anyone who comes near you. But I know you'll hate me for it."

The anger in his words made her shudder. He wasn't completely human right then. "I know what you'll do," she said as calmly as she could manage. "I've seen you do it."

And when she had, she'd left him—but neither of them dared to voice that punch line. Instead, it lurked in the shadows like a scrap of evil magic.

Banishing it required trust that their bond could survive if one of them made a mistake. He might let the wolf take over for a moment. She might run. They would have to forgive, pick up the pieces and carry on believing they'd do better the next time. Love was resilient enough that a bad day didn't matter.

Lexie knew that. She also knew they weren't there yet. She was balancing her past, the overwhelming present and any future she had with Faran—it felt like a precarious stack of precious china, and her nose was tickling for a sneeze. She could barely breathe.

Faran cleared his throat, seeming to calm himself back down to his usual size. She could tell it didn't come easily. She'd met his wolf that night in bed. But exciting as that had been, she wasn't in the mood to be dominated. Lexie craved a few hours alone. "I'm sorry."

"I'll see you in a couple of hours." Faran spun on his heel and left, closing the door quietly behind him. Alone.

Alone was exile for a pack animal, even a lone wolf. Lexie sat down on the bed, wretched and guilty.

Lexie was left with the problem of how to run without actually running.

Her head was aching, her heart hurt and feeling woebegone wasn't going to help a single thing. She needed to get a grip. But given the cramped quarters of her rooms, finding a fresh perspective on anything was impossible. Every time she looked at the door, she saw that wounded guard falling to the floor and the false Kyle striding in. Before long, her nerves were strained to the breaking point. She was claustrophobic, and whatever Faran said, there was no good reason to hide indoors if the villains had a habit of dropping in. She wasn't any safer here.

After a half hour she gave up and went out for fresh air. Tourists were everywhere. The sun was bright, turning the first shoots of the season a tender green. If the weather stayed warm, there would be early flowers by the time the royal wedding took place on Valentine's Day.

And despite everything, the ceremony was still on. As far as the public was concerned, everything at the palace was fine. Lexie couldn't help but wonder what else went on all around the world that nobody knew about. The Company had its hands full. By extension, Faran and his fellow Horsemen always had missions to perform.

She strolled past the ornamental pond, relishing the sun on her shoulders and the soft quacking of the ducks. *Where do I fit in this world-saving business?* The question would have seemed ridiculous a week ago. Now, not so much. *Wherever I can.* Lexie could see herself working with Faran. The Night World was his world, and she wanted to be part of his life.

Although he has to get over this urge to protect me all the time. He'd been doing pretty well with it until the business with Ambrose—but to be fair, things were getting pretty bizarre. *Speaking of which...*

Lexie walked past the croquet lawn, where Maurice—resplendent in acid-green coveralls and cat's-eye sunglasses—was being swarmed by press wanting to know the secrets of his special effects. She veered away, wanting to stay clear of that scene.

The maze was up ahead, the high, clipped yew hedges even more impressive in daylight than they had been last night. They stood a dozen feet tall, a solid mass of green except for the entrance, where a marble gate arched across the opening. Lexie paused. She could feel its power from where she stood, like an echo of her own essence.

Her feet were moving toward it before she realized what she was doing. Her first thought was to turn away. Mazes were meant to get one lost. But there were plenty of people on the walk, so she let herself approach.

The energy of the place prickled over her as lightly as snowflakes on bare skin. Maybe those who were only half fey couldn't always handle their awakened powers, but this felt comforting as the sound of a voice long forgotten. She could be content just to feel this source of strength. As for her supposed invisibility trick—she hadn't made up her mind. The idea of such abilities was interesting, maybe useful, but she'd lived this long without them and she had the feeling parlor tricks weren't the point. Every instinct said this power was about being in harmony with the natural world around her.

She slowed to a stop just inside the yew hedge. She could see the spreading branches of the old plane tree where she'd been with Faran last night, and her core heated at the memory. Around her, lawns and flower beds flowed beneath the intersecting hedges, early bulbs like spears of green against the dark soil. There had to be a touch of magic afoot, because winter was already fading inside the maze. The air was warm enough that she shed her jacket.

"A lovely place, isn't it?"

She knew the voice before she turned her head. Ambrose. Alarm sang through her, but she refused to show it. She knew his game now, and had no intention of playing. "Is the weather here the work of the fey?" she asked calmly.

He met her reasonable tone with his own. "Older magic, actually. All spellwork—dark, light, sorcery or anything else you can name—is really just a method of harnessing what the earth has to give. We call this kind of place a source. They are all over the world. Stonehenge. Delphi. People still flock to leave their offerings, even if it is just the price of admission to look at a tourist attraction."

Lexie swallowed, her throat tight and aching with apprehension. She felt trapped by her own stupidity, like the B-movie heroine who'd gone into the basement. And yet, she hadn't been careless. She was in a public place, in plain view. There were plenty of people around, strolling in groups with their cameras and guidebooks in hand. *I'm not helpless, and this is the perfect time to get some information.*

"Why are you here?" she asked. "Not for the souvenir T-shirt, I suppose."

She turned to study him, looking for something that marked him as more than human. She could see arrogance in his refined features, perhaps a faded beauty that would have awed the viewer once upon a time, but that was all. There was nothing—no pointed ears, no upswept brows, no fairy wings. Faran was right—the fey were impossible to distinguish from humans, at least at first glance.

He smiled, but it was only with his lips. "To work great magic, but you knew that. And maybe to share a few tidbits you might find of interest."

"You want to instruct me like you did Justin? No thanks." She took a step back, wanting airspace between them.

"Ah, Justin. I regret pushing him too young." He waved a gloved hand as if flicking away a regret. "You, on the other hand, will miss the benefit of an early education. I would have hoped for a happy medium, but what can you do?"

Someone bumped her from behind, forcing her to stumble forward. Ambrose caught her, and then cold metal clamped around her wrist. The prickling of the magic stopped dead, as if someone had thrown a switch.

The sudden muffling confused Lexie for a moment. She jerked away, spinning to call out to the man who had bumped her, but he was gone. Something pulled at her arm, nearly putting her off balance. Lexie wheeled with a snarl worthy of Faran. She looked down at her arm, panic flaring in her chest. A band of plain dark metal cuffed her like a bracelet, and a chain stretched from the bracelet to Ambrose's gloved hand.

She was caught. It had all happened in a split second.

"What is this?" she demanded, straining to yell, but it came out no more than a croak. Her voice was gone.

"Shh." He pulled her close, tucking her arm under his to hide the shackle. "You won't have time to learn much of your fey magic, but there will be room for a few object lessons."

He began to walk, and her feet followed him. She strained to pull away, but no part of her body would obey her will.

"Now that your magic is awakened, Alexis, you will find some things have changed. For instance, you are completely at the mercy of cold iron."

Chapter 26

Faran came back to the palace late, Sam in tow. The Company had decided to return to the city for the fireworks display. Their justification was that they weren't coming as Company soldiers, but instead playing things low-key, arriving for the night's celebration in twos and threes and dressed like any other member of the public. If nothing happened, they'd go home without so much as flashing a fang. If something did, they would be there to stop it.

But however they spun their story, they were disobeying orders—or at least bending the rules into pretzels. That hadn't been an easy decision to make. Fierce argument had raged among the members of the Company, and no one could drag out a debate like a bunch of vampires who had the rest of eternity to make their point.

Faran unlocked the door to the rooms where he was staying with Lexie. He set Lexie's replacement phone on the empty coffee table and blinked, realizing this was the first time he'd ever seen the table free of her junk. With dawning apprehension, he saw her cameras and computer were gone, too, as was the big duffel bag she carried them in. "I don't remember Lexie mentioning a job this afternoon."

"Are you sure she's here at all?" Sam asked. "I only see your stuff."

Faran glanced around to see it was true. Without a word, he stormed into the bedroom. All her clothes were gone, too, down to the last thong. For a long moment, Faran stood in front of the depleted closet, refusing to understand. "Where is she?"

Sam stood in the bedroom doorway, his face tight with grief. He might have said "On a plane" or "I told you so," but Sam wasn't that kind of man. Instead, it was his expression that said history was repeating itself and Lexie had walked out.

"Everything was going great," Faran said, his voice coming from some other Faran who could still form words. "We had a bit of an argument this afternoon, but still…"

A slow pain was working its way up his gut, sprouting tendrils as it went. *Of course she left. What did you expect? She had a perfectly happy human life and then she ran into you again and poof, she's sucked into the freak show again.* The voice kept going on and on until he slammed it down like a buzzing fly.

Sam shifted uneasily. "I can see you thinking. Keep your head in the game, Kenyon."

"How do you know it's not?" Faran snapped. He was feeling sick, as though he needed fresh air.

"I know that look. It has her name all over it."

Setting his jaw, Faran pushed past Sam into the front room. Something didn't make sense. She'd been talking about finding her father. Is that where she went? Had she gone to see her mother?

"Look," said Sam, "she's obviously left with all her things, which says to me she went under her own steam."

"Damn her!" Faran swept most of the wine bar onto the floor. The bottles and glasses smashed with a satisfying cascade of glass and scarlet wine. His chest heaved, fighting chains of anger and grief. "Last time *at least* she left a note."

Silence blanketed the room, broken only by wine glugging from a broken bottle. Faran felt as if he were shrinking, life leaving him atom by atom. It would make sense if she'd jumped ship again—he was still a werewolf, and she was still haunted by a past he was only beginning to understand. And yet, he believed she was stronger than she had been in Paris. He'd heard it in her voice. He'd felt it in their lovemaking. She was too fierce to run now.

"This isn't right," Faran said, his voice half-strangled. "She would say something, even just a couple of words."

"What do you think happened?"

Faran swallowed hard. "Lexie's in trouble. They just made it look like she left."

"Okay," Sam said, drawing himself to his full height, "then stopping the Five and their ceremony is the best way to make sure Lexie is safe. She was supposed to be part of it, right? If we find them, we find her."

That at least made sense. Faran scrambled for some shred of reason, some mask to hide the eroding mess inside him. "Fine. Let's end those freaks."

It wasn't exactly a dungeon, Lexie thought. The room didn't have that much style. It looked more like a pantry with manacles.

She was chained to the wall, the long iron fetters giving her enough slack to slump on the floor. There was a covered bucket and a bottle of water and nothing else in the room except rows and rows of glass jam jars on the opposite wall, where she couldn't reach. Half the jars were filled with what looked like thick-cut marmalade. Nothing like a homey touch. She crossed her legs, trying to get more comfortable. The chains rattled like Marley's Ghost.

Has Faran noticed I'm gone yet? She thought of their disagreement that morning. That seemed utterly stupid now. She'd wanted time alone, which was fair, but now she wanted nothing more than to feel his strong body next to her.

Exasperated. Lexie banged the back of her head against the wall. This was just great. So she was to star in a Dark Fey ritual. Hopefully they needed all her blood and wouldn't waste any on torture. Lexie's stomach rolled with pent-up nerves.

The door rattled, making her jump. Her heart began to pound so hard she felt dizzy. Instinct made her curl up tight, wrapping her arms around her knees.

Ambrose entered, locking the door behind him again. "Ms. Haven."

She didn't bother to answer.

He pulled up a stool and sat down, resting his gloved hands on his knees. He'd been scrupulously careful never to touch her chains with his bare skin, and she wondered if the effect of iron was worse on full-blood fey.

"I do have a few questions I'd like to ask about the events of yesterday," he said.

She closed her eyes, not wanting to see his face. "You asked me already."

"And I will continue asking. What did your friend do after he chased my companion?"

"He came to find me."

"Before that."

"I don't know. I wasn't there. Why don't you use your magic to find out?"

"You're half fey, more's the pity. Any magic strong enough to sift through your mind would kill you in the bargain, and I need your heart beating to take your blood." Ambrose leaned forward. "What did your friend tell you?"

"He got cut in a fight. Then we talked about the concert. He was more interested in that." Which was true, as far as it went. She knew he'd killed the fetch and had taken his wallet, but so far Ambrose hadn't asked that directly. She'd found it hard to lie to him, but she didn't have a problem withholding information.

"Did your friend find Princess Amelie's wedding band?" Ambrose asked, just as he'd asked twice before. "Look at me when you answer."

She opened her eyes reluctantly. It sounded as if the fetch had retrieved the blasted ring from the hotel and never passed it on. "There was no mention of the wedding band."

The fey's face grew dark with anger. He flushed until he appeared almost purple, his brown eyes flaring to a deep, coal-hot orange. "Tell me the truth!" he roared. "Tell me the truth or I will suck it from the marrow of your bones!"

Lexie stared. After Justin, it took a lot for a threat to impress her, but glowing eyes did the job. Ambrose grabbed her chains, pulling the huge iron staples from the walls with his bare hands. They fell to the floor with a crash and clatter. Then he dragged her to her feet, gripping her by the upper arms. "Tell me!"

At that, he tossed her across the room, chains and all. Superhuman strength sent her sailing. Lexie's limbs thrashed, desperate to catch herself. The only thing that saved her from smashing against the wall was the weight of all that iron. It dragged her to the ground in a painful, clanking heap.

"I don't know where the ring is!" She squeezed her eyes shut, closing him out again. Her voice had gone tiny. "Honestly, I don't."

"Do you think to hold out until your white knight rescues you?" Ambrose prowled from one side of the room to the other.

Lexie didn't respond. Nothing she could say would make a difference. Instead, she tried to gather her legs under her, grateful that she could still move.

"I wouldn't count on rescue. After all, you've walked away from him before. Allergic to dogs, are you?"

That made her look up, a chill sliding down her insides.

"Oh, yes, I know what Mr. Kenyon is and who he works for. The supernatural community isn't all that large, no matter what side you're on." Ambrose's smile was real, but it was malicious. "I cleaned everything out of your rooms. As far as he knows, you've run away, just like you did before."

"You can't do that!" she said before she could stop herself.

"I can and I did, Ms. Haven. If you want anything to change, you'll tell me what I want to know."

She was suddenly afraid—not of the usual things like death or pain, but of leaving that loose end dangling. She'd seen the pain that caused the first time, the complete breach of trust. *Don't let him think I left because of who he is.*

But she didn't know anything about the ring. "I can't help you."

Ambrose reached down, using her collar to haul her up. Cloth cut into her throat, choking off her air, but he kept going until she was dangling with her toes just brushing the floor. "I could kill him, you know. A silver bullet is all it would take. I could build a fetch with your face to do it."

Lexie clawed for air, fighting the heavy chains to scrabble at her throat.

But Ambrose just kept talking. "That's how Leopold meant to be rid of the princess and his brother. By Marcari law, not even Prince Kyle could escape execution once he's seen murdering his bride-to-be. No thanks to your lover, we have to start over on that one."

The fey hurled her to the floor. She cried out as she hit the ground, but the noise was drowned by the cascade of chains. Tears sprang to her eyes, part pain and part grief. Faran! She would save him any way she could, but she was trapped here, in cold iron, and she had no information to bargain with. Frustration welled up in her, a clawed, squirming savage thing. She began to sob, a deep racking wail of helpless rage.

"I can't tell you what I don't know!" she shrieked. It rang against the tiles like a curse.

This was the man who had destroyed her brother. Who had made her childhood a living hell. Lexie looped the chain on her right wrist around her hand, a primitive corner of her mind planning to beat Ambrose to death with her shackles.

His nostrils flared as if she smelled foul. "You know, I'm starting to believe you. Your brother never withstood me this long."

"He was a *child*!" Lexie screamed, and swung the chain with all her fury.

But physics were against her. The long chain made a savage clank against the floor, but she could barely scoot it across the ground. Ambrose sidestepped her attack with a look of distaste.

"Useless creature. I'll give you some time to think of an

answer that might save your life." With that, he slammed out of the room as abruptly as he'd come.

Lexie roared her wrath at the blank, motionless door.

When Sam and Faran reached the palace grounds, it became hard to think about anything but the crowds of people cramming the lawns. The pyrotechnic display being held tonight was an old tradition, dating back to a time when men wore curly wigs and women's skirts were as wide as sofas. And while the good old days might have seen Handel, Vivaldi and their contemporaries providing the entertainment, tonight's stage was graced by a series of acts, ending with a set by Maurice.

Although open to the public, the number of people admitted to the palace grounds was limited by lottery. Those who got in showed a token just like the one Faran had found in the anti-Kyle's wallet. And, not all of the grounds were open. The water garden and the maze were roped off for safety reasons.

Taking advantage of the growing darkness, Sam and Faran found their way past the security ropes to the maze. Sam motioned him to silence. Another figure was drifting through the darkness. Faran recognized the silhouette and felt his spirits lift a notch. It was Dr. Mark Winspear, the Horsemen they called Plague.

Never one for pleasantries, the doctor gave a curt nod. "I've been busy while you two have been buffing your nails. The plainclothes Company members are in place throughout the grounds."

They were standing on the west side of the maze, in the deep shadow formed by the great wall of yew and a boxwood topiary of an enormous lion. The two vampires seemed to merge into the darkness and, even though werewolves weren't on their grocery list, Faran couldn't help a primitive prickle of wariness. On nights like tonight, he was very glad to be on their side.

"So what about inside the maze?" Sam asked. "Have we eyes in there?"

"That will be us," said Mark. "I was looking at the red dots marked on the map Faran found. There are, not surprisingly, five of them. I believe those are the positions around the central sundial where the participants in this ritual are supposed to stand. They were the original positions of some ancient standing stones."

"They need the blood of the Haven line," Faran said, swallowing hard to keep his voice even. "They'll bring Lexie here."

"We think so," Mark replied. "But even with your information and what the Company has found out, we're guessing at a lot right now. We need to wait and watch."

Not what Faran felt like right then, but this was still his best chance at a rescue. Half levitating, half climbing, Mark and Sam melted into the shadowy treetops. Leaving his clothes under the yew hedge, Faran took wolf form and slunk through the trees, hunching beneath the bushes to watch the bare mosaic with its sundial in the middle of the maze.

Barely a minute later, a pair of security guards came through, walking quickly so they could leave the spooky paths again. As Faran heard their footfalls recede, the first band took the stage at the other end of the grounds. In the distance, the crowd roared approval.

Another handful of minutes passed, bringing his impatience to search for Lexie to a boil. There was little to see from his position under the dense branches. A tiny moth fluttered past his nose. And then he saw feet. Two men and a woman, by the shoes.

"Where is the fetch of the prince?" said a female voice

Faran didn't know. They were in the middle of a conversation that didn't sound friendly.

"Lost," the man said in a sulky tone. "The fetch was chased just before that fool Maurice's charity concert."

"Chased by whom?" asked the woman. From his hiding place, Faran couldn't make out her whole figure, but he saw she was carrying a basket. She dipped her hand into it and pulled out a tiny glass dish with a candle inside. She set it on the edge of the circle of mosaic tiles.

"The man sleeping with Haven's daughter. Kenyon. He bears watching," the man replied. "He is one of the Company."

So the fey know who I am. That was bad enough, and the reference to Lexie stung like hot silver.

The woman took out another candle and set it a few feet from the first, then repeated the gesture, working her way around the circle in quick, efficient movements. She'd clearly done this before.

"Ambrose believes this lover killed the fetch." This time it was the other man who spoke, and the voice turned Faran cold. There was no anger or urgency in it, but just the opposite. Cold. Inhuman. It was like listening to a glacier speak.

"Hello, hello." A fourth voice sang out.

Faran's ears pricked forward in surprise. *Maurice?*

"You're late," said the woman. She'd set candles all around the circle. Faran could see her fully now, a figure in a pale cloak. She snapped her fingers. The magic surged, making Faran twitch, and the candles lit in a single flare of flame. The tiny glass squares of the mosaic glistened like water, catching the candlelight and throwing it back to the night. The woman set the candle basket down and picked up a second, laying out implements in the middle of the circle. A scythe, a bowl, delicate silver manacles and a long-bladed knife.

Maurice was watching the woman's every move, but if the contents of the basket bothered him, he gave no sign. He clapped his hands, nail polish glittering. "Got the ring? Got the girl? Where's Leo? Let's keep this snappy. My set's at midnight."

Faran's ears went back. A crawling disbelief raised the hair of his ruff. He'd truly believed Maurice was on their side, but tonight was the night for disappointments. He thrust his nose forward a notch to see better. Maurice was pacing back and forth, his stage costume glimmering in the glow of the candles.

"You can be late. We are freeing a kingdom, fool," said the ice-voiced man.

"Tell that to my manager," said Maurice, the tiniest bit of ice in his own tone. "So, did you find the ring?"

Faran's head hurt. Maurice was the one who'd told him about the tourists finding the ring after Leo dropped it on the croquet lawn. Clearly he was playing both sides. Or neither side. Or his own side.

The sulky man answered. "We think the Haven girl knows where the ring is. Ambrose is questioning her."

Faran's limbs lost all feeling. Images flashed through his brain in rapid sequence—Lexie in chains, torture, dungeons. He barely stifled a snarl.

"Tell Ambrose to bring the girl and that fool Leopold," said the ice-voiced man. "My queen awaits, locked behind the iron gates of treachery. Let us do this thing and set the Dark Lady free."

"The Haven girl will not speak."

"I can make her talk," said the ice-voiced man. "Go tell Ambrose to bring her here, and be quick about it. We don't have much time."

Faran heard a long-suffering sigh. "Fine."

With that, the first man left at a walk, as if refusing to be cowed. Faran ghosted after him on silent paws, retribution in his heart.

Chapter 27

Lexie swore she'd never eat marmalade again. At some point during her violent encounter with Ambrose, several jars had fallen and smashed, permeating the air with the sticky-sweet smell. It clung to the back of her throat, making her cough.

She hurt all over, but at least nothing was broken. One good thing about Ambrose's temper tantrum was that he'd freed her chains from the wall. When she'd finally gathered her limbs and tried to move, she had been able to search the prison-pantry for a way out. It became immediately clear that the first step to freedom was getting out of the chains. They were insanely heavy.

The next twenty minutes she'd spent trying to pick the locks on the iron cuffs. So far she'd tried improvising a pick from an earring, and then the smashed-up lid of a marmalade jar. If she possessed any magic that could have helped, it was effectively blocked. The chains were pure cast iron, apparently forged for someone Faran's size, by the size and weight of the cuffs.

Lexie paused. *I've been thinking about this all wrong.* She knocked the wax out of the marmalade jar and scooped out a glob of the gooey orange stuff. If the room had smelled of Seville oranges before, now she choked on it. She slathered it over her hand, praying her idea would work. Soap or hand lotion worked to get rings off. Why not marmalade?

She folded her hand as small as it would go and tucked the cuff under her opposite arm. And then she pulled. The cuff slid down over her knuckles and then jammed, cramping her thumb. With a curse, she jerked and hauled. She felt skin scraping off her knuckles and hoped bitter orange was a good disinfectant. She pulled and pulled, eyes streaming with the pain, but she thought of facing Ambrose again. Anger helped. Then she thought of Faran walking into their rooms and finding her gone. The look on his face. It shrank the pain to a pinprick.

Her hand finally wriggled free. Lexie dropped the sticky, bloody cuff to the floor with a gasp, stuck her wounded hand in the marmalade jar, and started on the other side.

By the time she was free, she was exhausted and bruised, her eyes streaming from tears of pain. But she'd just taken the first step. The door was the next challenge. She picked up her collection of improvised lock picks and started to work, but it was hopeless. Nothing she had was strong enough to manipulate the ancient iron hardware.

Frustration got the better of her. Lexie slumped against the door, swearing under her breath. Her gaze roved over the room again, looking for an easier solution. And then it caught on a shadow she hadn't seen before.

She rose to investigate, running her hands along the

wall. This side of the room was wallpaper rather than tile, decorated in a faded geometric print. She could feel a bump just next to the shelving and about five feet off the ground. A panel. The print had all but hidden it.

Lexie knocked on the wall, ignoring the sticky feel of her hands. The panel sounded hollow. She knew they were somewhere in the palace, and the palace had secret passages. A flicker of excitement revived her. If this was a way out, it was worth a try.

She used the broken jar lid to cut the paper around the panel, and then pushed, hoping the wood was rotten enough to give way. To her surprise, a catch clicked and the panel swung open an inch. But only an inch. The hinges were rusted.

Lexie had to pull hard to make an opening big enough to crawl through, which was barely enough to admit any light from the pantry. Maybe that was a blessing. What she could see was a mass of cobwebs and dust that roiled her stomach. A shudder rolled over her as she ducked and plunged into the disgusting mess. But then—there was light far ahead. Light meant a way out.

She crept into the passage, not letting herself stop until the tiny passage merged with another. Here, her way was cleaner and not so cramped. The light ahead grew brighter. Soon enough, though, she saw what the light was. A lantern sat on the hard stone floor, and next to it sat Prince Leo, bound hand and foot and gagged with a piece of tape.

Shock surged through Lexie, and she froze in her tracks. She and Leo were in the same predicament, and whatever stupid things Leo had done, she was instantly on his side.

She crouched next to him. His eyes flared, telegraphing hope and a plea. Gone was the haughty, temperamental prince. He was scared out of his wits.

"Don't worry," she said. "I'll get you out of here." And she reached for the tape to free his mouth.

"I wouldn't do that if I were you," came a familiar voice.

Lexie spun around. It was her stranger from the concert hall, but this time he was facing her. She knew the body, the way he carried himself, but he was wearing a mask. Nothing fancy, just a black silk affair that covered his face from forehead to chin. A hooded sweatshirt covered his hair and neck. Whoever he was, he liked his privacy. The disguise did nothing for Lexie's nerves.

"What happened to you?" the man asked, sounding genuinely curious.

She ignored that and pointed at Leo. "Why is he here, like this?"

"He was Ambrose's prisoner. Now he's mine. What are you doing here?" He said it conversationally, as if they'd met at the grocery store. She'd seen just enough of the Company to know that was their way. Rescuing prisoners was just another day at the office—but was the stranger really a Company man? Was that something she dared question to his masked face?

She opted to play it safe. "Ambrose had me, too."

The stranger sucked in air with a hiss. "Thank God you got away."

"Yeah. It was exactly like you said. He wanted me for their ritual." She looked at Leo. "But why him?"

Leo's eyes tracked from Lexie to the man. They were wide enough to see white all around the iris.

"Prince Leopold was their dupe. They made him one of the Five long enough to get what they needed, and now they mean to use him as their puppet on the throne. I've been tempted to leave this idiot at their mercy." The masked figure reached down, slashing the ropes that bound Leo's ankles with one slice of a wicked-looking knife. "I didn't realize they'd caught you or I would have rescued you first."

Despite the strange circumstances, something about the way he said it amused her. "That's very kind."

He gave a slight, almost sarcastic, bow. "But, all things considered, you don't look like you need help."

"It's been touch and go, but thanks. It's good to know I have a man inside," she looked around. "Inside the walls, anyway."

He chuckled. "Now I need to get this fool to his father." Leo made a frantic noise—he clearly didn't want to see King Targon—but the masked man grabbed him by the collar and heaved him upright.

"Just one question," Lexie said.

The man paused. "Yes?"

"Do you know what happened to my father?"

The figure froze, as if he'd been caught in some illicit act. This man knew something about her father.

Then he gave a careless shrug. "Someday we'll talk about that, Little Red, but right now there are secrets to keep. I hope you can respect that. I hope you can keep mine."

Lexie's heart leaped in her throat. She fell back a step. "I can. I will."

And, in that moment, he'd let her know who he was. *Impossible*. But it was. All the small gestures, the tone of his voice, the set of his head suddenly clicked into the familiar place in her memory, and it explained so much. Her stranger definitely was a Company man, through and through.

And yet she couldn't let on what she'd just figured out. Not in front of the prince, who was watching them with voracious interest. He hadn't missed her moment of surprise.

Lexie cleared her throat. Ten thousand questions crashed

into her mind, but she went for the obvious. "By the way, how do I get out of here?"

He gave a short laugh. "Do you want the easy way or the smart way?"

The easy way was going with him, which he freely admitted might end in a confrontation with other members of the Five. They'd be looking for their missing prince. Lexie picked the smart way—a bit of a tour through the tunnels to emerge in the palace kitchens. How hard could that be?

Really hard, it turned out. It was a confusing, filthy warren. Lexie crawled through the tunnels for at least another half hour. By the time she reached what she thought was her destination, she almost yearned for the easy way, gunfire, black magic and all. But there was the secret panel to freedom, low in the wall just like the directions said.

But the moment she opened the secret panel, she knew she'd taken the wrong route. A wash of conversation swirled around her, along with the scent of hors d'oeuvres and expensive perfume. This wasn't the kitchens—she was back in the freshly repaired reception room where the ring had first been stolen and where Faran had leaped back into her life, hunting hounds on his tail.

And it was no quieter than it had been that first night. Outside the huge glass windows, fireworks fountained into the sky, snapping and cracking like gunfire. The room was packed with elegantly garbed men and women sipping champagne and watching the show. Lexie's only comfort was that the secret panel was behind the grand piano, which sat idle. She was able to close the passage behind her and find her feet before someone noticed she'd popped out of the wall.

She began to inch toward the door when she saw Chloe in a backless white dress fastened at the neck with a rhinestone collar. Lexie inched closer. "*Pst*! Chloe!"

Chloe turned, her eyes going wide at Lexie's appearance. She marched over, putting herself between the crowd and Lexie to shield her from curious stares. "What are you doing? You look like a chimney sweep! And what's that all over your hands?"

Lexie looked down. Her hands were gloved in filth-coated marmalade and blood. She squeezed her eyes shut and fought an inappropriate urge to giggle. "It's a long story. I need to find Faran and clean up."

"I'll get you to your room."

Chloe was using a gentle voice that said Lexie appeared to be having a breakdown—which sounded like a fine idea. Lexie grabbed Chloe's champagne glass and drained it in two swallows.

"Yeah, no," Lexie replied. "My room is a terrible idea because they know how to get in."

"They?" Chloe asked, her voice going hard. "You're in some kind of trouble, aren't you? Never mind. Whatever. Come with me."

Lexie didn't argue. She was too tired to launch into an explanation of strange men in the walls, not to mention blood rituals in the maze. She passed the glass to a slack-jawed waiter and obediently trailed after her friend, careful not to touch anything.

They'd nearly made it out when she saw a wolf run past the window. "Faran!"

Chloe had seen it, too. And then she saw Sam sprinting after, Maurice at his side. Chloe ran to one of the side doors and opened it. "Sam!"

"Let me past," Lexie demanded, and Chloe obliged. "Faran!"

Lexie stepped into the garden. Her shadow, backlit by the lights of the reception room, stretched like a giant across the lawn until another Roman candle exploded in the sky, washing everything away in lurid brightness. She looked around for a wolf, but there were none in sight.

Lexie wandered a little farther, grateful to the darkness that hid her filthy state. She was tired and dirty and bruised, but she was winning. She'd made it out of Ambrose's clutches, shed her chains and escaped to safety through secret passages. Not bad for a night's work.

Now all she could think of was telling Faran that he'd been tricked, that she was here and waiting for him and wanting him by her side. Then everything would be perfect.

Another barrage of fireworks went off in the sky, making a bouquet of chrysanthemums. In the flare of light she saw Ambrose leaning against the wall, breathing hard. He saw her and his lips peeled back in a grimace. "You have more lives than a cat, Alexis."

"So it was you my friends were chasing," she guessed.

"They caught my servant as he came to look for me, but that is all. The truly important among us escaped, and we'll have our revenge on that turncoat musician. No one crosses the fey and lives long to brag of it."

Lexie had no idea what he was talking about, but she was really tired of this guy. She cupped her hands around her mouth and yelled at the top of her lungs. "Hey, Faran, Sam, over here!"

Ambrose hissed, a noise that no one with a human face should ever make. And as he did, he raised his hand and clutched it tight, making a fist so tight it shook with the strain of his muscles.

Lexie stopped breathing. Her hands flew to her throat, but there was nothing to grab and pull loose. She clawed at the invisible bonds that strangled her, but the world got darker. She was aware of Chloe running across the lawn in her bare feet, white dress billowing like an angel's robes.

Lexie dropped to her knees, losing strength. She'd wanted to talk to Faran, but the reason for it was getting blurry. Everything was spinning now, her heart thudding in her ears, her lungs aching and burning like nothing she'd ever felt before. A stray thought flitted past, wondering if this was what drowning was like.

She was dying. She'd had close calls, but nothing like this. She'd wanted to disappear when Ambrose was chasing her, and it had happened. And now she desperately yearned to fight back.

Lexie's power went to the one source she knew well—the maze. She couldn't say how she called to it, but she did and it answered. The tingling, sparkling power surged under the earth to where she knelt and boiled up inside her. Ambrose's spell fell away and she gasped in air, sucking sweet relief into her tortured lungs. And then she thrust out a hand, releasing a blast of magic that slammed him into the stone wall of the palace with enough force that she heard bones crack.

The next instant, a bullet of gray fur flashed past her, so close she felt the rush of wind. There was a snarl that was half a human scream, and the sound of wet and tearing flesh. Lexie collapsed, another glorious breath whooping in, and then another. The borrowed magic drained out of her in a rush, leaving her giddy. She scrunched her eyes closed as another barrage of fireworks flashed across the sky.

Gradually the world stopped spinning enough for her to roll to her knees, though her head still pounded like the fireworks had moved inside her skull. Slowly, Lexie rose up, pushing her hair out of her face, and looked around.

Faran, still in wolf form, crouched over Ambrose. The fey was clearly dead, throat bloody, arms splayed as he fell. Lexie's stomach dropped and she looked away, glad she hadn't eaten for hours. She squeezed her eyes shut a moment, swallowing down her queasiness. After another breath, she managed to look back at the scene.

The wolf's yellow eyes were fixed on her, watching her every move. Lexie remained very still, not sure what to do. Suddenly, she was back in Paris, in the alley, watching a wolf stand over the body of a man. They'd come full circle.

Faran stood, head and tail low. She took a breath, wanting to say the right thing, not finding the words because no matter how much she logically grasped, it didn't stop the horror in front of her. He'd done what he could to protect her, but that meant claws and teeth. He was a wolf. Despite Faran's kindness and humor and the incredible sex, it was like loving lightning—a terrible force of nature.

But now, Lexie finally got it. She'd felt that protective rage when she'd been in chains and Ambrose had threatened Faran. And she'd just called her newborn power to slam the fey into the wall. The battle of light and dark wasn't pretty, but there were times when pretty wasn't on the menu.

Faran turned, taking a last look at Ambrose, and began padding into the dark. The moment was running like water through Lexie's fingers. *I don't need pretty, or easy, or comfortable. I need Faran.*

"Wait!" she said. "Don't go."

Faran's ears swiveled forward as he swung his massive shaggy head around. The yellow eyes were guarded. Lexie's mouth went dry. The moment he'd jumped through the window had felt just like this, balanced on a knife-edge where they would either connect or drift apart.

But this time Lexie knew exactly what she wanted. "Get over here. Neither of us gets to walk away anymore. We're stuck with each other."

With a huff, Faran trotted a few steps and then broke into a bouncing run. Lexie flung her arms around his neck, burying her face in the rough, wiry fur. The wagging tail thumped against her knee as the warm, solid bundle of wolf all but enveloped her. After so much darkness and fear that night, the unchecked joy of it was too much. Lexie started to cry. "Thank you, thank you, I love you."

And then suddenly she was holding a lot of hot, delicious naked man. "Whoa!"

"I love you, Lexie," he murmured in her ear. Her heart sang in that moment. There was nothing, *nothing*, she had wanted so much to hear.

"Oh, *please*, Kenyon," said Sam from where he stood beside Chloe a few yards away. The vampire held a hand up to his eyes. "*Please* put some clothes on."

Chapter 28

Later, Lexie stood in the burning hot shower wondering if any part of her wasn't bruised. It wasn't just her body she was wondering about. The sound of Ambrose hitting the wall kept replaying in her mind, and every time she flinched. That sound, if nothing else, would keep her from ever abusing any magical skills she might develop. She'd done what she had to do, but there were real consequences and few easy answers. This wasn't some cartoon with superheroes and capes.

The rings of the shower curtain squeaked on the rod, and cold air wafted in. "Hey!" she protested.

The rings squeaked again, shutting out the cold, and then Faran was behind her, wrapping one arm possessively around her middle. "What are you thinking about?"

When she didn't answer at once, he nibbled on her shoulder. She felt her mind spin away, but snagged it back for a single, final item. "One question and then we'll close the subject of Ambrose for the night."

"What?" Faran asked softly.

She swallowed around a lump. "Did I kill him?"

"No."

That meant Faran had. "It was necessary," she said.

"Yeah."

The hot water pounded on her as she turned around and rested her cheek on his chest. She had to take the sting out of the moment, and tried to think what one of the Company men would say. They relied a lot on dark humor, and now she knew why. "I hope he tasted better than he looked."

"Eh, not so much."

Faran tilted her chin up and kissed her on the mouth. That was fine with her, because that meant there was no more need for awkward words. There was just the two of them, their skin and heat and unspoken understanding.

He broke the kiss and lifted her hands, cradling them gently. She'd scrubbed the filth off them and could see the damage from the cuffs now—savage scrapes where the skin had been sacrificed for freedom. He pressed his lips to them, at first reverently, but then nipping at her fingertips. The featherlight touches of teeth were weirdly erotic, as was the quick stroke of his tongue against the inside of her wrist. His lick was rough, not quite human, but it was arousing.

Her free hand slid down the hard, wet curve of his chest, circling the flat bud of his nipple. Faran leaned into her touch, bracing one hand against the tiles on either side of her. She nibbled on his jaw, tugging his earlobe with her teeth. He groaned and with one hand hit the shower controls, turning off the water.

The noise level dropped, leaving nothing but the bathroom fan and the dripping of water from their bodies. Faran slid his hands behind her, caressing the small of her back before he hoisted her upward as easily as if she was a doll. Lexie hooked her legs over his hips and hung on to his shoulders. The shower curtain slid away in a billow of steam. Faran stepped out of the shower, carrying Lexie with him.

They'd gone to a hotel—a place with no bad memories. The bed was luxurious, piled high with down quilts and cool linens. Faran laid her down, heedless of their wet skin and the long tangle of her hair. The air was cold, puckering her nipples, but wherever Faran touched was warm. And he just kept kissing her, his lips and tongue moving over her skin as if he was drinking every trace of moisture the shower had left behind.

And then he parted her knees at the edge of the bed, letting the cool air touch the inside of her thighs. Lexie felt wildly vulnerable, and wildly heated. His tongue, wet and rough, slid up the soft skin of her hip, traveling ever closer to where she wanted that touch. She shivered, ordering herself to keep her shoulders against the quilt. Sometimes a girl just had to surrender.

She inhaled as he put his tongue to work on her sex, as if this was what her body had hungered for all her life. A flame sprang to life somewhere deep in her belly. Lexie made a noise, part trepidation and part delight. A slow conquest of wet, rough pleasure was taking place, every lick making her breasts heave with her helpless gasps. Faran took his time, savoring her, leaving nothing untouched. And when the nuzzling and licking left off, suction began. Lexie's fingers dug into the covers, holding herself down, tearing with the urge to squirm.

His blue eyes danced with mischief, and something darker, as her breathing began to lose control. He rose up over her, stroking his thumbs up her abdomen in a twin arc of pressure. She shuddered under his touch, moaning as his hot, wet mouth found her nipple. Sore and flushed

and needy, the flash of sensation connected every body
part in a twist of erotic pleasure.

"Oh, God," she cried.

"Give it up," he coaxed, moving to the other breast.

And she did. Lexie arched beneath him, straining so
hard she thought her spine would crack. But she was
greedy, as if she had been starving and he'd just offered
her one bite of a delectable meal. "More."

With a low chuckle, he seemed to spring, rather than
climb onto the bed. Lexie nearly came again just at the
look on his face. His eyes had gone golden, the wolf fully
present. He moved sinuously, body loose and coiled at
once. Prowling. Lexie rose up on her elbows, still throb-
bing. The sight of him, the hard muscles sliding under his
skin, did nothing to cool her desire. This time she was
more than ready for his beast.

He grasped her waist, pulling her to where he wanted
her. He was fully aroused, long and hard and glistening
with anticipation. A condom went on and then her legs
were around his waist, and he was inside, stretching her
until she thought he had filled her whole body. Already
primed, it was all she could do to hold on.

Faran wasn't having any of that. In one long stroke, he
had her, her body erupting around him. He knew her too
well and knew just what angle to use. Her nails found his
shoulders this time, doing to his flesh what she'd done to
the bedclothes before. He made a noise of pain and triumph, but he wasn't stopping there. His rhythm became
faster and harder, winding the tension inside Lexie one
more time. She writhed beneath him, her breathing now
just a ragged gasp. It was like a wild ride, every swoop-
ing, dropping, flying moment of it different than the last.
And he was sending her into space again, as hard and far
as he could manage.

The blazing heat between them finally hit nova. Every nerve in Lexie short-circuited at once. Faran snarled as he spilled into her and her body milked him, sealing them together in a long, sweet agony of pleasure.

Afterward, they lay curled together, bundled under the wealth of luxurious covers. Lexie was spooned against Faran, her fingers laced through his. She could feel him wake from a doze, a stirring and resettling she recognized from their time together in Paris.

"So is the Company back on duty?" she asked softly.

"Yup."

"And you're staying here until after the wedding?"

His arm tightened around her. "Mmm-hmm."

For a moment she thought he was sleep talking—making the sort of agreeable dialogue people do when they're just trying to doze off again. She stopped speaking, figuring it would be better to let him rest.

But then he asked, "What about you? Where are you going after the ceremony is over?"

She swallowed. "Um. That depends. I have a few jobs lined up but…"

"But?"

"Will you stay in Marcari with me?" she asked quickly, getting the words out before she could stop herself.

She felt him rise up to look down on her. "Why Marcari?"

Lexie turned her head to look up at him, but she didn't have a wolf's eyes. In the dark, he was all but invisible. "I need you to keep a secret."

"What?"

"I saw my mystery man again tonight."

"Yeah, in the walls with Prince Leo." She'd told him that much.

"I have to find him again. He knows what happened to my father."

She heard Faran's breath catch. "Okay then. I can see why you want to talk to him."

"But that's not all. I think I've guessed his secret."

"His secret?" Faran asked dubiously.

"Yeah, and I probably shouldn't say anything," Lexie added, feeling her heart start to pound—but this was one thing she couldn't keep from Faran. "I know who he is, and his cover probably depends on us keeping our mouths shut. He asked me not to say anything."

Faran must have sensed her tension, because he stroked her hair in a reassuring gesture. "Who is he?"

"He called me Little Red. He always used to do that. And then I recognized him—his voice, the way he stood, everything. Until that moment, I couldn't place who he was."

"Who?" Faran asked more urgently.

"Jack Anderson. He's not dead. He's deep, deep undercover, and he seems to know all about what's going on with the fey."

Faran said nothing for a long moment. She could only imagine what was going on in his mind. Jack had let everyone who loved him believe he was dead.

When Faran spoke at last, it was with bloody satisfaction. "I'm so going to kick his ass."

A dinner party came three nights later. King Renault announced it was to celebrate Amelie's full recovery, but everyone knew it was also in honor of foiling the Five's plot.

It wasn't a vast affair like the banquet. Instead, it was just Kyle's and Amelie's immediate family and the few close friends. The dinner didn't appear on the official palace timetable, and the press never knew about it. Lexie's belongings had mysteriously reappeared—she suspected

Jack had found them somewhere in the bowels of the palace—but she left her cameras behind when she sat down to dinner. This was a time for the royals to be just people.

Faran cooked. Lexie knew it wasn't something he did often, which was a shame because he obviously enjoyed himself. Dish after fabulous dish came out of the kitchen, starting with the crispy shrimp she loved so much. There was a delicate cold soup and lobster salad, quail done to perfection and…Lexie just lost track. When Faran was in a very good mood, he liked to feed people. Judging by the menu, he was ecstatic.

Her one regret was that Faran couldn't be in two places at once, because she wasn't in the mood to do without him for a minute, to say nothing of an entire formal dinner with him tied up in the kitchen. She'd rather have him tied up someplace more private, but that would have to happen later.

In the meantime, she sat with Chloe and Sam and Mark Winspear and his partner, Bree Meadows, who turned out to know Prince Kyle and his infamous cousin, Maurice.

"Do you mean Maurice was here?" Bree exclaimed. "I haven't seen him for years. How is he?"

"He left yesterday for who-knows-where," said Lexie. "He wouldn't say more than that he wanted some quiet time for songwriting." She suspected he was actually laying low for a while to keep off the Dark Fey's radar.

"I don't understand what was going on with him," Chloe said in an undertone.

"He caught word of the plot some time ago and volunteered to act as a double agent," Sam said just as quietly. "I don't know who his handler was."

Actually, Lexie could make a very good guess, but couldn't say anything. The news that Jack was alive had thrilled Faran, but he'd agreed they should keep the fact quiet. It was hard. Chloe was his niece, and the other Horsemen had looked to Jack as a friend and leader. But Jack had asked Lexie to keep his secret, and an incautious word could get him killed.

"What I don't get," said Lexie, "is if the gates are locked on the Dark Fey, who is helping them from the outside?"

Sam shrugged. "I guess they missed a few. Probably the original Five, and over time some of those five had to be replaced with other suckers."

"Loose ends," Mark Winspear grumbled. He was the tall, dark and sardonic type. "Ambrose and Prince Leopold were caught, Maurice was one of ours, but the other two escaped."

Lexie winced. Leo was under King Targon's lock and key until a suitable trial could be arranged. Since he had been plotting to murder Kyle and Amelie—not to mention every other kind of treason—it was unlikely he would walk free ever again.

Sam raised his glass. "Well, here's to 60 percent fewer bad guys."

They could all drink to that.

Dessert came. Faran, dressed in clean whites, brought it in himself, amid a chorus of "oohs" and sincere applause. It was a *croquembouche,* a beautiful tower of choux pastry balls held together with strings of caramel and decorated with ribbon and candied flowers. It reminded Lexie of a Christmas tree, but it was a traditional dish for weddings in this part of the world.

Faran set it before Amelie and Kyle with a bow. There was a moment of silence and then Amelie picked something from the top of the tower of spun caramel and pastry.

"It's my ring!" she cried, racing around the table to kiss the cook, then Kyle and then her father. "How did you find it?"

Lexie gasped, thinking back to that night in Ambrose's makeshift dungeon. She'd been tortured for that ring.

Faran gave a wolfish grin. "I've had it since I caught the fetch on the rooftop, but if no one knew where it was, it couldn't get stolen again."

At that moment, his eyes found hers. They held apology, but also triumph. Lexie understood. If she'd known where the ring was, the night might have ended with her death and the success of the ritual. She was brave, but she had no illusions.

Amelie flushed, oblivious to everything but her happiness. "You horrible man! Captain Valois will be so utterly cross with you." She slid it onto her finger and cradled her hand against her chest. "But I adore you for taking care of it for me!"

Prince Kyle rose, raising his glass. "I give you Faran Kenyon, our most faithful servant."

The company rose, happy to acknowledge a man who had not only caught a poisoner, uncovered a plot and saved the ring, but also cooked a very fine meal.

Then Princess Amelie raised her glass. "And I give you Lexie Haven, whom I've noticed being every bit as clever and resourceful as our Company members. We owe her much of the happiness in this room."

"Hear, hear," said the Horsemen in chorus. "So say we all!"

Sam winked. "I underestimated you. If you ever want a seat at the Company table, just let me know."

"One step at a time, gentlemen," Lexie said with an arched brow. "I'm not sure your benefit plan covers half the hazards I've seen these last few days."

"Oh, come on," said Chloe. "You're cohabiting with a werewolf. After that kind of vacuuming, how much worse could it be?"

* * *

Lexie found her way to the kitchens much later that night. The fabric of her long taffeta skirts swished as she walked, the sea-green color luminous in the dim light of the palace hallways. She was stuffed to bursting with so much good food and wine and laughter, she was about ready to collapse right where she was and sleep for a month. In fact, as she pushed through the swinging doors and saw the stainless steel tables gleaming in the overhead lights, she thought they might do as an impromptu bed. Who knew eating could be so exhausting?

Everyone but Faran had left. The kitchen was spotlessly clean, every dish washed and put away, and every surface scrubbed. It was quiet, nothing but the hum of the refrigerators filling the air.

He was leaning against one of the workstations, arms folded across his broad chest, and staring at the table before him. On the table sat a single chocolate cupcake on a plain white plate.

Lexie drifted slowly between the worktables toward him, her sequined flats tapping softly on the tiles. The air was still warm from the ovens, and she let her silky shawl slip from her shoulders to dangle from her elbows.

"Are you going to eat it or interrogate it?" she asked, drawing near. "I've never seen a cupcake tremble like that before."

His mouth quirked, but it wasn't quite a smile. "Do you know why they call me Famine?"

She leaned next to him, her arm touching his. "Because you eat a lot?"

He took a breath. "It's the horseman I fear the most. It's not just food. It's scarcity. Of family, of community, of everything that makes the pack work. The alphas of the pack keep order, but they also make sure all systems are working. If their world is going right, there is enough to go around. No famine."

She put a hand on his arm, feeling the hard muscle beneath his sleeve. "They're providers."

"Wolves have a complex society. I'm on my own now. My pack is gone. But that doesn't mean I lack the instinct to keep a community safe."

There was a lot he still hadn't said about his past, but it was coming out in bits and pieces. Lexie didn't push for details, but gathered scraps like this one up. One day there would be enough to quilt together the story of his childhood. They were coming more frequently now as the trust between them grew.

He put an arm around her shoulders. "You look gorgeous tonight."

Lexie leaned her head against him. "You wowed your audience."

"Do you like the cupcake?"

"It's a very nice cupcake."

"I made it for you. Chocolate on chocolate."

She really thought she might faint if she ate anything more. "It's lovely but I'm stuffed."

"One bite?" He looked pleading, his blue eyes almost childlike.

Heaven help her, she couldn't say no to those eyes. "Do you have a fork?"

He looked around the kitchen. "One or two." And then he handed her one that had been sitting next to him all along. His movements were a little too quick, as if he was nervous.

Those nerves found an answering flutter in her stomach. Something was afoot.

A little apprehensive, Lexie plunged the fork into the cupcake. It sundered the dessert in a rich waft of chocolate.

The frosting quickly buried the fork, the layer of butter and cocoa thick without being too much. The cake sprang apart, just the right balance between fluffy and fudgy. It was a masterpiece.

The two halves of the cupcake parted, one half falling with a crinkle of paper frill. Lexie lifted the fork to lick it clean, but something caught on the tines.

It was a diamond ring, smudged with chocolate. Lexie's heart squeezed, seeming to leap inside her with a flutter of panic and delight. She tipped the ring from the fork to her hand, turning the gems to the light. "Oh, my gosh."

Fire sparked from the stones, one white diamond flanked by two smoky ones. Dark and light. Man and wolf. Woman and fey. It was…perfect.

"Amelie's wasn't the only ring I've been keeping," he said quietly. "I was going to give this to you a long time ago."

"There was a reason it had to wait," she said, a lump in her throat crowding her words. "I wasn't there yet. I didn't know who I was. Or who you really were."

"We both had more to learn," he said gently.

Tears filled Lexie's eyes and she had to bite her lips to keep them from trembling. She sniffed, trying to pull herself together while Faran watched with a bemused expression.

With brisk movements, she dusted the crumbs from the ring, licking them from her fingers. The dark, sweet taste burst on her tongue like a benediction. *Sweet heavens, can he bake!*

She passed him the ring. "Here, you put it on me."

For the first time ever, his fingers felt cold against hers. When he fumbled the tiny gold band, she knew it was nerves. That just made her love him the more.

He didn't need to worry. It fit perfectly. It suited her

hand perfectly. The design and quality were impeccable. He could bake and he knew jewelry, too. "Faran, it's beautiful."

"Um, will you marry me?" he asked. "I think I was supposed to do that part first."

Lexie gave a hiccuping kind of laugh. She slid her arms around his neck and rested her cheek against his chest, listening to his heartbeat. She wanted to be near him, to be warmed by him and held close in the circle of his arms. Always. "Yes."

"I love you," he said, tilting her head up for a kiss. It was long and luxuriant, sweet and dark and not unlike the cupcake.

Which they shared, even if Lexie already had eaten too much. There's always room for chocolate, especially the grand chocolate ganache of love.

No cupcake was ever so significant, or so admired as the one Lexie and Faran consumed in the Marcari palace kitchens at two o'clock that January morning. It was the first of a spectacular history of cupcakes between them.

* * * * *

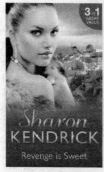

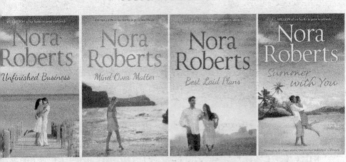
15_ST_11

MILLS & BOON®

It's Got to be Perfect

* cover in development

When Ellie Rigby throws her three-carat engagement ring into the gutter, she is certain of only one thing. She has yet to know true love!

Fed up with disastrous internet dates and conflicting advice from her friends, Ellie decides to take matters into her own hands. Starting a dating agency, Ellie becomes an expert in love. Well, that is until a match with one of her clients, charming, infuriating Nick, has her questioning everything she's ever thought about love…

Order yours today at
www.millsandboon.co.uk

MILLS & BOON®

The Thirty List

* cover in development

At thirty, Rachel has slid down every ladder she has ever climbed. Jobless, broke and ditched by her husband, she has to move in with grumpy Patrick and his four-year-old son.

Patrick is also getting divorced, so to cheer themselves up the two decide to draw up bucket lists. Soon they are learning to tango, abseiling, trying stand-up comedy and more. But, as she gets closer to Patrick, Rachel wonders if their relationship is too good to be true…

**Order yours today at
www.millsandboon.co.uk/Thethirtylist**

MILLS & BOON®

nocturne™

AN EXHILARATING UNDERWORLD OF DARK DESIRES